DEATH IN A PALE HUE

AN ART CENTER MYSTERY

SUSAN VAN KIRK

LEVEL
BEST BOOKS

Praise for Death in a Pale Hue

"Death in a Pale Hue is alive with vibrant small town characters, buried secrets, and a sleuth up for the challenge of solving a murder close to home!"—Molly MacRae, award-winning, national bestselling author of the Highland Bookshop mysteries and the Haunted Yarn Shop mysteries

"An art center brings new life to Apple Grove—until it brings death. A buried skeleton, a stolen sculpture, and a surprise murderer mark an auspicious debut for a new series. Susan Van Kirk once again brings a small, Midwestern town to life."—Judy Alter, *Saving Irene*

"In *Death in a Pale Hue*, thirty-year-old Jill Madison returns to her hometown to bring a new community art center, named in honor of her late mother, to life. Her mantra, "I will show them success," is challenged by a burglary, the discovery of a corpse, and a board president who sends constant messages of criticism. Author Susan Van Kirk does an excellent job of mixing intrigue with Jill's balancing of her job, her first big art event, and the actions of the killer who plans to permanently paint her out of the picture.

"This is the first in a new series, but it won't be the last. Jill and her friends are characters readers will want to spend more time with than *Death in a Pale Hue* offers. For now, though, I highly recommend *Death in a Pale Hue* for an easy and enjoyable read. Disclaimer: I received an ARC of this book, but that did not influence my review."—Debra H. Goldstein, Kensington's Sarah Blair mysteries

"A charming cozy with a sensitive young artist heroine, Jill Madison, who returns to her small town with the best of intentions—to develop a nonprofit art center to serve the community—only to discover an old murder that will pull the community apart before it can mend. With a rich cast of secondary characters—including Jill's intuitive detective brother Tom, the dour board member Ivan who constantly doubts Jill's management abilities, and a range of suspects—it's an entertaining read and a wonderful start to what I hope will be a series!"—Karen Odden, *USA Today* bestselling author of *Down a Dark River*

"This was a well-written and evenly paced whodunit that I could not put down, quickly becoming a page-turner as I had to know who was doing what to whom. We are introduced to Jill Madison, whose new beginning is marred when a sculpture is stolen, and a body is discovered on the premise of her art center. Wanting to find the truth, Jill starts to investigate and finds herself in the crosshair of a killer who wants to remain hidden.

"The author did a great job in staging this multi-plot drama that had everything I love in a mystery – a solid plot, a likable cast of characters, and a small-town setting. With a small suspect pool, the author took the time to add a bit of backstory that helped in gathering clues to determine the killer's identity. The author knows how to tell a story that pulled me in with visually descriptive narrative and engaging dialogue that would point us in the right direction. There were a few strategically placed twists that ratcheted up the pacing and the suspense and I couldn't put the book down until all was said and done. Overall, this was a terrific read and I can't wait for the next book in this pleasantly appealing new series."—Dru Ann Love, Author Champion, Book Advocate, MWA Raven Award Winner

"There's nothing pale about this book—vivid prose, colorful characters, and small-town secrets!"—Kaye George, award-winning, national bestselling author of mysteries with a twist

"The journey of artistic protagonist Jill Madison and the small town she's determined to turn into a thriving arts center infuses every page of this compelling mystery with warmth and gentle humor."—Ellen Byron, Agatha and Lefty Award-Winning Author

"A stolen sculpture and the discovery of a corpse threaten to prevent Jill Marsden from opening her newly created art center. A cast of zany characters make this a rollicking adventure of a spirited new series."—Marilyn Levinson *aka* Allison Brook, author of the Haunted Library series

"A break-in, a stolen piece of treasured sculpture, and a buried body introduce mystery lovers to Susan Van Kirk's talented young artist, Jill Madison. Will Jill's grit unearth the dirty deeds that threaten her town's art center opening? Or will her plans to honor her mother's name get painted out? A strong debut with a very likeable lead character."—Judy L Murray, Agatha finalist and IPPY Silver Medalist, *Murder in the Master* - A Chesapeake Bay Mystery

Chapter One

In the heartless cruelty of my sixth-grade year, I sat behind Ned Fisher in English class, joining in the snickers of my friends. Ned had ears that stuck out from his head like Dumbo the elephant, and he probably wished he could fly away. Now, decades later, I found myself once again occupying a seat behind Ned Fisher.

But this time I was in the back of his police car.

I wasn't laughing.

He had pounded on my door at six in the morning, a summons that led to this race across town to check on a break-in at the art center. He politely called me Ms. Madison. Guilt—it never died. I thanked him for his help, hoping he'd forgotten our mutual past. My heart pounded because I oversaw the renovation and management of the art center and reported to a board that wasn't quite sure an artistically talented but business-challenged thirty-year-old could handle this job.

We pulled up outside the art center on the public square as my detective brother, Tom, drove up beside us and parked his unmarked car. The art center's façade had been updated in the first phase of construction, and my heart swelled to see my mother's professional name in the signage above the second-floor windows. The Adele Marsden Center for the Arts. My dream. The cream paint on the wall provided a rich contrast to the dark viridian green trim and letters. I sighed as I took in the sight. My gaze followed the architectural details down to the entrance, where I saw a small, broken windowpane in the door next to the handle.

Louise stood in front of one of the new windows, texting away.

Thank God she's safe.

Louise Sandoval, my office manager, stood there pushing her hair back behind her ears as she always did while typing messages on her phone. I scooted out of the car and walked over to her.

She looked up from her phone screen. "Thank God you're here, Jill. I called nine-one-one after I noticed the damage. I was just texting you." She glanced at the policeman. "Oh, don't worry. I didn't touch anything, Officer. I've seen enough of those *CSI* shows, so I wasn't about to pick up the knife or the gun. That poor sucker is always the one charged."

I whispered, "Don't think we have a murder here, Louise."

"Have we been inside yet?" she whispered back.

I recognized Chad Simmons, the policeman at the front door. When Tom got out of his car and walked toward us, Chad relaxed, his shoulders less rigid and his scowl turning to relief. My brother had that effect on people. "Dominic and I did a perimeter check. Side door on the alley's locked, but this window was broken and the door's unlocked."

"Did you check inside yet?"

"No, we were waiting for you."

I looked at both men. "The door has an alarm. Didn't it go off?"

Simmons shook his head. "No record of the alarm company notifying our dispatcher."

"That's strange." I was mentally rethinking last night when I left. Only Louise and I had keys. The key in the lock disarmed the alarm—old-fashioned, cheap, and not exactly cutting-edge twenty-first century.

Louise turned to me. "Don't worry, Jill. My nephew, JoJo, is in a building trades class at the high school. He can fix it. Cheap."

"Thanks. Cheap is in our financial range. Does he know anything about glass repair?"

"Now that's a good question. I'm sure he can Google it."

The price was right. JoJo would have to do.

Tom looked at me. "Any cameras?"

"No. We have those on our wish list, but we need to wait until the budget catches up with our wants." Maybe in twenty years. I scratched my head.

"I can't understand why the alarm didn't go off. I set it every night when I leave."

Tom turned to me. "Stay close to me. We don't know what's happened yet or when it happened. You're my kid sister—got to keep you safe. We'll go around to the alley door and I'll have you unlock it."

I followed Tom around the building to the alley, watching his confident walk and his broad shoulders. Next to my dad, he was the John Wayne of my life. Always dependable. Louise trotted along right behind me. Dominic Aubrey, the other cop, was standing there, waiting.

Tom looked at us. "Aubrey, we'll go first and see if anyone's inside or if there's any damage. You two wait here. Do you keep money on the premises?"

Louise nodded. "I have a cash box in my file cabinet used for purchases at the gift shop, but most people pay with credit cards. We rarely have much cash. Hardly enough to pay for gas to drive twelve miles to Edgington."

"All right. We'll clear the building first and make sure it's safe. Once I come out, Jill, I'll have you walk through the building. Make sure nothing is missing. However, don't touch a thing. I want you in the center long enough to inspect the exhibit. That's all."

Maybe I should mention my fingerprints and Louise's were all over the center but, well, this was Tom. He liked to go "by the book."

"What will you do?"

"Once we clear the building, I'll check the alarm system. See what's up with it."

The Adele Marsden Center for the Arts shared a wall with a pet shop on the north side, but an alley on the south side separated it from an insurance company. Our side of the alley had a door that employees often used, and Tom pronounced the alley door untouched and locked. I produced my key, unlocked it, and watched him and Aubrey walk in. The endless, painful minutes stretched out so long I wondered if Louise was right and there was a dead body.

While Tom was gone, I thought about my board of directors and how I was going to explain this. One thing I knew for sure, the board who hired me was more conservative than the Spanish Inquisition. They'd made it clear we needed only good publicity, like the story in the *Ledger* about our renovation.

Tom returned and pointed to me. "Don't touch anything. No one's inside, but I'm afraid there's damage."

Almost as if he'd heard my thoughts, the board president's number came up on my phone. Ivan Truelove. What a misnomer of a name and the bane of my existence. With great satisfaction, I tapped the "decline" button. Sometimes it was better to put off unpleasantness.

I dashed through the exhibit of my mother's sculptures, a mixture of bronze and mixed-media pieces. My mother had often worked in themes about nature—its patterns, its contradictions. I blew out a long breath. They were all accounted for.

The last piece was *Mother and Child* at the end of the room under a glass cover. Only it wasn't. I walked to the display, missing now, the cover lying on the floor. I tiptoed over to it, took in the empty pedestal, and fell to my knees. "Oh, my God," I whispered. "What am I going to do?" Tears began to seep from my eyes and roll down my cheeks.

My mother had left it to me in her will, so its sentimental value alone was priceless. It was a sculpture of us. When I was three, I played in my mother's studio while she wrestled beauty and meaning from clay. *Mother and Child* displayed her willowy arms, strong hands, beautifully chiseled cheeks, and soft, gentle eyes—eyes that gazed at me with love as I sat in her lap and held a bouquet of daisies. Priceless. Missing.

My mind raced. We had insurance to cover each piece of art to a certain point. *Mother and Child* had its own policy, but it was irreplaceable. Aside from sentiment, it was also valuable in financial terms since it had won the Brookington Award, one of the most prestigious prizes in the sculpture world. Normally, it was stored at the college archives under lock and key, safer than my house. But I had borrowed it for this temporary exhibit.

The voice mail jingled on my phone. Sorry, Ivan. Busy having tea.

I moved over to the front door, where Tom was examining the alarm, his glasses perched on his nose. They were always sliding down. *Why didn't the alarm go off?* repeated on a continuous loop. Louise tiptoed in and stood perfectly still.

Tom glanced at me. "Looks to me like maybe the alarm wasn't set last night."

"What?" I gasped.

My brother shook his head. "Do you remember if you set it?"

Why did my face get hot while my heart galloped when I screwed up? "Must have been me. I didn't get home last night until nine-thirty after I had started the morning at seven. It was a long, exhausting day. I'm not making excuses, but I could have forgotten to set it." Taking another deep breath, I shook my head again. "I am so stupid."

Tom fussed with the alarm. "Hey, we all make mistakes. You can learn from this. Simply make sure you change your pattern to set the alarm, no matter what, before you go out any door for the night. Mistakes happen. We'll do better next time."

"Tom. *Mother and Child.* It's gone."

That was when he turned to me, pity in his eyes. "I saw that, I'm afraid."

"It's gone."

He pulled me close in a hug, a gesture that loosened a new flood of tears.

"What can I do? It was priceless. Mom, me. Now it's gone, could be forever."

He released me and put both his hands on my shoulders. "We'll find it. We'll get it back." His intense eyes softened. "Do you have a photo of it?"

"Of…of course."

"I'll need it ASAP. We'll get it out to regional art dealers and hope the thief shows up, wanting to sell it on the quiet. Art dealers hear things, and a rumor might surface that indicates someone has the sculpture to sell."

"The black-market art industry is huge. We may never see it again." I wiped away a few stray tears on my cheeks.

"We don't know that. We'll do everything we can to find it. They also took cash from Louise's office. I hope they don't know the value of Mom's sculpture and grabbed it because of the glass covering, figuring it was worth more than the others. They may not know what they have. Meanwhile, until you get security cameras, you might consider a sign on the front door that says you don't keep cash on the premises. Then make a deposit each day."

"We can make that happen." I looked at him, my thoughts swirling. My artist brain kicked in. "A small, tasteful sign at the front. Maybe Cerulean blue with black lettering."

"Yes. Tasteful. Burglars like tasteful."

I smiled through my tears, remembering everyone said he was a brilliant detective. Louise walked over to me and patted my shoulder.

My brother stared at the ceiling, lost in thought. "Could be it was kids. They'd not have much use for a sculpture. Hate to say this, but we'll need to have you and Louise come to the station to give us your fingerprints."

"Why?"

"We need to be able to exclude you from what we find. Problem is, I imagine this place has lots of prints of people coming and going. I'm not sure how much good it will do, but it's worth a try. Maybe they left prints on the cash box. We'll call in the crime scene people who'll be here for a while, so you don't have to worry about the door locks at this point. We'll get everything done so you can get back to work. You'll have to close to the public for a few days."

"Tom, please tell your people to be careful. We have artwork everywhere." He nodded.

I turned to Louise and we both sighed, thinking of all we had to do for our first regional exhibit, Home in the Heartland. Dealing with a board that wasn't keen on my lack of business experience, I had adopted the mantra, *I will show them success.* But now my mantra grew fainter. Ivan the Terrible, my nemesis, would be all over this.

I took a deep breath, straightened my back, and clicked on his voice mail.

"Ms. Madison. This is Ivan Truelove, president of your board—a board to whom you are woefully accountable. Police sirens? Scanner reports of a break-in? I'm sure you have a satisfactory explanation. Looking out my window a short time ago, I saw and heard emergency vehicles, which appeared to be dashing toward the art center location. My scanner confirms. I expect you to return my call. Quick. Efficient. SOON."

Then there was a pause, as if he were wiping some distasteful thing from his mouth.

"It goes without saying this disaster will be discussed at our upcoming meeting, along with your job status. Good day."

"This is weird. I thought my fingers would be all black with ink—you know, the way they do it in the movies when they stick your fingers on an ink pad and press them on a card."

The morning was flying by. My watch said it was almost ten as Louise and I were walking back from the police station. It was a hop, skip, and a jump from the art center, past the downtown stores, and around two quadrants of the square. "You've watched too many police shows. Those glass plates they use now give the police a scan of your prints to compare on their computers. Tom says even here in Apple Grove we're up with the times." I glanced at the parking meters. "Well, mostly."

We had a four-block walk to the art center, the temperature was perfect in the high 70s, and a light breeze stirred around us. I looked up for a moment at the blue skies and fluffy clouds, and my heart lifted as if my shoulders felt a heavy burden gone. This was the kind of summer day I remembered. We took our time, meandered along, and I studied buildings and cracked sidewalks that took me back to the years when I grew up in Apple Grove. It was no longer the bustling town I remembered. Many of the old stores like the Five and Dime were gone, and the movie theater had closed during the economic downturn in 2007. I glanced at the Tiny Tots Clothing Store window and gently nudged Louise toward the display. "Look at those kids' coloring papers in the window. It's a July 4th contest. Just think, Louise, those are our future students for our art classes."

"Judging from their final products, they'll need us."

I laughed and stared across the street at the electronic sign on the Citizen's Bank of Apple Grove. "Oh, look. They have us on their sign. 'Coming Soon…Home in the Heartland exhibit at the Adele Marsden Center for the Arts.'" Despite the June heat, a shiver coursed through my whole body. This made it real.

When I'd returned home to Apple Grove six months ago, I'd been hired to oversee the building remodel and become the executive director for this art center named for our sculptor mother. Moving back after nine years of experience in the art scene amid the chilly winters and glorious summers of Chicago, I was still feeling my way with this new job. I simply had to succeed. Seeing this bank sign was another encouraging push in the right direction.

Louise must've felt it too. "It's like a sign from heaven, Jill. We'll pull this off."

We both turned and strolled again, nearing the town square. Next to the bank was WHIM, the local radio station, and Talbert's Pharmacy.

Donna Filbert appeared in the doorway of the pharmacy looking back at someone. Then she turned and saw us on the sidewalk. "Hi, you two. Isn't it a gorgeous day?"

Louise walked over to her. "Yes, the sky is beautiful."

Donna's red curls bobbed up and down around her face as they often did when she was excited. "I've come up with ideas for two glass fusing classes. I could teach one in late August, and we'll make flags since Labor Day is in early September."

"Great idea. Louise and I were just saying it was time to line up the class schedule."

"I'm all in, and I thought in December we'd make snowmen ornaments. The kids always love to do things like that so they can give them to their parents for Christmas."

I turned the calendar in my head to late summer, trying to figure out how each class would click into place. "We're kicking things off with a beginning watercolor class and already have twenty-five people signed up for the first one. Paige Lemon, the elementary school art teacher, is going to teach three classes on consecutive Saturdays, so we could put yours on the last Saturday of August."

"Perfect. I'm so excited, you guys. I've been thinking about this for weeks. Your mom and dad would be so impressed and proud of you, Jill. A place to make art, a transformative experience for so many kids in the area." Her art teacher eyes went to some hazy place beyond my shoulder on that last statement, but I knew what she meant.

"I'm making a mental note on my calendar, and I'll write it down when I get back to work."

Donna smiled at Louise, shifting a large sack she carried. "I heard all the sirens this morning. What happened? Do you know?"

"It was the art center. We had some unwanted company overnight." Louise downplayed the situation, a script we'd agreed on should anyone ask. "A burglary, but not a big deal. Tom Madison's already been in with the police, and we're headed back now to work on our first exhibit."

"Oh, my gosh, Jill, you just got home and now this happened?"

I nodded. "It's fine. Not a problem." I looked at my watch. "We'd better get going back to work. I'll be in touch, Donna."

"Sure thing."

We said our goodbyes. I was so thrilled when she said she'd teach classes in the fall. Our autumn lineup of classes was rapidly filling up. We'd had offers from possible teachers and hundreds of hits on our new website checking for classes, and the *Apple Grove Ledger* had given us great coverage.

Louise's phone played Selena Gomez's "Bad Liar," and I wondered who that song might describe in her life.

"Hang on a minute." She moved a few feet away and sat down on a bench in front of the insurance company. This northwest quadrant of the square was a part of the town as I remembered it when I was growing up. Across the street, Sharon's Sewing Center advertised a Summer Spectacular Crafter's Sale. In front of her store windows were tubs and baskets of plastic flowers, small flags, roles of gingham and calico, and red, white, and blue garden pinwheels. My mom brought me here to make a costume for a parade I was in as a kid. In fact, it might've been the 4th of July parade.

Louise talked softly into her phone while I moved out near the curb and gazed across at the square. Eight huge American flags billowed in the breeze on the square's circular green grass. Several benches surrounded them, and, stretched between poles, a white plastic banner announced Summer Bible School at the Episcopalian Church. Despite that lovely thought, the veiled threat of Ivan Truelove lurked at the back of my mind. I pushed it away and looked across the street at the collection of different architectural styles of the stores.

Sharon Green came out of her sewing shop with an armload of artificial flowers to put in a huge wooden tub. While Louise was on the phone, I figured I'd stop over and talk with her. A few weeks ago we'd discussed a space in our art center for the weaver's guild. They'd lost their "home" in the library's back room because the librarian needed the space for a new collection donated from an estate sale.

She saw me crossing the street and walked over to meet me. "Hi, Jill. Your offer still open to use a room in your art center for our weaving?"

"Absolutely. We'd love to have you there, and I have space in the back room where you can set up your looms and meet on whatever day you choose."

"I talked with our group and they were so excited they were ready to move in before you even opened up. You're a sign from heaven at a time when we were feeling orphaned. Are you sure we won't be in the way? Those looms take a lot of room, and I know you're just getting started. I'd hate to cause you any growing pains."

"Are you kidding? Your weaving projects would be a huge plus. I'm already thinking about how we could not only display some of your fabric pieces but also have an event designated where you could show the public your craft. Think that might work?"

Sharon's eyes twinkled and her smile sparkled. "It's been a long time since we've had any kind of programs or even places to teach and explain what we do. I imagine you're thinking about working with the schools in the area too?"

"We are. I'm trying not to get ahead of myself. First, an exhibit. Next, we start classes, and finally, we plan for school connections and big events. I think I'd like to start a group of seniors too. Maybe a monthly meeting with various kinds of discussions and speakers who work in different art fields. We have a good-sized senior population."

"Well, you're thinking up a storm, aren't you? We haven't had such excitement since Jim Ruskin started his cooking school and caught the building on fire."

My reaction must have been obvious because she put her hands out and came closer. "Oh, no. I didn't mean your art center might catch fire. I meant it's exciting to know we'll have so many artsy, craftsy things to see and do."

"After Jim Ruskin's story, I'll check the fire extinguishers as soon as I walk in the door. Thanks, Sharon." I turned and looked across the street. Louise and I had better get moving.

"See you soon, and I'll get in touch about the weaving guild."

"Thanks, Jill. Can't wait."

Louise was ending her conversation as I showed up. "Don't call again, please," and she stood to walk the half block with me back to the center.

"Everything okay?"

Louise blew out a long breath and shook her head. "A guy I met on a dating site."

"Good news or bad?"

"Yesterday's news. I expected a six-foot-two, dark-haired hunk who was a weightlifter, and I got a frog—a five-foot-seven, white-haired, overweight, former hippie with lots of chains around his neck."

"Does this mean you're done with the dating-site battleground?"

"Heck no. You never know. Could be the frog will be prince charming next time. You know, hope springs eternal."

We crossed the street and walked past the yellow-taped window of the art center to the alley door. As we entered, we drew determination from each other to work our little fingers off the rest of the day. I'd make this center a success, and if it meant dealing with Ivan, I'd remember my goal—to honor my parents with art possibilities for the people of our little town. After talking to Donna and Sharon, I straightened my shoulders and lifted my chin. *Bring it on, Ivan!*

Chapter Two

The crime scene people were finishing up. Tom had told us to scan the building and see if we could see anything else out of place or absent.

"Louise." I'd walked all through the gallery, and I was at the back, past the offices and restrooms. "Would you please clean up that fingerprint powder now that they're done?"

"Yes. Anything else?" came from the far end of the hallway.

"Now that I think of it, did you leave the door to the basement open? Have you been down there?"

"No."

"Maybe it was the crime scene people. I'm sure I closed it last night. Why would they go to the basement? It's empty."

"I'll wait here if you want to check."

I considered my feelings about the gloomy area. "You know how I love to go into the basement. No windows. Musty smell. Dark. Scary. Want to flip for it?"

Her laughter was clear. "Nah. You're the boss. If you want, I'll wait up at the top of the stairs."

I gritted my teeth. "Fine. I'll check." I hated dark, musty-smelling places. Something about this basement gave me the creeps. I envisioned a murder victim bricked up behind a wall like Poe's "The Cask of Amontillado," a story I remembered reading in high school.

Five minutes later, I was back upstairs again. I couldn't imagine anyone would believe we kept artwork or money in the basement. It was mostly cement floor and empty space. Perhaps someday we'd be able to make it usable. A light had been left on in the farthest area from the stairway. Must have been the crime scene technicians. I always turned off lights. I heard Dad's voice. "Do you think money grows on trees? Turn off the lights."

Time to work on the Heartland exhibit. I stood at my office door, staring in dismay. Boxes, files, sculptures, and books overflowed the shelves. My desk was cluttered with folders accompanied by odd objects with a relationship to my past week. A whiteboard on one wall listed my jobs for the week and the month. My eyes scanned it momentarily.

The first exhibit was only a start, but, for the board it was a test to see if I could do the job. My mom's center would be open to the small town of Apple Grove, a town of 15,000 souls and a small piece of heaven surrounded by corn and bean fields. But my parents and I believed man couldn't live on corn and beans alone. My art center would be a teaching hub for the children and adults of the town to learn about the arts. Sure, we also had an art gallery for enjoyment, but the main thrust of my plan was education. Classes, exhibits, plays, movies, an artist-in-residence, and programs for various ages.

I sat in my chair and thought about yesterday. I'd had grants to write, phone calls to make, websites to research for grant information, calls to set up meetings with possible sponsors, rules to write for the regional exhibit, crumbs on the children's room carpet to clean up after cracker-eating children, and separate interviews with three of the people on the center board about hiring an accountant.

By nine, I'd missed two meals and was cleaning the toilets in the restrooms. While people might think "curator" sounded classy, in this case, a curator was a circus juggler. Someday, somehow, we'd be able to afford a custodian. An accountant for a year, maybe, would also help, until we were on our feet. I tapped my fingers on my desk and thought about the burglary. I might lose my job because of my forgetfulness. Mid-self-flagellation, I was staring at the whiteboard when I heard music. Strange.

It was my cell phone cheerfully singing, "Welcome to the Jungle," and I picked it up from my love seat.

"Andy?"

"Yeah, sweet sister. It is I, your amazingly young and terribly successful entrepreneur-brother."

I smiled and mentally rewrote his description. My perpetually adolescent, occasionally irresponsible, thirty-six-year-old brother always cheered me up. He and his partner, Lance Hughes, owned a popular gift shop in town, and I was sure he was calling me from work. A bit of silliness from my brother would be welcome right now.

"Andy. Hope you're having a better day than I am." Translation...no police, no burglary, and no Ivan Truelove phone sermons.

"Inventory sucks. I hate it. I wish your burglar would break in and steal the ugly chartreuse vase Lance decided would be perfect for the store." He paused. "You all right, Sis?"

"I'd be better if you knew any fences in town who might sell *Mother and Child* back to me."

"I'll check with my underworld contacts. Still coming to the pub tonight?"

"Wouldn't miss it, despite a burglary and construction workers showing up today to begin tearing things down around me."

"The *Apple Grove Ledger* had a featured article today about your work at the art center. I didn't realize the Lowry Building was so old. They quoted you as saying you'd have to 'ramp up the structural integrity of the old building.' I didn't know you knew phrases like 'structural integrity.' When did that happen? Thirty years old but you talk like a veteran of 'structural integrity?'"

"I got a degree, remember? An Arts Management degree."

"Not a degree in building renovation? I must admit the information about how you'll turn the building into a twenty-first-century safe structure was kind of interesting. Besides, the description of the impending work in the basement sounded impossible. Totally."

"Andy Madison, I need a little respect here. I'm not your five-year-old sister. I'm grown up, and I'm confident this will all work out." *Now, that was a whopper.*

"I'm just kidding. I've got your back. In fact, we'll play a song just for you tonight."

"Oh." I smiled and brightened at his generosity. "One of my favorites?"

"I believe the hugely popular country hit, 'The Board Fired Me, but Now I'm Free.'"

"Very funny." I smiled, despite myself. "I'll be there."

I punched off, noting the date on my phone screen. June 10. I'd looked forward to this day all week because I'd planned to continue working on my first art exhibit ever, and then it would be off to my friend Angie's pub, where Andy was performing with his band. Still plenty of time before the first exhibit. At times, my brother could be ridiculously difficult...but other times he was my wonderful brother. Families.

I shook my head. This break-in was a distraction. Ivan could stick his head in a bucket. Tom would do his job and find my mother's sculpture. The Home in the Heartland exhibit should be my priority—kind of sentimental since I was home too.

I studied the photograph of *Mother and Child*. My mother gazed at me. It was her eyes. So much love. I grabbed a tissue, wiped my face, and blew my nose. Enough. My gaze moved to the calendar on my wall. The board meeting was scheduled on the twenty-first, eleven days from now, and it promised to be a doozy after today. Eleven days. Tom might find the sculpture by then. My mood brightened. I took a deep breath, squared my shoulders, and repeated to myself, *I will show them success.*

Chapter Three

After I hurried back from an early lunch, I focused on the information about the basement and the second part of the renovation. I had hired a company located an hour away. Not only had their references checked out, but they also specialized in preservation of sites with historical value. Once they finished in the basement, I would have a few months' reprieve before they came back to work on the second floor. That was exactly what I needed.

I texted Tom to ask if he had any leads yet on my mother's sculpture. After several minutes, he texted me back, **not yet.** A man of few words was my brother, so texting suited him well. Ivan the Terrible should have such talent.

My conversation with the construction general manager, Jim Blackstone, had been several weeks ago when he came to inspect the site before bidding on the job. I spent another ten minutes reacquainting myself with the plans we'd discussed over the phone and the notes I'd taken. The Lowry Building. Tom and his wife, Mary, used it as bait to persuade me to return. The crumbling building was vacant and—voila!—they had me. How could I resist an art center that would give back to Apple Grove in the form of art education while it kept my mother's name alive? It involved mountains of work and sleepless nights, but I loved it.

Louise knocked on my door. She stuck her head in, and when I turned around because I sensed she was still there, her expression and hand gesture indicated "Ooo, la, la."

I expected a group of construction men, so I wasn't surprised. Walking into the hallway, I figured we'd better talk outside my tiny office. I could see why Louise was ahhing. The four muscular guys were eye candy.

"It's finally nice to meet you and put a person to your voice," said the oldest of the four. "I'm Matthew Brandise, the site manager."

They stood in a semicircle as each of them introduced himself.

"Nice to meet you, Matthew." I put my hand out and hoped he would be gentle. He was.

"I'm Mark."

"I'm Luke."

"I'm Jesse."

"And I'm surprised. They don't call you John?" I imagine they'd heard that reaction before, especially since Jesse's face turned bright red. Cute. A grown man blushing. I looked from one to the other and thought *every muscle in the western world is in my art center*. Matthew was taller than I'd expected since I imagined he might have to navigate tiny openings underground in some jobs. Maybe six-foot, with auburn hair—a lovely carmine with an ivory black tint pulled into a ponytail I'd noticed when he turned toward Jesse.

Mark was short and built like a fire hydrant. Luke, dark stubble on his chin, seemed the youngest, with a Cubs hat turned backward over his dark, curly hair. Jesse was obviously a weightlifter. He was maybe thirty or so with massive arms bulging with muscles.

I took a deep breath. "Well. Let's get to it. Follow me. I'll show you the worksite." I led the four to the back of the building, past the offices, and down a small set of stairs to a door. "This is the only door to the basement. These stairs are the original wooden planks from the eighteen hundreds. No handrail, so you'll have to be careful." Taking another deep breath, I straightened my back and tried to ignore my usual feeling of dread. I stopped on the landing at the top of the stairs and switched on an overhead bulb to illuminate a set of six steps with wide boards and, as advertised, no railing. With heels on, I had to be cautious. "Watch your head."

Once the four of them reached the bottom of the stairs, I moved to the side of the sizable but colorless room and pulled on the chain of another light bulb.

"The lighting isn't great, but I figure you'll bring your own light equipment."

"Yes, ma'am." Matthew looked around, his eyes opening wider as he examined the end of the room, closest to the street. "This is quite an old building. When did you say it was built?"

"Eighteen seventy, right after the Civil War. At first, it was a mercantile exchange that sold everything, kind of like a department store. Before that, the land had been an apple orchard."

The four men fanned out through the musty, airless room, checking out the stone walls. They were 19th-century brick, clinging together with 1870s plaster, now pushed out in gray, cloud-like shapes. The apostles, as I'd decided to call them, paid attention to several windows that had been near ground level but, at some time, had been bricked up. The building had settled considerably on the south side. The guys examined various spots where newer plaster had been added between rows of bricks.

Matthew turned to me. "We'll try to keep the original in mind as we work to reinforce it. Probably metal plates and wood beams, as Jim discussed."

"Perfect. I'd like it to have structural integrity but also honor the past."

He pointed at the plaster in one section of the wall. "This is like a topographical map of one hundred fifty years of wear, tear, and the ravages of nature. Like the lines and wrinkles in an elderly person's face, remembering what happened in each of those years."

"Exactly. That's why I hired you."

He had an eye for line and shadow detail like I did.

They sized up the job ahead and touched various plaster parts of the walls. Their examination done, they all gathered again in the middle of the room.

Matthew said, "Well, Ms. Madison—"

"Jill."

"Jill. I know Blackstone talked with you extensively. I agree with him this will be a lot tougher without paperwork. No blueprints or diagrams of the building."

Anxiety crept into my chest again...a tightness as if I couldn't breathe. "I understand. I've already dealt with too many unknowns in the front sidewalk. Jim Blackstone handled it all so well. He never budged an inch from his original statement saying *we* would deal with whatever came along.

He was much calmer than I was. Problems cropped up we didn't expect, and I'm still bruised and battered."

Matthew turned to me, shaking his head. "I see. Get ready for more of the same. Without plans, we don't know what's behind the brick. Maybe structural beams, maybe spaces, maybe nothing."

Maybe a dead body a la Edgar Allan Poe. This didn't make me feel confident. Not a step about the renovation of this huge building had worked the way we originally figured. "I could use some positive news. Next week my board will meet, and I'd like to be able to tell them we know what we're doing. I need to say all is well. On time. Under budget." I laughed with them on that one. "No, seriously. It would be nice to have a positive report to give them."

They had no idea how essential good news would be. I had held my breath on the front sidewalk project, and now I was doing the same over the start of this part. Unbidden, the pointy bald skull of Ivan the Terrible came into my thoughts but no words escaped his mouth. It was just his usual look of dismay plus a deliberate shake of his head. I would need good news to counterbalance the burglary.

Matthew nodded. "We'll bring equipment in through the back entrance upstairs and the heavy-duty stuff tomorrow."

"Perfect." I turned to leave, and as I ascended the stairs, the sounds of their voices discussing where to start digging gradually faded away.

Back in my office, I checked my whiteboard with my jobs for the day. I needed to write a prospectus with rules for the exhibit, list the prizes from sponsors, find a juror to judge entries, and add all to the prospectus so it could go to the printer for a proof. That was all. I would write as much as possible before I contacted the juror I had in mind. We needed to work on an exhibit poster to be strategically placed in locations around town. I should also keep working on the upcoming class schedule. The apostles' voices in the basement, and sometimes their footsteps echoed as they went up and down the stairs with equipment, but the noise wasn't deafening yet.

I reached for my phone...and couldn't find it. This happened a lot. Walking next door to Louise's office, I pointed. She handed me her phone. I texted my friend, Angie, and she located my phone at the front of the building because it appeared to be in the street. Her cell phone could find the approximate location of my phone with GPS, saving me on too many occasions to count. We both figured it was the best idea we ever had. Chalk up another favor I owed her.

As I headed down the hallway, I noticed the framed art arranged on the wall. One was slightly off balance, so I stopped to fix it. My OCD self. These were paintings and photographs by local people we featured throughout our art center. We sold their work on consignment in our gift shop near the front as people walked in, and Louise handled the sales of local art pieces.

An oil painting by a local artist, Anne Metcalfe, made me think about my own artwork. I'd used oils since I was a teenager, but now I hadn't painted for several years. I couldn't deal with the emotions painting conjured up. Too much had happened. Staying away from a canvas kept all of that at bay. Still, this morning I had walked past the family room at home, where I'd stored the tubes of pigments and canvases I'd brought back from Chicago. They were taped closed, brooding at my absence, putting a bit of pressure on me to go back to my old emotional outlet. For now, they brooded on without me.

A few minutes later I went back to my office, phone in hand, smiling in amusement as I thought about the first names of the construction workers. I glanced at the end of the hallway, where the door to the basement was open, and suddenly I heard loud voices. They must be arguing. Then silence.

I walked over to the doorway and stuck my head in the opening. "Everything all right, Matthew?"

Silence.

"I think you'd better come here, Ms. Madison."

Really? He had called me Jill. Now this. Something was up. "I'm coming."

I started down the stairs, wondering what they could have been arguing about. Picking my steps with care, I imagined the headlines. *Woman Found Dead in Art Center Basement. Cause of Death Poor Shoe Selection.* It was eerily quiet now. When I successfully reached the floor once again, without a broken neck, all four guys stood at the far end of the room, where the cement floor ended and the dirt floor began. Matthew looked up, signaling me to come over.

My heels clicked on the cement, stopping when I tiptoed onto the dirt floor. The workers stepped aside and pointed. I glanced into the hole they'd dug, wondering why on earth they needed me. Then my eyes focused on what appeared to be long, skeletal fingers, white with a bit of ivory black, lying just out of the dirt. I leaned over and stared, squinting. A few inches farther was the top of what could be a skull.

"Oh, my God—" I managed to say, and Matthew caught me as I became lightheaded.

Chapter Four

I was swimming. My eyes were shut tight to keep out the murky water. Gray, cadmium yellow light, with a bit of ivory black mixed in. Somewhere, far away, I heard Tom's voice. I didn't want to open my eyes because I was afraid. Falling, falling deeper into the pond on my grandparents' farm. I was six. It was restful, but I realized I had to struggle to get back to my brother. I heard his voice and forced my eyes to open a little. Everything was blurry, so I closed them again. Someone patted my arm. Opening my eyes a tiny slit, I saw Tom, then Louise. I closed my eyes again. Then, opening them, I recognized my desk across the room. I was in my office at the art center. Louise patted my arm, her expression worried.

I stared at Tom, who stood over me, concern in his eyes. "What? What happened?"

"You'll be fine. You got lightheaded and passed out."

I scrunched up my eyes and tried to remember. "I did?"

"Yes."

"How? How did you get here?" I took a couple of shallow breaths. "Why are you here?" My mind went in multiple directions, as if I were in a maze, confused by every corner.

I saw him glance at Louise, who sat next to me in a chair pulled over to the love seat. They must have moved an awful lot of stuff to put me on this love seat.

Louise leaned over. "Tom's here because I called him when one of the guys brought you up from the basement." She smiled broadly. "You didn't have to faint to get Jesse to carry you upstairs in those gorgeous, muscular arms."

"Oh, I missed that?"

Now Tom smiled, concern gone, his "brother look" back again. "The workers found a body in the basement. Buried. Do you remember?"

I nodded slowly. "Sounds familiar. I seem to recall skeleton fingers. Halloween? How could we have a dead body in my basement? Who would be so inconsiderate?"

"Just take it easy. I think you're still recovering from the shock. Whoever this person was, he didn't walk down there and bury himself. I came after the nine-one-one call from Louise and sent for the coroner, Abe Calipher. He's in the basement now. I'll go down and see what I can do since I know you'll be fine. Louise, you're in charge."

"I'm getting really experienced at calling nine-one-one. I've never had such an exciting job. Two emergencies in less than a week. I may have to ask for hazard pay."

She glanced at Tom and made a gesture that meant he could leave. They both looked at me. Tom left to go downstairs, and Louise muttered, "I think I'll go grab you a bottle of water."

I pulled myself to an upright position and stood up to test my legs. They were fine. Where was everybody? Peeking out my doorway, I saw yellow tape on the front windows at the other end of the building. Just then, Louise came back with water and a cookie.

I sat down. "Where are the guys?"

"Tom questioned them. All they knew is that they stopped digging quickly when they saw those fingers. He sent them off to lunch, telling them you'd let them know when they could work again. I suppose he mostly wanted them out of the way since there isn't much room to stand around the—the body or skeleton or whatever you call a person like that." She handed me the cookie after I took a couple of swallows of water. "Here, eat this."

"I'm fine, Louise. I didn't faint because I felt hungry." I bit my lower lip and thought about this skeleton. It must be someone from a long time ago since the building hadn't been occupied for twenty years before I moved in. I saw what looked like a skeleton hand sticking out of the ground. Thank goodness I didn't see the rest. I'd never seen a dead person who'd been buried a long time. My phone rang. I recognized, once again, the number for Ivan Truelove. I needed to go to his house at night, find that scanner, and bury it. Sighing, I punched the "accept" button.

"Hello again, Mr. Truelove."

"Ms. Madison. What in the name of…of…" he sputtered, "of all that's holy is happening at our art center? All I've heard this morning are alarms and sirens. What have you done now?"

Why would he think this was my fault? I took a deep breath. "Well, Mr. Truelove, you see, it's like this—"

"If this newest emergency doesn't involve a murder, I won't understand why the nine-one-one calls seem to be emanating from your art center. Did someone walk in and threaten to destroy the place?"

"Well, Mr. Truelove…It's a bit messier than that."

Louise rolled her eyes.

"Messier? Have you been invaded by armed terrorists? I warn you that I'm losing my patience. Do I have to come over there?"

I panicked. That was the last thing we needed, this hissing snake of an accountant with his bald head, spindly legs, sensible shoes, and polka-dotted bow tie over here putting himself in charge. I remembered the silence. He was still waiting. "Ah, no, Mr. Truelove."

"No, what?"

"No, you don't need to come over. Everything is under control." I heard Tom and the coroner ascending the basement stairs. "I—uh—have friends over here to help. Professionals. It's all good. I must go now. Goodbye." I tapped the end button but figured soon he would hear about the body in the basement. How could I make this sound less catastrophic?

My board of directors was divided over their confidence in me. Even though Mom and Dad had had banker friends in town, my attempts to yank a renovation loan from their clenched fists hadn't been easy. Because I was thirty, I think I scared them when I decided to tackle the 19th-century Lowry Building for a new art center. That was exactly what I had encountered on this whole project. People of little faith. I took a calming breath. I'd show them.

24

While I was considering this, Tom came back upstairs with Doctor Calipher. I'd never seen the doc without a carryout cup of coffee and immaculate clothing. His most noticeable features were a pair of dark, bushy eyebrows like caterpillars over pale blue eyes and a small gold stud in his left ear. I'd known Abe's name for ages because he was a local doctor that everyone liked, and he'd been coroner since before my parents died.

They were just outside my office door, so Louise and I shamelessly eavesdropped.

Abe's expression was serious. "We have an unattended, unidentified body. I called the state police. Should be on their way. They'll take over the death scene until they clear it to you and me."

Unattended? Someone had to be there to bury the guy. I suppressed a giggle at that thought. Louise and I both listened, staring at each other, not saying a word.

"When do you think that will be?"

"Don't know yet. I left it as is. The state boys will work the scene and release it to me for an autopsy. They'll document it all, shoot video and photos, and write a description of the burial area. If any evidence needs to be taken to the lab, they'll do it. Oh, and check for fingerprints."

I started to giggle again but caught myself and stuck my fist in my mouth. Fingerprints? Where did they hope to find fingerprints? On a shovel I hadn't noticed conveniently left in the basement?

"Thanks, Doc. We don't normally dig up bodies in buildings around here."

"Not since I've been coroner. Accidents, like your parents—sadly—yes. No murders. Could this anonymous person need a space to bury a body but he didn't have the money to pay a funeral home or cemetery? Strange, but it happens."

"Have you ruled out murder?"

"Haven't ruled out a single possibility. We'll have a more definitive picture once the autopsy's done. Like I said, who knows?"

"Where are we on procedure after they're done?"

"Once they're done, they'll release the body to me. I'll take more photos and move it out on a gurney. Brought a body bag, and my technician will show up soon. It's your crime scene, so you can give the all-clear when you finish."

"Fair enough. I'll talk with my sister. The workers will have to wait through the weekend at least to come back to work."

"Your sister?"

"She runs the art center. Seems odd, I know, but I'm the only detective on the police force, and the body was found in her space. Can't be helped she's part of my family. She's not involved."

The coroner nodded. "I'll go out to the alley and wait for the state police." He crushed his paper cup and dropped it in the wastebasket by the alley door on his way out.

I quickly ended my eavesdropping, moved away from the door, and sat on the love seat.

Tom entered my office. "Great. Your face has a bit more animation, isn't quite so pale, and I'd say you're able to talk now."

"Louise and I would like to know what happens next."

Tom studied us, and his calm, detective-like demeanor settled around us. "Well, here's the bottom line." He moved over to my desk and sat down. "They'll have the body out by later this afternoon, and when the workers return, you can talk with them to make arrangements."

"What arrangements can I make? When will they be able to come back to work?"

"Today and tomorrow are out of the question. Monday will be the earliest you can open. The art center will have to be closed the rest of today and tomorrow. That doesn't mean you and Louise can't be here. You can work as long as you don't go into the basement."

Louise started laughing. "Like Jill loves to go into the basement anyway."

I narrowed my eyes and pursed my lips. "I knew something was scary about our basement. Every time I went down there, my heart sped up and my arms began to shake."

My brother smiled. "Well, I don't know about that. Could be the body's been there a long time. I think Calipher will decide to release it to Bloomington, where they have a forensic pathologist, and if they need an expert to deal with old bones—which they will—they'll call in a forensic anthropologist. Once they figure out the age, the sex, how long it's been buried, the manner of death and the cause, they'll try to identify who it is."

"How can they identify someone who's been buried who knows how long?"

"Dental records, DNA, any broken bones, various databases of missing persons. They'll work with me here locally. Once we have an ID—if we get one—we'll have to talk with anyone still alive who's related."

"How long will that search take?"

He seemed to tick off all those ideas in his head. "Databases a week or so. DNA longer—maybe four."

"Weeks?" My impatience was obvious. "Tom. Once the newspapers get this, the publicity will be terrible for the art center. We're a fledgling organization here."

He shook his head. "Sorry, Jill. We have to approach things methodically."

I sighed, shaking my head. I loved my brother. He was a great detective, but speed wasn't his strongest trait. Dotting the I's and crossing the T's. Meanwhile, the board would hear "dead body" and they wouldn't buy the suggestion it was an art installation. I already figured Ivan the Terrible would show up when he heard the news.

Louise stood up. "Maybe Jill and I should leave, get coffee, and come back."

"Sounds like a plan," Tom agreed. "Take your time. Doc and I will be here all day. I'd guess they'll get the body out by this evening."

"Thanks, Tom, for coming here fast." I felt almost normal now, my lightheadedness gone and my giggling subsided. Shock. I must have been in shock. "Louise is right. We'll leave and come back."

He turned toward me and pointed. "The side door through the alley. The front is locked with crime scene tape for a day or two."

He left for the basement, and Louise went to get her purse in her office. That left me alone with my thoughts. Looking at the photo of my parents, I shook my head. *Oh, my God. The theft of my irreplaceable piece of sculpture connecting me to you, Mom. A dead person in the basement. A meeting with my board in a little over a week. An exhibit in five weeks. What's next? A plague of locusts?*

After the coffee shop, I was ready for a quiet afternoon. Tom told me the state police had come and finished their work, but he was still poking around in the basement, dealing with evidence and documenting the scene while he waited for the coroner to return. Louise and I worked on the list of items we needed to get done, some for the exhibit, others for the general operation of the art center. I worked on grants we'd use for specific projects with school districts and sponsorships. Only a few times did I think about those skeletal fingers.

With all this work, the afternoon moved fast. By four, I told Louise I'd lock up and she could go home early and have time with her kids. I was all alone and practically jumped out of my chair when my phone vibrated and began playing, "Welcome to the Jungle." Andy.

"Hi, Andy."

"Just called to find out if any more people are dying to get into your art center." His voice was perfectly solemn.

I took a deep breath. "Andy, this is nothing to joke about. Tom already lectured me on my inappropriate behavior. Where did you hear about this?"

"I heard about the big excitement from a customer, and my little sister's in the middle of it all. Way to go!"

I sat back. "Oh, my gosh. What can I do? It'll be all over town, and you can bet the board—including 'Keep it Under Control' Ivan—will hear about it."

"I called to see how you are, little sis."

I thought about his motive for a moment. This was a new Andy, worried about me. "It's horrifying. Poor soul. No clue about who might have wanted to bury a body in our basement. I don't want to seem unkind, but I also wonder how this publicity will affect the art center."

"Hasn't been a great week, has it? Despite the body in the basement, I think we have one piece of exceptional news."

"Oh? What's that?"

"I've heard it said no publicity is bad publicity."

"You mean you think a dead body will entice people in?"

"Of course. How often do we have a murder in town? You could sell tickets for a tour of the basement, or you could have a dinner theater production of

'The Body in the Basement.' Very Agatha Christie-like."

"They haven't called this a murder, but if there were a production, I know who I'll volunteer for the corpse."

"Oh, a certain board president? It means I'm off the hook for a change."

"Maybe for now. We'll see."

We both hung up and I glanced at the photo of my family. How could I have two such different brothers—John Wayne versus Looney Toons? I focused on their pictures. Tom, his face white like our father's, and Andy, his skin tones a soft honey like mine. Both of us favored the ebony coloring of our mother. We didn't look much like other families in town when I was growing up. Two older brothers. Andy provided comic relief when I sorely needed it, and Tom's protectiveness toward me had tightened over the past few years. I often had to remind him I was an adult.

About that time, I heard the door to the alley open. I guessed it was the coroner again with his aide, or whatever he called the guy. When I went out to lunch with Louise, people had been gathered at the front of the building staring in through the windows between swaths of police tape. Maybe Andy was right. Once we reopened, we might see an increase in people checking us out, but not for art gifts.

I turned as a crash reverberated on the side of my office wall. It was Dr. Abe, who somewhat clumsily turned the corner with a gurney and black body bag he and his helper were taking down to the basement. A brown tarp sat folded on top of it. They carried a mixture of dark colors in their articles of death. I walked over to the door, silently watching their progress.

A cheerful Abe looked over at me. "Shouldn't be too long now. We'll be out of here in no time."

Why are coroners always cheerful?

Tom was still in the basement. I didn't even like the air in the basement, and now I shivered as I considered the times I'd gone downstairs walking near, and maybe over, a dead body. That raised goosebumps.

I went back to my desk to work, but my phone rang again, this time with the "Anytime You Need a Friend" ringtone. Happy party memories from summers in high school, and always there when we needed each other, Angie.

"Hi, Angie."

"OMG, Jill. Are you all right?" Her voice was a shade lower than hysteria. "I heard about the sirens from one of the customers. Rumors abound. There was a dead body in your basement. True?"

I sat back, touched by her concern. Ugly news traveled faster than the internet in small towns. "Oh, Angie. Why did I ever decide to be the curator at this art center? And yes, they found someone buried in my basement."

"You need me to come over there? I will. Right now."

I hesitated and thought how much better I'd feel with Angie here. I'd sent Louise home an hour ago. After a few seconds, I decided I was being selfish. I glanced at the clock on the wall. It was five, and she'd need to be with her husband, Wiley, at their bar business. "Nah. I'm fine."

"If you want me to come over to your house after work, I can. All ears. I can listen."

"Thanks. You're my best bud."

"Jill Madison, I hear a quiver in your voice."

"No, it's gone now. Seriously, I'll be fine. If I'm up to it, I'll come by after work. I had planned to before all—all this."

"Sure. You know where to find me. I'm only a phone call away, well, that is, if you can find your phone."

I heard footsteps, heavy, slow ones, on the basement stairs. "Gotta go. I think they're taking the body out." Words I never thought I'd hear myself say.

I stood in the doorway and Tom's back emerged first; next, the gurney and Abe's helper on the other end, the tarp thrown over the body bag. I rushed ahead of them to open the alley door. Evidently, the local television station had a reporter outside with a camera operator. Once they'd moved the gurney out and put it in the coroner's van, Tom came back in.

My eyes scanned his face for worry and exhaustion. "What can I do to help you, Tom?"

He brushed his hand through his hair and wiped the sweat from his forehead with his other hand. "I think we're finished for now. I need to put tape across the door to the basement. No one—and I mean no one—goes down there."

"Got it. Don't worry. I'll tell Louise when she comes in tomorrow."

"I need to go downstairs first and pick up an evidence bag. Jewelry." He walked past me down the hallway, headed for the basement door.

"Do you mean it was a woman? Or was it a man's ring or watch?" I called to him as he came back up the steps.

"Don't know yet, but we'll see what the autopsy says." Tom sighed and collected the evidence bag from the floor after he taped the door shut. The tape said "No entry by order of the Apple Grove PD."

"Autopsy results will be next. I'm headed back to the station. Lock up well tonight."

"Why more than any other night? Do you think more dead people are down there waiting to get out?"

He turned, staring at me as if he didn't know me. I had pushed it too far, and he was exhausted. Uh oh. I knew that look. A lecture.

"Jill. You're my sister, and I love you. I want to keep you as far away from this as possible." He paused. That moment told me he was thinking of his wife, Mary, who would scold him for what he was about to say next, and I could see the wheels shift in his head. "I don't know who was buried in your basement. I pray it's no one from town, nor anyone any of us would know. A person from a long time ago. This is what I think. Everyone will work hard to put the pieces together and bring justice to this victim, no matter who he was."

"Justice?" I thought for a second. "Yes, you're right since someone must have buried her or him. I'm sorry. I should have been more respectful. You're right." I dropped my guilty head.

"I'm tired. We have a lot of pieces of the puzzle to put together—dental records, DNA, identification, I hope. People to interview. If you keep your eyes on the prize, your exhibit, and use tomorrow to get quality time in without interruptions from the public, you'll find your life will get back to normal again by Monday. We'll leave you in peace, but the crime scene needs to stay as it is until Monday when I'm done."

That was one thing I loved about Tom. Mr. Sober Sides. Never missed a chance to give me helpful advice. Really. Not sure I was excited about his ridiculously 1950s overprotective male attitude toward me—a woman who could take care of herself. However, I walked over to him and gave him a hug. "Thanks, Tom."

"Are you ready to go? Why don't we lock up and call it a day?"

He waited while I gathered my things and took one look back at the basement door.

I glanced at the glass in the alley door, the ever-present television cameras waiting for any change, and I muttered to myself, "News at Eleven. Like we need this."

Chapter Five

I parked my car, checked the time on my phone, and walked toward the heavy metal and glass doors at Angie and her husband's bar. It was called Priscilla's Pub after their pet Akita. Her husband, Wiley Emerson, had designed and built a place of honor—a pink sleep bed with a mixture of white and rose red shag faux fur—near the end of the bar for princess Priscilla. Their business had done well for seven years now.

The façade of the bar had two plate glass windows. The left one had been broken and replaced a few times. A pink neon "Open" sign hung in the window next to the front door.

Once inside, I stood for a moment and let my eyes get accustomed to the glowing soft lights. The buzz of conversations was loud. The crowd was the usual blue-collar group, a mix of millennials and thirty-somethings. They were scattered along the bar, but the back booths and tables were filled with customers squeezed into them, swigging beers and eating peanuts.

Many of these drinkers were employed by small stores or businesses around Apple Grove. We didn't have huge corporations or warehouses, so we were a town of small businesses. What we did have were welders, body shop workers, electricians, plumbers, carpenters, tree removers, landscapers, various college employees, and clerks and salespeople for a decent range of businesses downtown.

Several circles of people gathered in the dance area by the booths, talking in small groups. Blue jeans, shorts, T-shirts, or vintage pieces were the uniform of the day. Lots of red jerseys for Cardinal fans and blue hats for Cub fans. Near the bar, people sat or stood, waiting for drinks from Wiley or a young man they'd hired for the summer.

Seldom did I have rules in my life. However, one was for sure. I never went to a bar I'd call a dive. I defined "dive" as a place where it was dark when I walked in, but if I saw it in the light of day, I might throw up because the darkness hid the dirt and various stains and ugliness that defied naming. My own standard had stood the test of time. Angie called it my puke rule.

That wasn't the way I'd ever describe Angie and Wiley's bar. The crystal glasses shone, and the garnish trays, stemware racks, and sinks were polished to perfection. Various sizes, shapes, and colors of liquor bottles were lined neatly along the brick wall behind the bar. Napkin holders were placed at intervals, and clean towels hung within reach. Metal stools with wooden seats matched the highly polished cherrywood bar.

Priscilla's had five beers on tap—the taps lined up like soldiers—halfway down the bar. My eyes were drawn to the walls where the flat-screen televisions were tuned to sports. At intervals between them, framed photos of the hometown teams stood out from the brick wall. A small-town Apple Grove atmosphere. We weren't in Chicago anymore, Toto.

Strolling over to the bar, I sat on a nearby stool, setting my slate blue clutch on the bar's shiny-smooth surface. Angie was talking to a couple of people at the other end, all of them laughing. She could talk to anyone while I was a bit more reticent. I caught Wiley's eye, and he sauntered toward me with a glass of my favorite beer. He smiled and pushed the tall glass across the bar in front of me. "Hi, beautiful!"

I still remembered the first time I met Wiley. I was home on a visit that summer from upper Iowa, where I was in college, and Angie went with me to the county fair. She brought along this tall drink of a guy. Wiley Emerson. Angie was working at the front desk of the *Apple Grove Ledger*, one of a series of jobs she'd suffered through after high school, and Wiley had gone in wanting to place an ad. Angie was smitten, but she was also ready to settle down. Unlike me, she'd never wanted to leave Apple Grove. Marriage was on her docket. I was about to finish college, and she was looking for romance.

"Like a lightning strike," she'd told me. "I know we've cynically pooh-

poohed stupidity in our fellow humans, but I'm telling you, Jill, love happens in a split second. I have to eat my words since I made fun of other people who claimed that."

I'd asked all the appropriate questions a best friend and possible future maid-of-honor should ask, and I hoped against hope Angie wouldn't decide on a pink-netting-and-ruffled concoction for the bridesmaids' dresses at her future wedding. I could see Cupid's arrow had hit the target. Wiley was a charmer who ticked all the right boxes. Our friend, Carolyn, was supposed to be in the wedding too, the third of "the three musketeers" from high school, but she'd left town. A year later, we walked down the aisle, me in the ugly pink dress with, yes, pink netting and ruffles. Angie was in a long, tapered, too-low-cut bridal gown, stepping on pink and white rose petals. I tried not to laugh at that picture. Instead, I liked to think of it as a noble sacrifice I made for my friend.

I shook the overwhelmingly pink picture out of my head. "Wiley, my love, how's business?"

Wiley put his finger to his lips, his smile widening beneath his bushy brown moustache. He reminded me of a young Sam Elliott, a movie star my mom had often pointed out. "Shh. Don't let my wife hear you call me that. I'm on her good side for the moment. You could ruin me for life, or at least till next week. I believe she made sure the sofa was the most uncomfortable, scratchy, lumpy place to sleep on purpose."

I laughed, gave his hand a brief squeeze, and then let go to take a sip of beer. It was velvety smooth sliding down my throat, and I set it on the bar and sighed. Glancing over to the stage, where Andy, Lance, and two others were playing, I asked, "My brother giving you any trouble?"

"Good Lord, no. Look at the booths and tables back there. Jam-packed with music-loving, beer-drinking, *paying* customers. Those boys bring 'em in."

"Glad to hear. They should be on a break soon before a new set."

Wiley went through the motions of wiping off the bar. Then he glanced up. "Heard about the body in your basement. What's with that? Do the police have any idea who it was?"

I shook my head. "Tom's on it."

"Kind of a shock, I'd guess."

"Horrifying."

He glanced down the bar toward his wife. "Well, hope they get it all sorted out. I'm sure Angie will be here to see ya as soon as she can shake loose. We've been steady since six-thirty. Enjoy!" Walking away down the bar, he leaned over to take another order from two guys who were way ahead of me on their beer consumption.

Unbidden, my brain flashed back to those skeletal fingers reaching out, grasping the dirt. What a nightmare. I sat still and stared into space, thinking about how terrifying it had been when I leaned over that dark hole. Time to distract my thoughts.

I wandered back near the small stage. I'd missed most of the band's first set. Usually, they played classic rock, some 90s nostalgia, and a final set of country. A small table sat empty a few yards from the stage, and I settled in a chair to watch the end of the first set. I loved to hear my brother sing. He'd played guitar and piano for years, unlike me who decided to play the piano for a while but then quit. For some reason, I couldn't pull up enthusiasm tonight. Maybe it was because of my exhausting day. Shivering, I kept seeing that skeleton, those fingers looking to claw their way out of forever.

Eventually, the band put their guitars on stands to take a ten-minute break. Andy and Lance grabbed beers from Wiley and ambled over to my table, pulling out chairs.

My brother took several swallows of his beer. "How'd we sound?"

"Perfect. Like you're ready for the big time."

"Yes!" Lance took a long pull on his beer, set it down, and left to go to the restroom. Lance was the yin to Andy's yang. He had a talent for knowing their gift-buying customers, and he could find precisely the right objects.

Andy took care of the books for The Gift Gallery and boosted sales with his charming personality. On occasion, thank goodness, Lance reined Andy in.

I clicked my beer bottle with my brother's. "Better times ahead!"

Lance reappeared and sat across from me while Andy took a long chug and sat back, his eyes scanning the bar. "How are things at the house, now Andy and I have vacated to our new home?"

"The house" he referred to was Mom and Dad's house, where Andy and Lance had been staying since our parents died. I was living there now after the boys moved out to their own place. The two frat boys lived, well, you know, like guys in a frat house. I did much of the distasteful pitching of unwanted stuff. "I haven't changed a thing except for the basketball hoop over the door in the dining room." I glared pointedly at my crazy brother. When he didn't defend himself, I added, "You may pick it up any time, Andy."

"Thought you might find an ingenious artsy use for it. Maybe make one of those artistic installations with flowers and basketballs?"

I rolled my eyes.

Then he looked at me more closely. "How are you after they found that dead body?"

"It wasn't my finest hour. I passed out. Next thing I knew, Tom was there. The more I think about it, the more worried I am about the bad publicity for the art center. Already had a call from Ivan the Terrible, demanding to know if a floor had collapsed. For some reason, he's been obsessed with floors collapsing lately. I swear the man believes I'm totally incompetent."

Lance focused in on my face. "I seem to notice a few dark circles under your eyes, and I counted your yawns while we played the last song. What's up?"

As if on cue, I yawned. "I haven't slept well, and when I'm awake, I spend way too much time worrying about what will happen if this art center tanks. People count on me. What if we put all this building renovation into play and I show up for work one day only to see a huge pile of rubble?" My voice broke momentarily, struggling to find itself. "Some days I'm confident I can do this. Other days the naysayers win out. Right now, I can see the blocks falling into place, but who knows what catastrophe lurks around the corner."

Andy leaned toward me. "Don't listen to the negative people. Mom and Dad would tell you that."

I looked into his eyes. "It's hard not to. This job's too important to me, and to our family. It's a chance to keep our mother's name alive. Between the burglary and surprise in the basement, I'm so worried the board will get rid of me or maybe close the center. I've worked so hard and now a dead person appears and might take it all away from me."

Lance chimed in. "Come on. You can't be blamed for the corpse in the basement. Knowing Tom, it will take time. He's smart, you know. He'll get the right criminal. And speaking of time—" He pointed to his phone screen. "It's time, dude."

They stood, drained their beers, and left to start another set. About then, Angie showed up.

The band belted out "Joy to the World," and we had to yell to hear each other.

"How are things at the art center? Figure this burglary and dead body will get solved?"

"Tom's confident. Me, I want his investigation wrapped up with a bow as soon as possible. Once the police arrest a suspect, a person who has nothing to do with the art center, all will go back to normal, and the board will be happy. I've a mind to investigate myself—to speed things up. Oh, don't think me callous, but I'll be glad when it's behind us." Thank goodness the song ended. My throat was getting hoarse from yelling.

"I understand. You know if you need volunteer help with anything, I'm your woman. Well, when I don't have to work."

I nodded. "Yes, and thank you, my friend. Right now, I could sure use an accountant, someone who would deal with the books for a year or more. Then I wouldn't have to so I could concentrate on the building renovation and the exhibits."

She looked at me. "An accountant, you say. Let me think about that a minute." While her eyes darted back and forth, her hands tapped the beat to Lance's latest song, and her lips mouthed the words. As if a light bulb went off in her head, she turned from her lyrics with the band. "You know, I think I have an idea."

"Really? Who? Please don't tell me it's Louise's brother's uncle's sister-in-law who has a degree from night school."

She laughed, briefly patting both her hands on the sides of my face. "What would we do without Louise and her relatives?" She paused. "I've got an idea. Remember Mr. Wyatt, dreamy math teacher in high school?"

"Mr. W?"

"The very one."

"Doesn't he still teach?"

"No. He works as a CPA for Stran Industries. Comes in here occasionally for a beer with several of his friends from work."

"He isn't a teacher anymore?"

She shook her head. "Hasn't taught for some time. Remember, you've been gone. He went back to school and got his degree to be a CPA. Guess he couldn't make enough money as a teacher to support the little lady plus the two kids."

"I find that sad. I thought he was a good teacher. Very enthusiastic."

"Not to mention good-looking. He comes in here quite often. Should I tell him you need accounting help to get by for a while until you get the center in order?"

I considered Mr. Wyatt. Sure, he'd be okay, but I didn't know if I could pay him enough to make it worth his time. "As long as he knows I can't pay him much. We'd almost be a charity case. Gotta love nonprofits."

Angie stood, patted me on the head, and nodded. "You got it. I'll send him around if he's agreeable."

"Thanks, Angie. You always have my back."

She smiled and pointed both hands at me like six shooters. "Back at ya." Then she returned to the bar.

Andy and Lance had moved into their 90s numbers. They finished a Def Leppard song and began playing Pearl Jam's "Daughter." People were up on the dance floor, and I watched them for a while before considering another beer. I didn't know how long the *Ledger* would hold off with the story about the unidentified body, but I felt uneasy about all the negatives. Despite Andy's words of wisdom, no one liked bad publicity, least of all Ivan-Who-Keeps-the-Ship-Away-from-Icebergs.

Chapter Six

I texted Louise **I m on my way** because I overslept after yesterday's workload and last night's late hours. It would be a long Saturday.

Louise texted back. **Bo orpblen Im hare**

Shaking my head, I deciphered, "No problem, I'm here." Louise had a hard time texting. Not sure whether it was her coordination, her speed, or her busy life between work and children. Fortunately, an office manager didn't need to text well, and Louise was a thoroughly competent manager. She'd dealt with local artists whose work we sold, sent out invoices, checked on deadlines, watched over my shoulder, and helped me with the creative side, like designing posters for the exhibit. Our personalities complemented one another. She talked with the people who didn't recognize deadlines and took that unpleasant task out of my life.

Our parents' house was only four blocks from the Marsden Center, so I decided to walk this morning, as I often did since the weather was beautiful. It was a color-feast for my eyes: crimsons, yellow-greens, raw siennas, and medium yellows. The world was full of such gorgeous hues. I waved at Jim Taylor, a former classmate from Apple Grove High School, who was on a ladder cleaning the gutters on a two-story house owned by Mrs. Mapley. She must be in her eighties by now and sharp as a tack the last time I spoke with her at the art center opening.

Jim waved back and yelled, "Hi, Jill. Welcome home!"

Walking down the sidewalk to work, I mused about these neighborhoods where I'd grown up and people like Jim, who knew I'd come back. Unlike the Chicago suburbs, with their cookie-cutter apartment complexes and identical houses, Apple Grove's streets boasted all sorts of architecture. I hadn't appreciated that when I was young. On the corner was Ms. Evans's home, a two-story frame house with a huge, wrap-around front porch. On rainy or snowy days, she let us wait under her porch roof for the school bus when we went to junior high, a kindness I now appreciated.

A few doors down from Ms. Evans's house was Mr. Atherton's, the meanest man on the block. He had black, beady eyes and was gigantic. I swore the ground rumbled when he came out on his porch. Well, I was a kid back then, so maybe he was more normal-sized than I thought. If we cut through his yard, he yelled at us. After a while, he constructed a fence so we couldn't go through. Andy egged his windows one Halloween. I doubted Mr. Atherton was alive anymore, and the fence was gone now. I'd like to think someone kinder was in the one-story, ranch-style house. I hoped, if I was right about him, they'd reinforced the floors. Whoever it was, they'd recently painted the wood siding light blue with black shutters and trim. Looked much friendlier.

It was a comfort to be home, like a clean canvas I could use to paint whatever…like starting over again. I would build a new life for myself here, in this familiar place. Unfortunately, my actual canvases were still at home, packed in boxes in the family room, but they could wait. Clean canvases meant…possibilities.

I unlocked the alley door of the Marsden Center since the front was still covered with crime tape. We had a long list of work to do today on the publicity for the Heartland exhibit, and it would be much more focused without all the noise from the Four Apostles, Matthew, Mark, Luke, and Jesse, in the basement.

Louise was organizing items in the children's area. "Intern in your office." Louise never missed a beat or even checked to see if it was me. I was sure she had my footsteps memorized, but then the doors were locked. "I figured we could let her in, despite the crime scene tape."

I moved along to my office. Through the open door, I saw Jordan Grant, the intern I'd hired for the summer. I'd been able to secure a grant from the state arts council because the money was available for students ages 14-19.

Jordan was 16, African American, and didn't know much about art. A lack of knowledge about art was fine. Besides doing mundane chores like cleaning, she needed to have problem-solving skills, social media knowledge, and computer savvy. Her interview had been flawless.

I thought about the morning she'd come in to see me, answering an ad I'd put on social media. It was almost as if my mother had laid a hand on her shoulder and sent her to me.

Jordan had been upfront about her lack of art knowledge. She was enthusiastic to work with people. She'd sung in the school choir for three years, was involved in school clubs—including the computer coding group—and could talk with anyone, according to the teacher references she'd brought. When I asked her why she wanted the job, she said she had a dream to go to college, get a degree, and run a nonprofit. I thought about myself when I was sixteen. I hadn't even heard the word "nonprofit." I would have figured it was a failing business. For a moment, I believed I was listening to a twenty-five-year-old. She was far more mature than I had been, which put me at a loss for words. An idealistic teenager. Perfect.

I understood my mother's philosophy about people and art. Louise, Jordan, and I would represent the welcoming faces of the art center at least for this summer. My mom believed art could bring people together, no matter how rich or poor; no matter what race, ethnicity, or gender; and no matter what age. The mission statement of the Adele Marsden Center for the Arts said exactly that. Jordan would fit in here, no question.

"Good morning, Jordan!" I walked into my office and set my blue and white tote on the floor, motioning her to sit. On my desk, I spied a yellow memo sheet, another ridiculous reminder from Ivan the Terrible. Later. I would deal with him later.

"Hi, Ms. Madison." She held her hand out to shake mine. Another social grace I might not have thought about at age sixteen.

"This seems like a perfect day to get you started, despite the crime scene decorations. However, we'll need to be much less formal. You can call me Jill. Have you met Louise?"

"Oh, yes. She already showed me around so I would know where everything is. Actually, Louise is related by marriage through my great-grandmother. We're cousins, I guess."

Of course. Someday I'd like to see Louise's family tree.

"I love the sculptures." She glanced past my head at the photographs she could have memorized while she waited for my late self. "Are those people your parents?"

I turned around to see where she looked. Hanging behind my desk were six 20" x 24" photographs, taken by me but developed by my brother Andy. They were photos of my family, my parents, the family house, my siblings, the art center, and my now missing sculpture, *Mother and Child*.

"Yes. My mom and dad. The center is named for her. I hope it's a place where we can do great work for the town."

She nodded. "Her skin tone is darker than mine."

"She was from Jamaica. Met my dad in Chicago. Long story. Lots of stares from people back in the eighties."

"I heard about the burglary and the dead person. I'm sorry."

"That's kind of you. We hope to get my mom's sculpture back and figure out who the body belonged to. I tell myself they're temporary distractions." I reached across my desk for my latest list. "Now, I have a list of jobs I plan to have you do to get started today. Seldom is one day like any other around here. We'll talk about the details later like paychecks, what to wear, hours, days off—you know, all the nitty-gritty. I'm interested in putting you on social media and our website, but we won't start there today. Your first job is construction."

A puzzled look crossed her face. "Construction?"

"How are you with a screwdriver?"

"I've used one on occasion. Phillips or standard?"

Seriously? She knew about screwdrivers too? How old was this woman? "Good. You pass the first test. In the children's room, you'll find a large box that contains a new exhibit, a dollhouse. Once it's done, you'll see a small table to put it on. It may take you a while to put it together, but it should be fun if you love to solve problems. Instructions, I'm sure, are inside. If you need anything else, ask Louise. She'll be around or in her office." I checked my watch. "Take a break from ten-thirty to ten forty-five. It's beautiful out on the plaza, and you'll find benches to sit on if you want to go outside. Just knock on the alley door to get back in. We'll hear you. Clear?"

"Yes, crystal. And," she paused, "thank you Ms.—Jill—for giving me this chance."

Back in my office, I grabbed Ivan's memo. He emailed them daily, it seemed. Louise often printed them to have a record. They appeared in bunches, depending on how his day was progressing. This was only the first today.

Ms. Madison. Despite your recent ineptitude with locks, make sure you lock up the art center EVERY NIGHT. DOUBLE CHECK. We CANNOT afford a new alarm system. DO NOT EVEN ASK. Ivan F. Truelove III.

Ivan adored capital letters. In this case, I stuck the printed email in the shredder. So much for Ivan.

I sat at my desk and considered the photograph of my parents, a typical studio photo they'd had taken. My mother was lovely, her graceful hands folded in her lap. Sitting next to her, my father had his usual humorous expression. He'd always kept us happy and hopeful with his corny jokes and upbeat humor. Five years after their deaths, I was able to speak of them without tears immediately springing to my eyes. Paint, no. I wasn't sure I could paint again. The very process brought out too many emotions. Coming home, at least, had given me hope I might be able to move forward, and managing this art center was the giant step I took that would make it happen.

Coming home also meant I had stopped running away from the strange, unfamiliar family configuration—Tom and Mary wanting to protect me, Andy and Lance making sure I smiled, and me, the baby. Now I was thirty, a baby no more. I had to envision a new family without our parents' generation at the top. I smiled, looked away from my photographs, and swore I'd move ahead. Things would get better.

After dealing with paperwork, I spent the next hour conferring with Louise on the Heartland project. I had settled on a first exhibit of regional artists that would run eight weeks. Anyone who now resided in the area or who had lived here in the past could send their work. No one would be turned away, plus, it would give these artists an opportunity to add to their portfolios, garner reviews, and get exposure to the competitive art world.

Taking a break, I decided to check on Jordan.

Quietly, I stuck my head in the doorway of the children's room. Amazing! She had the house almost finished. She sat on the floor, fully focused.

"Great job, Jordan. You didn't tell me how handy you are."

"I like to solve problems, so this has been a lot of fun."

I turned and was almost out the door.

"Jill—"

I stuck my head back in the doorway.

"This is really cool. I'm astonished. These figures for the house. Some are black like me and others have biracial or white skin. How come?"

I considered my answer. "You know, when I was growing up, it was rare to see anyone who looked like me in this town, well, other than my brother Andy. When I ordered the dollhouse, I thought about children playing with it, and I decided it would be more honest to show them people come in various shades of skin color. I reasoned if they could see dolls in the house who looked like them, they'd see themselves as part of the greater world."

"Makes sense. By the way, I know your brothers too. When you were growing up, I imagine people used to stare at your family."

I moved into the room and sat on a small stool. "When Tom introduced me to someone as his sister, they looked at me as if to say, 'you don't look alike.' I think it was code for 'what are you?' After a while, I got used to it."

"For the first time, I figure it's better to be me. You must have to constantly listen to people who are puzzled by your heritage. Everyone wants you to be one thing or the other. It's obvious I'm Black."

"You know, one of my favorite artists, Leonardo da Vinci, once said something like this. 'When you lay a transparent color on top of another color of a different nature, the result will be a mixture different from the simple ones that created it.' I like to think it's the story of my family."

She smiled and nodded. "What a neat way to look at it."

"I think you're miles ahead of where I was at your age." I stood up. "Well, back to work."

I was about to go to my office when there was a knock on the alley door. Craning my neck around the corner of my office, I saw Tom and walked out into the hallway to let him in.

He looked up, saw me, and smiled. "Just coming in to deal with details in the basement."

"Have you figured out who it is—was—yet?" I asked.

"Not yet. The databases have yielded no one who's missing in our area who might fit the description, and the autopsy isn't finished yet."

"Do you even know if the victim was male or female?"

"That I do know. Female. However, if anyone comes to ask questions or snoop around from the newspaper, you don't know anything."

"Got it." I thought about asking him to speed up the investigation but figured I might be able to get more information since he was in such an expansive mood.

"You know, I find it kinda strange someone would bury a body in the Lowry Building basement. I mean, if they were simply looking for space to avoid funeral expenses, they could go out to the countryside and bury the body there. Done."

He had started toward the basement stairs but turned around and nodded. "You're right." Leaning against the hallway wall, he crossed one leg over the other and folded his arms in front of him. "I haven't spent much time dealing with deaths here in Apple Grove, but I've had plenty of training. It appears the hyoid bone might be broken, and that wouldn't be good news."

"What do you mean? What's a hyoid?"

"It's in the middle of the neck between the chin and the thyroid cartilage."

"Why's it so important?"

"Only one way it breaks—strangulation."

"Seriously? Possibly a murder?"

"Not possibly."

"Oh, Tom. That's even worse. Can't you make this go away? Soon? I've already had a message from Judge Spivey—you know, Mom and Dad's friend who's treasurer of the art center board. He wants me to call him back. Ivan has texted or called like a fired-up bill collector with a deadline of yesterday. Constantly, he sends memos with opinions and directions. On top of that, the breaking news keeps coming. Can't you find these criminals faster?"

"I have to be careful. Otherwise, if we do catch them, they slip through the judicial fingers."

I considered his theory for a moment. "Need help? I'm smart. Angie and I could do some footwork to speed things up."

He smiled at me and chuckled. "You two on a murder investigation? I understand your concern, but I think you should call the judge back. We do the best we can, slowly but surely. Stick with your art center work and leave the bad guys to the police."

Chapter Seven

After work on Wednesday, I had my niece's softball game. I grabbed my tote and figured I'd wear my dark navy shorts and a white sleeveless T-shirt to the game.

I dug through the contents of my favorite tote made of woven straw, making sure I hadn't forgotten the bug spray. It was a symbol of my belief in over-preparedness. Yup, insect repellant. Sunscreen, a sandwich, a water bottle, my favorite baseball hat, Band-Aids, antibiotic wipes, driver's license, cash, my cell phone, and a towel to place on the bleachers. God only knew how many crows had flown over those bleachers dropping a load of bombs. I was ready.

Tom always reminded us to lock our doors and windows because the days of small towns, where we could leave everything unlocked, were gone forever. Locking the house, I drove out to the Little League park, where I'd made my own debut in center field at age nine. Certain to see lots of action, I was sadly disappointed when few of my friends could even hit it to center field. Weight training—that was what we'd needed back then. I stuck with it until I was eleven, when I discovered painting. My focus shifted, and I was all in with summer art programs through the Y and occasional school time spent on art. But it was never enough.

It was that memory I revisited when I took Tom's advice to manage the art center. Softball's loss, the town's gain. I didn't see myself making sports history. I could have lain in the grass and read a book in centerfield. Despite my decision to relax and forget the art center, I still couldn't get my mind off the conversation with Tom. A murder victim? A woman? How did she end up in the Lowry Building basement? The place had sat empty for at least twenty years. Was this body buried when the building still had a business or during all the years it had sat idle?

Parking my car at least a half-block away to prevent lucky fly balls from sailing through my windshield, I dragged my tote out of the back seat and walked over to where the Jackson Electronics dugout was emptied of players who were warming up. I could see my eleven-year-old niece Emily in the outfield catching balls. After all, she was Tom's kid, and he was the athlete in the family. She looked cute in her zinc yellow shirt and white pants. I waved at her and headed over to the bleachers, where my family sat as they watched the warm-ups and talked. I landed next to Lance, laid my towel on the bleacher, and pulled a sandwich out of my bag, along with the bottle of water.

At the far end of the field, Angie walked in our direction from her car. Angie was always loyal and showed up, even if only for a brief appearance. During the game, she was more likely to be using an Emory board on her nails and talking about the latest gossip from the bar. Always loyal Angie. While I watched her approach, I wondered how Tom could ever identify the body in the basement. I still considered the possibility I should help Tom investigate to move this bad news away faster, but where to start? Maybe newspapers for missing persons at the library?

Lance tapped my arm. "There's your partner in crime headed our way."

"That's the perfect name for her."

He looked over at Tom and lowered his voice. "You know, with all the stuff that's gone on lately, I hope you and Angie are holding yourselves in check."

"And to what are you referring?"

"Oh, sister. I remember all the crazy high school just-over-the-line-slightly-against-the-rules situations you two got into, and Andy or I helped you hide the consequences from your parents or Tom. Or all three."

"Why, whatever do you mean?"

He laughed and turned to me. "Look, you're grown up now with a responsible job and, just because you're home, don't let Angie drag you into some of her crazy schemes."

"Actually, I think I was the one who designed the plan to put the dead fish in the boy's locker room."

"Exactly. Time to grow up. You have enough problems with other people putting dead bodies in your art center."

"Hmm. Did Tom put you up to this lecture?"

"No. It's in the interests of self-preservation. I have enough trouble keeping Andy out of hot water without having to keep track of you and Angie. Your homecoming has increased my oversight responsibility."

"I'll make an effort to give you a rest. My partner in crime, I can't promise you."

Angie was almost here, and I looked at the crowd in the bleachers. Quite a few spectators lined the seats. Some were parents and siblings of players, and others were people I'd known since they'd been in high school ahead of me.

"Hi, Madison family." Angie made her way up the bleachers and plopped down next to me, set her soda on the seat, and unwrapped a sandwich. "Told you I'd be here. Couldn't miss Em's first game."

"Fantastic. How long you got?"

She glanced at her phone. "I can stay an hour. Then I need to get to the pub. It's slow the first hour, so Wiley can do without me. Hi, Lance, Andy, Mary, and Tom." She shaded her eyes and peered toward the outfield. "Wow. Eye-catching outfits. Would you call those shirts neon yellow?"

I moved her soda to a safer spot as Lance explained, "I think it's their strategy. Electric yellow to blind the batters."

"First game of the season." Andy turned to us. "She's ready, I'm sure. Notice her correct stance and eagle eye as she catches those balls in the outfield. She's been listening to her uncle. Oops, missed that one." He shouted, "It's okay, Em. You'll get the next one." As if she could hear him.

Lance and I looked at each other and shook our heads. We had been instructed, by Emily, to keep Uncle Andy in the bleachers and pull him back down when he yelled something at the umpire, which could result in his getting ejected from the game. This was the embarrassment factor to Emily, who, at eleven, was keenly aware of social pressure. Andy and Lance were her favorites—all right, only—uncles, and she championed them fiercely, except if Andy embarrassed her. I'd been here last summer for a couple of games, but I realized, as I was sure Lance did also, it was a full-time job to keep Andy on the straight and narrow.

In the calm before the game, Tom gave Mary his usual instructions. "Now remember, honey, it's just a game. If anything happens, like a ball hits her, let the coach take care of it. Stay here, don't worry, and it will all be fine. At this age, they can't throw hard enough to do much damage."

Mary nodded, turned toward us, and rolled her eyes.

We stood for the National Anthem and the coin toss. As the players took the field, I scanned the dugout and saw my old math teacher, Neal Wyatt, coaching. When he first started teaching, we tormented him, but then we settled in and gave him a chance. He turned out to be a satisfactory teacher, although way too easy, and since he was young, we girls daydreamed about him. You know, every school had at least one of those starting teachers who wasn't a lot older than his students. That was Mr. Wyatt.

I had to admit he'd aged well, but he wasn't the twenty-something anymore. He still had his hair, he hadn't put on weight, and, from a distance, he didn't look like he'd turned gray. Well, he was probably only in his mid-forties. Angie had told me his kids were now pre-teens, and one, Bree, was a shortstop on this team with Emily.

"Angie, did you ask Wyatt about working part-time for me?"

"Yeah. He was in yesterday, and he said he'd think about it. Ask the wife. You know. All the usual stuff."

"Gee. Remember when we thought he was cool. He must have been a young teacher, especially compared to Mr. Heckly and Miss Weston. They were ancient back then. At least forty."

Maybe after the game I'd have a chance to catch Mr. W and see if he'd decided. I turned my attention back to the diamond and saw Emily in the on-deck circle. Andy had already turned on the juice, and I listened to him whistle and shout field chatter at the opposing team. Emily walked over to home plate. The first two pitches were balls, high and outside.

Whack! Emily gave the next pitch a solid hit, possibly a double. Wow! Where had that come from? If she'd followed in the Jill Madison tradition, she'd already have struck out and been trotting back to the dugout. Now I was on my feet cheering with the rest of the family. Emily crouched with a slight smile and led off the base, watching the pitcher. I was sure her smile was aimed at her uncle's voice.

"Tom, where did you get this child? Are you sure she's a Madison?"

"Of course. She's not just a Madison. Mary was a short stop in her day."

Before we could stop him, Andy made his way down the bleachers and walked over to the fence near the first baseline to see and yell advice to Em. I could hear him each time the next batter lined up her stance. By the time she had a full count, I was nervous.

Then we saw a low, inside pitch and, miraculously, number twenty-five hit it. Line drive out to the right fielder. Coach Wyatt, near third base, signaled Emily to run, and we all stood up as the ball wound its way to third. She slid into third base and knocked over the third baseman, who landed on top of Emily and the base in the dust. A tangle of arms and legs, a cloud of brown dust, and the umpire's arms signaled "safe." A cheer went up from the crowd, but when the dust settled, we could see my niece lying on her back, clutching her right leg and rolling around in pain.

I turned to Mary and Tom, and they, too, stared out at the cloud of dust. Andy was already running around the fence toward third base. Suddenly, Tom moved people in front of him, parting them like the Red Sea when they saw it was the Apple Grove police detective. Once he hit the ground, he ran over to the third-base line and literally jumped the fence, heading for Emily.

Mary turned to me and shook her head. "I knew it. All this time he's told me to stay out of it, to sit in the bleachers, and the coach will take care of it, and who's the first one on the field? Her father. Thank goodness he didn't sprain his ankle jumping the fence. I'd have to nurse them both."

Concerned comments about Emily mixed with a few chuckles at Mary's nursing thought.

We stared over at third base, where Emily was still on the ground, the other players looking at her, and Coach Wyatt's assistant walked over there while

Wyatt checked what looked like her ankle. The audience in the bleachers had become quiet, and several people turned around to Mary and told her not to worry. After what seemed like a long time, Tom and Coach Wyatt pulled her off the ground, and she put an arm over each of their shoulders while she hopped on one foot over to the dugout. Everyone stood and clapped to honor her courage. Small town, good sports. When I lived in much bigger places, the parents fought over the calls, charged the umpire, and starred in the ten-o'clock news. Much more exciting, but not so admirable.

That was how we all ended up at Apple Grove Cottage Hospital in the waiting room while Emily had her ankle X-rayed. Angie had left for the pub but made me promise to call or text her. Mary was with Emily, and Tom nervously paced around the waiting room. I always said if we had a family emergency, Mary was the one to handle it. She was the laid-back, calm person we all relied on, never rattled.

We were still waiting when Neal Wyatt walked in and asked what progress had been made.

Tom stopped his pacing. "None. Still waiting."

"Oh, hi, Jill." Mr. Wyatt stuck his hand out to shake mine.

"Hi, Mr. Wyatt."

"I think you can call me Neal now. We're all adults."

"Sure." Mentally I thought, *Not in my lifetime.*

Coach Wyatt sat down, determined to wait with us, and explained his assistant had taken over and we were ahead seven to two when he left. Tom continued his pacing, Andy went to search for a coffee machine, Lance examined a magazine, and I was left with Neal.

"I think Emily will be fine. Looked like a sprain to me. She's a tough kid—ice and a generic anti-inflammatory should help." He paused. "Angie asked me about some accounting work for your art center."

"Have you had time to think about it?"

"Sure. I'll be glad to do it. You'll have to let me know what you want. My firm encourages pro bono work in the community, and you'd give me an opportunity to rack up some hours. You're a nonprofit, right?"

I nodded. "Thanks. I'll be at work most days if you'd like to stop in and discuss possibilities."

"Sounds good. I'll stop by after work in the next few days."

"Thanks, Mr.—Neal."

"By the way, I don't know that much about your business plan. How did you end up in the Lowry Building, and how are you organized with a board of directors?"

"When my parents died, their wills set up a memorial trust to provide a center that would educate people in the arts and allow them opportunities to enjoy art. It took quite a while for the wheels to turn. The family lawyer set up a not-for-profit center chartered by the State of Illinois. Then he selected volunteers and helped them write policies and bylaws for the new art center. They also had to investigate and buy a building and deal with the red tape. The Lowry Building was empty and centrally located but needed a lot of work. Enter me. I was hired by the board of directors who meet monthly and listen to my best advice, but they can also fire me. I'm working really hard not to have that last thing happen. Oh, the doctor's back."

The doctor came in, still in his shirtsleeves, no white coat. Mary explained to us that Emily had a sprain but no broken bones. She'd be off the ankle for a few days and he'd wrapped it. I called Angie to give her the news and then, as quickly as it had begun, the evening ended. We all split up and went our own ways. Tom and Mary took Emily home. As I walked down the hospital's waxed and polished hallway, I realized how tired I was. A burglary, a dead body, and Tom's announcement of murder. I had a lot to think about.

On the way to my car, I considered another idea. Despite my concern at Emily's sprained ankle, I realized what I'd missed in those years I'd been away. Andy went to college, majoring in music and parties, and Tom left for college and the police academy. They both came home, Andy to buy the gift store, and Tom to work his way up from patrolman to detective. They hadn't left for a period of time like I had when I lived in Chicago.

Oh, sure, I'd been back for Christmas or Easter and a few times in between. Now, for the first time, I was home more permanently and found myself back in the community as an adult. It was such fun to watch Emily play softball with the family all cheering her on. Her brother, Jim, was away at camp, but he'd be home in a few weeks too.

For the first time, it seemed I might fit in here, part of a five-adult family, without the presence of our parents. I couldn't change their deaths, so I might as well make my peace with the situation. Being home again made me see I was finally doing exactly that.

Chapter Eight

On Friday morning, I was relieved that we could finally keep the alley door unlocked so I wouldn't have to let people in while I was trying to work. I asked Louise, "Did we get the prospectus proof back from the printers?"

"Yes. I have it on my desk. Just a minute." She left my office, where we'd gone over the list of jobs we had to organize for the Home in the Heartland exhibit in another five weeks.

I'd found a juror, Debra Montiero, who lived in a city two hours away, a woman who knew the Midwest but wouldn't be familiar with these regional artists. The juror would award the prizes, and I was waiting for her bio to put in the prospectus—a two-sided paper that went out to artists with the rules for the exhibit.

Louise walked to my office and put a paper on my desk. "Here it is. Oh, and yet the fourth message today from your esteemed board president." She dropped it on top of the prospectus.

Ms. Madison. A ~~suggestion~~ item for the consent agenda. Place multiple articles in the local newspaper about the new safety improvements at the building. It will encourage visitors if they realize no upper floors will collapse on their heads. Ivan F. Truelove III.

I shook my head, crumpled it up, and moved on. Examining the proof, I turned it over and found a couple of minor mistakes. I circled them and placed the paper on the corner of my desk to await Debra's bio. "We'll get this to the printer today. I may have to remind Debra with a text. They should come back, printed, tomorrow so we can send them out to artists and area businesses." Then the wait would begin. I prayed we'd get entries. This was the first time we'd put on an exhibit. My mom's sculpture had been mostly a placeholder, an expensive placeholder, as it turned out. I woke at night, pencil and paper by my bedside, only to remember another job we needed to do.

"—and start Jordan making social media posts?" Louise looked at me expectantly.

Startled, I realized I had been thinking about my nightmare about no entries instead of listening to Louise. "Yes, she can start them anytime."

"She's amazing on a computer. I can't wait to have you see the ads she's finished."

"Excellent."

Louise looked at me silently.

"What?"

"You seem a little distracted."

"A little?" I started to laugh. "I'm surprised it's only a little. Frankly, I'm still having anxiety and nightmares about the body in the basement. However, this is helpful, this work on the list of what we must accomplish over the next four weeks. I'm on top of it, honest. This helps me keep focused." *And moves my mind off the murder victim and bad publicity.*

"Gotcha, Boss. I'll go check on Jordan's progress and see what I can do to round up volunteers for the hanging and lighting of the entries. The board has given me a list of names, and if even half of them say 'yes,' we'll be in great shape." She paused. "Mr. Truelove called about one minute after we opened."

Oh, no. I was late for work because I'd stopped by the bank.

"I told him you were away on a consultation with my brother's ex-sister-in-law about certain legal matters. She's an attorney."

"Really?"

"No, but I thought it sounded good. I crossed my fingers."

"Did he buy that?"

"He muttered an ominous threat about getting your resume in order."

Two could play this game. Maybe I should text him and say the workers found termites in the basement. No, that would bring him over here—a situation I tried to discourage.

After Louise left my office, I moved back to my computer and began to check on the information I needed for a grant. I hoped to have our first class in early August, after the Home in the Heartland exhibit had been juried. My bracelet didn't play well with my computer touchpad, and I took it off, laying it on the desk. *Ah, much better.*

When I glanced at the clock, I'd been working for a solid two hours. I didn't think I imagined a male voice behind me, and it wasn't my brother's. Not either brother.

I turned around to see Neal.

"Thought I should stop in. I wanted to double-check what Louise needs for your board meeting next Tuesday. I'm pleased. I think this pro bono work is a great idea. I feel like I'm helping you two, and I can easily do it."

"Your help is a relief to both of us. We need to get this exhibit up, and the real pressure hits soon. Anything you can do to work with the numbers and free Louise for the exhibit is wonderful. Thanks, Mr.—Neal."

"You're welcome." He started to leave then turned back. "I hear you've had excitement around here. Read the story this morning in the paper."

I sighed because I figured he was referring to the story about the unidentified body in our basement. It was only a short blurb since no one really knew any facts yet. "I suppose you could call it that. It's been horribly unsettling, but I think the police have it under control."

"Do they know who the unfortunate person was?"

I shook my head. "Don't think so. I imagine it will take a while to deal with missing persons' reports, DNA, and whatever else a search involves. My guess is whoever it was has been buried here a long time, and I don't know how much luck the police will have."

"You may be right. Very well. Headed to Louise's office."

"Thanks again."

On my desk were some crumbs from a cookie I'd eaten. I remembered I'd meant to send a text to Mary to thank her for the banana bread I found on my kitchen table last night after I got home. She always equated love with food, so Tom was well fed these days. Smiling at that thought, I texted her and went back to my grant research. I was into a crucial juncture when I heard the alley door open and close. I peeked out of my office doorway.

Tom walked down the hallway. "Hi, Jill. Making progress?"

"Absolutely. We made a real head start on Saturday, and today we're moving ahead. Any news on the uninvited corpse?" Too late, I remembered his lecture about solemnity from yesterday. This time he only gave me a pained expression.

He turned and saw Louise and Neal listening from the doorway. "Not yet."

"I hope they find out who the poor soul was. Thanks for your difficult work," said Louise.

"My job, Louise. I love it. If we can return this body to the family, I'll be thankful they'll be able to bury the person in a cemetery with a ceremony."

Louise and Neal left for her office. We had gift shop invoices and payments, and all the information had to be included in the monthly totals for the board report. Next Tuesday, I reminded myself. Five days away. Anxiety had found a permanent home in my chest. A burglary to answer for and a dead body.

Tom stared at my desk.

I tried to lift his spirits. "Tell Mary I said thanks for the banana bread. I texted her, but sometimes those cyber messages go astray. Her surprise was thoughtful...that's your Mary."

He walked over next to me and picked up my bracelet from my desk as if he hadn't even heard me. "Is this yours?"

"Yes."

"What can you tell me about it?"

"What do you mean?"

"How did you happen to buy this? Or was it a present?"

I chuckled, remembering our plan. "Angie, Carolyn, and I each ordered an identical bracelet when we graduated from high school. Don't you remember? I was leaving for college, but Angie and Carolyn were staying here. We wanted to have a special memento to remember our friendship by—you know, the three musketeers—so we each bought one of these bracelets. See the three stones in the silver circle? Each one is a birthstone. April for me, June for Angie, October for Carolyn. It's special, but it doesn't play well with my computer keyboard, so I took it off."

Tom still studied my bracelet, holding up the circle with the birthstones attached. I watched his face while he stared at the birthstones as if he were memorizing them.

"Tom?"

He didn't answer me immediately. What he did do was walk over to my office door and close it. I thought he'd answer me. Instead, he was silent momentarily, and then he turned and said softly, "I think I have an identical bracelet in my office."

"How could you? They were special-ordered."

"Does Angie still have hers?"

"Yeah. She had it on the last time I saw her at the ballgame."

"And that leaves—"

"Oh, my God. The bracelet at your office?"

"—was found with the corpse." He must have seen the disbelief on my face followed by shock, because this time he reached out to hold my arm as I stared at him, comprehension setting in.

"Oh, no. It can't. It can't be—"

He nodded his head.

I couldn't breathe and felt panicky. Tom gently pulled my arm and moved me over to the love seat, knocking off a pile of art magazines and several crumpled-up advertisements. I watched as he grabbed my water bottle and put it up to my lips. "Drink."

Chapter Nine

I gazed at several couples as they danced to the jukebox music, laughing, a two-step moving them around in circles. How could they smile when my heart was broken? Angie was working, but she knew I needed to talk with her. One beer down and halfway through my second. I glanced at my phone, which said seven, and I took another swig of my beer. It wasn't too busy tonight at the bar. Earlier, I'd left work and stopped at home for a while. Drinking a beer, I'd spent quiet time in a chair at the kitchen table as I remembered Carolyn. None of this made sense. Maybe someone had stolen her bracelet.

At Priscilla's, I traced the lines in the wooden tabletop with my finger, thinking about all the times Angie, Carolyn, and I had used fake IDs to buy two six-packs at the package liquor store on South Main, taking them to the lake. I sniffled and watched the dancers again, killing time until I could break Angie's heart too. Not that I meant to do it, but we were in this together. The only difference for Angie was, well, she didn't know yet. I had to be the one to tell her.

Angie grabbed the other chair at the table and wiped her forehead with a towel from the bar. "We're not too busy tonight, so Wiley said to take time off, a break, kinda, and see what's happening with you. Ever since you called to say you were coming, I figured it was good. After the week you've had, you should relax. Talk. I can listen." She put the towel on her lap and encouraged me to venture right into the muck of the week. That was my Angie.

"It has been a crummy week. First my mom's sculpture—which Tom thinks he can find, but I don't know—and now this body in the basement."

"Yeah. What's the news on the dead person? Tom must be investigating. Has he said anything new? Do they have any clues about what happened?"

"That's just it, Angie." I paused, trying to figure out how to get into this without shocking her immediately. I drained my second beer and looked for courage. I would slide in slowly so she could keep her bearings. "It's pretty bad. The worst kind of bad." I swallowed. "You remember those bracelets we special-ordered for high school graduation?"

"Sure. Mine's in my jewelry box. Doesn't work too well to wear it at the bar since I pour beer and wipe up all night. Why? What does it have to do with anything? Did you lose yours? It would be all right if you did. I wouldn't be upset, even though we promised we'd still have them at our fiftieth high school reunion." She put her hand in mine and leaned toward me, a worried look.

"It's the third one."

"The third one? Carolyn's?"

"Yeah. Uh, Tom found it."

"Weird. Carolyn hasn't been here for years. Did she lose it somewhere before she left?"

"No, not exactly." I swallowed again. "Angie. She never left."

Her face was a mask of confusion. "Never left? Of course she did. She sent postcards. Remember? Dallas, New York, and wherever else they went."

"She didn't. It wasn't her."

"That's crazy. It had to be her. Why are you talking about this?"

"The body, Angie. The basement of my art center. The bracelet was with the body."

Her face went from concern to disbelief to shock. Precisely what I felt when Tom told me.

"No, it wasn't. How? How could that be? We all know she left with the college actor guy. The postcards she sent us from all over the country. The note she left for her mom." She stopped a minute. "What are you telling me?"

"She's dead, Angie. I know it. I feel it. The bracelet proves it, well, until they get dental records. I knew who her dentist was, and I told Tom. He'll have Dr. Anderson fax her records to the pathologist in Bloomington. No one knows yet. We can't tell. Once the ID is for sure, Tom will have to go tell her mother." I paused a minute, pursing my lips in displeasure. "And her ugly stepdad." I looked at Angie and raised one eyebrow.

Angie sat back and took a deep breath. Her face was still a mask of confusion, but even as I watched, her mouth began to quiver, her eyes screwed into a taut line, and tears began to leak out. I leaned over, grabbed both of her hands, took in a deep, sobbing breath, and let her go to it as I cried too.

"Follow me." I stood up, marched down the bar area, and headed out the front door. Angie grabbed two beers on the fly, not spilling an ounce. Once we were in the parking lot, we hugged and hugged and couldn't stop. Carolyn. A piece of us was gone, a shared history and an imagined future had ended. When our tears subsided, we checked each other. Angie had grabbed a clean towel along with the two beers.

"I can't believe this." She handed me one of the beers. "All those years I pictured her off in an exotic place with the college guy. I figured they'd settled down and maybe he was a teacher and they had a couple kids."

I waited for her to process this. Watching her face, I could see her leave the emotional wreckage of my announcement and head into all the questions that had plagued me since Tom explained.

"The thing is, I always wondered why she didn't call, didn't come back. It seemed weird, but then, Carolyn was a little different. I mean, even the way she took off like she did. I know she wouldn't have a reason to come back and see her mom or Stupid, but what about us?"

"Well, it explains why we couldn't find her on social media. Every time we thought about it, she was nowhere to be found. And she never contacted us. We both figured it was unusual, even for Carolyn. We loved each other. We shared memories and dreams and history."

She joined me, sitting on a cement parking curb.

I took a couple more swallows of my beer. "Remember when we sneaked out to the quarry and dove into the water? Carolyn was the first one in while we watched and considered?"

Angie laughed. "Sure. That was Carolyn. Always ready to jump off a cliff."

I searched my mind because we had so many memories about time spent with Carolyn. "Cheerleading. Practicing crazy pyramids, throwing her into the air."

"And her broken ankle when we missed." The ankle story brought a chuckle from Angie too.

"Yeah. Took her a long time to talk to us after we missed. She did get us back since we had to pick her up for school and carry her stuff all day for weeks."

We were silent.

I pondered my memory of her disaster. "You know, she always believed things would get better. Do you suppose her life would have been different if her real father had lived?"

"Don't know. Her relationship with her stepdad was terrible. He was a piece of work. Still is, actually."

"I never knew her dad."

Angie looked at me. "She had a picture of him from when she was little. She said he died in a construction accident. Her mom talked about him as if he were a knight in shining armor. I had the impression they loved each other, and Carolyn's years before we met her in school were happy. I always thought she changed in junior high after her mom remarried. She seemed less carefree."

We sat a few minutes, once again in silence.

"Remind me again what happened after I left for college?" While I waited for Angie's answer, I squashed an ant climbing up my leg.

"Awful. It was like the breakup of the Beatles, only more colossal. Our threesome was together all through school, and then you were gone. Carolyn was still working. In fact, she wandered from one job to another, like me. Unlike me, because she was so gorgeous, men hit on her all the time. She could be choosy, and I had the feeling she was waiting for her prince charming to take her away." Angie reached down and checked the buckle on her sandal, adjusting it. "I met Wiley and didn't see her as much. I knew she was dating and partying at the local college. I tried to connect with her, honest."

"She wrote a lot of letters to me that summer when I stayed at my college. Said it helped her clear her mind and solve her problems. Then, nothing. I probably threw them away. When was the last time you saw her?" I set my empty beer bottle on the cement beside me.

"I hadn't seen her for, maybe, two months. Then she called out of the blue. We went to a play at Apple Grove College. It was the fall after you left for your junior year. The play was outdoors, and one of the guys invited us to a party afterward. A little weed. Booze. Then we went to the bar—the Rusty Nail. I know she got home because I walked there with her before I went to my own house. She had to babysit the next night and told me she would see this guy from the college later. It was the last night the traveling rep company was in town, and then he'd leave with them. I tried to talk her out of it. She said they'd dated a couple of months."

"What was it about the college guy?"

"Oh, you know. Early twenties. Great looking and in amazing shape. Carolyn's type. A real talker. I bet he had a 'woman in every port.' You know Carolyn. She was 'in love' and believed everything he said. The next day, I saw her early in the day, but the day after that, she was gone. She'd left a note at her apartment that said she was leaving with a guy. Finally, a ticket out of town, she'd told me. You could see the stars in her eyes when she mentioned him. I thought maybe it's why she called to go to the play so we could see each other one more time before she left. I remember her mom was devastated. End of story."

Almost as if on cue, a huge truck lumbered into the parking lot, and we watched as Mitch Payson got out and walked into the bar. He was still good-looking and smoked a cigarette he flicked on the ground and stomped out before going inside. Dark-haired, T-shirt with the sleeves rolled up over big muscles, three-o'clock shadow on his chin. He had an auto body shop downtown. My dad took our car there one time when it was hit in a parking lot by someone who didn't bother to leave a note. Payson's was the place to go if you had car trouble. Mitch could fix anything.

Angie watched him saunter past us into the bar, the door closing behind him. "Speak of the devil. Now he might be a possible suspect, along with the college guy."

"Did she still see Mitch that summer?"

"Of course. On again, off again. I never understood his patience with her. She'd have a fling and then go back to him. Every time."

We sat in silence once again.

"I wonder how a person could get into the Lowry Building after it closed."

"An old building like that? I'd bet a lot of people could get in with a lock-picking tool." After a few minutes, Angie asked, "How did she die? Does Tom know?"

"He thinks she was strangled."

Angie let out a terrible sound and put a hand on her neck. "I shouldn't have asked. Oh, Jill. Our Carolyn."

We both started to cry again. After another bath of teary saltwater, we managed to pull ourselves together.

Angie blew out a deep breath.

I stared at Mitch Payson's truck, my breaths coming faster and faster, my heart pounding. "We have to find out who killed her." I grabbed her arm. "Angie!"

"What?"

"You and me. She was one of us, and someone kept her from ever being in our lives again. No wedding, no kids, no reunions with us. No future. Whoever did this took away her life. We had plans. She was going to be in our weddings. Even have one of her own. Why? Why would someone end all that?"

"I don't know. I've never known anyone who was murdered. I can't imagine. Carolyn. Strangled. What can we do?"

"We can find him and turn him over to Tom."

"How?"

"Investigate. We're smart. We're the ones who knew her best. Much better than Tom. We can do this. That murderer must pay a price—go to prison or be executed. What kind of friends are we to just let this go? He killed her."

"How can we do that? It was ten years ago. That's a pretty huge long shot."

"We can help Tom investigate. Maybe we can do some sleuthing on our own. We knew her and can somehow trace her last days. You were even with her then."

Angie's tears had dried and her face went from a mushy, tear-laden mess to a determined, decisive, look of anger. "You're right. We can do this. Whoever killed her can't get away with it. We need to get justice for our Carolyn."

"Darn right."

"But what about Tom?"

"Well, that's a stumbling block. He'll say we're too young. To leave it to the police."

Angie pursed her lips. "Maybe he's right?"

"Angie! We must persuade him we can help. We knew her best. Come on. Put your hands on mine."

We grabbed hands like we used to when the volleyball huddle broke up. "Justice for Carolyn!"

Angie repeated after me. Then we both said it together, a new resolution in our voices.

Angie stood. "You've had enough to drink. Give me your keys. You're slurring your words. We'll get Andy to come pick you up. No, Lance. He's the responsible one." She helped me get on my feet. "I'm in. All in. Starting tomorrow, the Carolyn Anders Murder Investigation gets underway."

She was right. I was blitzed. "You're absolutely, unconditionally, definitely, and without a doubt, right. We can do this. We can find justice for our third musketeer. And woe be to whoever murdered our Carolyn."

Chapter Ten

Coffee and a couple of aspirin started my morning. My headache was a mixture of Naples yellow and cerulean blue. All in all, an ugly shade of green. I hadn't drunk so much in a long time. Remembering I had an exhibit to oversee, I vowed it couldn't happen again. Angie returned my car in the middle of the night after they closed and left the car keys in my mailbox. That solved one problem.

Despite my little Austin mini in the driveway, I walked to work again since it would clear my head. Carolyn was on my mind, and my determination to find her killer hadn't wavered, drunk or sober. It was still impossible to believe that skeleton, those grasping fingers belonged to my best friend. Since the construction workers usually arrived before me, I had set my alarm to beat them so I could look at the place where Carolyn's body had rested for the last time prior to a cold, metal gurney at the medical examiner's. I took a deep breath and closed my eyes for a second with that thought. As I walked to the art center in the first light of dawn, my headache lessened but my anger toward Carolyn's murder increased. I needed to get control of my feelings or I wouldn't get any work done.

My emotions were connected to why I couldn't paint. After my parents died, I was often too critical, my paintings reflecting my anxiety. A brushstroke here, a brushstroke there, and I saw on the canvas the barometer of my confidence, or rather the lack of it. Strangely, even now I found myself painting in my mind during the day, the Winston and Newton tubes of pigment, the gesso to prepare the canvas, the palette knives, and brushes, an image in my head. Then my critical self said, *No, Jill. You can't do this.* Now, here I was again, my best friend pulling at my heart. I looked at the door to the art center and figured I'd put one foot in front of the other and lose myself in a long list of deadlines.

I unlocked the alley door and noticed the crime tape had disappeared. It was totally quiet inside, except for the sound of the air-conditioner. Leaving everything in my office, I faced the prospect of my next task. Tom had taken the tape away from the basement door, and I peered into the darkness. Pulling on the light chain over the stairs, I took a deep breath. *I can do this.*

I tiptoed carefully down the steps. At the bottom, I pulled light bulb chains as I crossed the room, figuring I'd leave them lit for the apostles. When I reached the end of the concrete, I saw the area they'd dug to begin with, and all the equipment and timber lying on the floor. They'd planned to use the wood to fortify the first and second floors. Over at the side of the room was a cluster of little white flags, the kind the power company inserts in the ground to signal underground lines. I guessed the coroner had planted them, and maybe Tom had removed them. I peered into the remaining depression.

Standing there in the silence, I closed my eyes and said a prayer, hoping God had taken her in His arms, and only that set of bones was left on this earth, in this existence. I prayed her last few moments had not been as horrific as I'd imagined them. Maybe she was with my parents now. I hoped so. I stared at the dirt and remembered Angie and me last night. "Justice," I whispered. We would help Tom find her killer. He would pay.

Turning, I walked back upstairs since the workers would be here soon. Louise was due in a half-hour with Jordan on her heels. We'd get through this day.

I'd already put in a halfhearted hour on radio and newspaper ads before the guys showed up. I figured it would be comforting to have people in the basement making noise. They trooped down the steps like they were on a mission, helping me feel as if life was back to normal for now. A smiling Louise arrived next, her arms filled with coffee and donuts. "My aunt's favorite donut recipe." She could always pull me out of my gloomy thoughts.

I'd had time to check on Jordan's social media plans for the Heartland exhibit, and they were as imaginative as Louise had predicted. When my intern came in the alley door, I told her I loved her designs. "Today, keep working on the internet ads, and we'll also have you write a note to send to volunteers for the hanging and lighting of the exhibit. A reminder to them about the time."

Jordan nodded. "I can do that."

"I think we'll have a meeting closer to the opening—you, me, Louise—to discuss our plans for the weeks up to the opening. It's important you understand what we're doing if you plan to run your own nonprofit someday." I winked at her. "We're trying to be very 'hands on.'"

Louise was working on the volunteer list in her office as I stuck my head in the doorway. "How's it coming?"

"Going great guns. I've already heard back from six volunteers. Six should be enough, even if we don't hear from others."

"You're putting a smile in my day." Returning to my office, I pulled out a couple more files and grabbed my pen. I'd make myself concentrate.

Before I could start on them, my bracelet clinked, reminding me of Carolyn. That single small noise took me back to our past. She'd been the first one to go on a real date when she was fifteen. Of course, she'd sneaked out of the house to meet him. It was a joyous two hours at the drive-in theater, all the romantic details recounted to Angie and me like a legendary first. A swashbuckling, romantic evening by her account. Unfortunately, when she sneaked back in her bedroom window, her stepfather was sitting in her room, and they had a huge argument. Our Carolyn. Never could keep her mouth shut. She always threw it up to him that he wasn't her real father. Her weak, downtrodden mother had abdicated the discipline in the house much earlier. Despite being grounded for a month, Carolyn told us it had been worth it to meet the boy.

I sighed, the mental picture dissolving, and I reminded myself to focus on the exhibit.

Before lunch, Louise stopped in my office, her hands behind her back. "I brought you a gift."

"What's the occasion?"

"Didn't need one. It's a mental health and sanity gift."

I brightened. "Oh, that's the best kind. Must I guess which hand?"

"No." She brought out her hands. "You got yet another memo from the board prez in the email inbox."

"From my considerate friend, Ivan?"

"Yes. I found a spindle to collect them. See, you stab them with the pointed metal piece."

"Perfect."

On the wooden base was a newspaper photo of Ivan the Terrible, the spindle through his bow tie. "Wow. This could get a lot of use."

She nodded her head. "Here's the memo that came this morning. Your turn."

I grabbed the usual yellow missive with his official name at the top and slammed it onto the spindle. I'd read it later. "I love this. You sure know how to please a girl."

By afternoon, our group of three was working like a well-oiled machine. Closing in on the weekend, we'd accomplished most of what I'd planned for the week. We were on schedule, and a great weight was lifted from my shoulders. Of course, we still didn't know if we'd see an avalanche of entries, but I reminded myself it was out of my hands. This was a satisfactory day.

Late in the afternoon, Tom stopped to see me. I rescued a pile of folders that had mysteriously commuted to my love seat and indicated he should sit. He asked how my day had gone, but I knew he wasn't simply here to make small talk.

Eventually, he took a deep breath and blew it out. "I know Carolyn was your friend, and I'll tell you what I can about her. Most of this will be in the newspaper once I tell her parents."

"Her poor mother. I always liked Ruth Anders. Her stepdad, not so much."

He looked at me expectantly as if he thought I'd say more about her stepfather. "It might be better if you heard this from me instead of reading about it in the paper."

"You are kind. Thanks."

"Autopsy's back, but we're still awaiting DNA results. The dental records matched. You had the key. She wasn't listed as missing because no one

71

figured she was."

"No doubt it was Carolyn?"

"Correct. It was homicide—strangulation—about ten years ago."

"Right." A moment passed. "Don't soft-pedal it, Tom. I'm not a hothouse flower that will wilt. Carolyn was Angie's and my best friend, so we want to know everything. I know you think I'm still a kid, but I'm not. After Mom and Dad died, nothing worse can happen."

Tom looked at me silently and must have come to a decision. "This, what I tell you now, is between you and me and maybe Angie. The body was wrapped in a heavy plastic called visqueen so appendages, like the hands were on the outside, but the core was somewhat mummified because it was protected."

"What do you mean?"

"Hair, clothing, and parts of the core were still there. It wasn't simply a skeleton."

"Oh, my God." *No nausea. Keep calm. Act adult. Think about a calm shade of white and permanent blue.*

Tom agreed. "I felt it was weird too. Some soft tissue was protected by the wrapping, and we had the teeth to compare to records."

Looking at me, he must have recognized my composure. "Tom. Angie and I have talked this over. We think we could be helpful, maybe use what we know about Carolyn to aid your investigation."

He sat on the love seat quietly. Then his protective brother face appeared again. "I don't want either of you anywhere near this. For all we know, the killer's still out there."

"All the better for us to help with the theory work. We knew Carolyn, and we could help you identify suspects."

"If suspects are still here, it's all the better to keep you away."

"You didn't listen to me, Bro. Theory. You do the footwork, and Angie and I'll send you in the right direction."

Tom reached over and took a couple of tissues from the table near the love seat. He blew his nose, dropped the tissues in the wastebasket, and looked thoughtfully at me. Maybe, just maybe he'd listened. "There's something you don't know. We're keeping the bracelet and one other item out of the news coverage."

"What?"

"She was eight-to-ten weeks pregnant."

"What?"

"Yes. Pregnant."

"I—we—Angie and I—didn't know." *Poor Carolyn.* What else didn't we know? "Do you think this was the motive?"

"Perhaps. Who might the father have been? The autopsy can't give us the DNA on the baby. Too tiny and too long ago."

While I was thinking about that, Tom took out a small notebook and began to write notes.

Then I remembered. "Angie met a college guy Carolyn had been seeing when she disappeared."

"I'll check it out with Angie and go over to the college. Anyone else? How about Mitch Payson?"

I remembered seeing him in Angie's parking lot. "I can't imagine Mitch would be involved in this. I know him. He wouldn't have hurt Carolyn."

Tom looked at me, skepticism in his eyes. He gently shook his head. "That's the thing. You can't let your personal feelings get in the way. As I remember, they dated off and on. What if he found out Carolyn was pregnant? What if he knew it wasn't his? No telling what he might have done if he thought she was carrying another guy's baby." He paused a moment. "I hate to mention it because I know you like Mitch, but you've been gone for several years. He's developed anger management issues, behavior that was brewing under the surface years ago. Drinking way too much."

I focused hard on my recollection of the past. Thinking about him, I wondered if his drinking began with Carolyn's disappearance. "You know, Angie and I got postcards from her for at least a year after Angie last saw her."

"Do you still have them?"

"I don't think so. I doubt Angie would have kept them either."

Tom wrote in his notebook again. "What were they about?"

"Different cities they'd been to. Places she and this college guy had seen."

He shook his head. "Too bad. They might have given us clues because the killer wrote them. All right. You and Angie keep putting your thoughts together. Let me deal with the interviews."

This killer sounded organized, clever, and determined. A scary combination. I was disappointed. Here was Angie's and my chance to help find Carolyn's killer, and Tom was keeping us in the outfield. Maybe we could show him we were more helpful than that. "Tom, please. We really want—need—to help you out. Maybe you could find us a non-threatening job. We want to help. It's our Carolyn."

Tom sighed. "How about this? You can talk to Cindy Lanphere. She's safe. Cindy was living in an apartment with Carolyn before the murder. She might be able to tell you what was happening with Carolyn at that time. Think you could pull some information out of her?"

"Of course. Angie and I can collaborate on interview questions. I don't know why I didn't think of Cindy. We'll put our heads together and figure this out."

"We need to know what was happening in her life just before her death. You can talk to Cindy after we inform Carolyn's parents. But don't mention the bracelet or the pregnancy."

"No, of course not."

A surge of excitement went through me. Tom had said "we."

Chapter Eleven

I spent the rest of the weekend with rather mundane tasks, like cleaning my house and ignoring my paint canvases. They sat in the family room and dared me to touch them. I didn't. By Monday, the newspaper had a full story on the murder and Carolyn's identity. The publicity irritated me, and the board wouldn't be happy with the media's flippant name for her killer. They'd dubbed the murderer, "The Art Center Strangler." As if my art center had a role in her death. Leave it to the media to sensationalize everything. This was terrible with a board meeting coming up. They hated bad publicity.

Tuesday came quickly, and I ignored my anxiety by thinking about all the items on my to-do list. The one I dreaded most was this night, the monthly board meeting, where they'd have lots of difficult questions for me. I didn't have a good answer for my forgetting to lock the art center door. I whispered my mantra.

The art center board was composed of fifteen people from all walks of life. They were chosen for exactly that reason, and each served three-year terms. The mix included businessmen, teachers and professors, stay-at-home moms, and bankers. I inherited this board, but, as time went by, I'd replace some of them after their terms ended. Still, I was their employee, and they could fire me. And "they" included Ivan Truelove.

I heard the apostles at work in the basement and voices on this floor. Louise and Jordan were deep in conversation halfway down the hallway. They had hauled the *Mother and Child* pedestal back to the storeroom. Tom said he was at work on the theft, but the murder took precedence. I'd talked to him on the phone last night. We began with the guys in Carolyn's life near the time of her death.

"She was dating Mitch Payson, her on-again-off-again boyfriend about the time she would've gotten pregnant, but I don't know if she had anyone else in the picture other than the college guy."

"Both of those are viable suspects."

"I see." Instead of listening, I formulated a plan in my head to stake out Payson's garage with Angie to see what went on there. I hadn't seen Mitch Payson up close for years, so we would only observe. Since Carolyn's body had been discovered, I might find a way to get him to talk to me because we knew each other way back then through her.

"On another note, I went to the house to talk with her parents and let them know we'd found her. Needed to do that before the newspaper report came out."

I sat up straighter in my chair and rubbed my eyes. "Well, how did it go?"

"It was quite strange, as you might guess."

I grimaced. "We know what kind of household it was. I'm not sure we know the whole of it, although Angie and I heard a lot. Carolyn's stepfather went from the chief disciplinarian to an alcoholic toad who, I think, might have hit her on occasion."

"My suspicion too. Her mother was stoic, not a facial expression or a reaction. That might have changed after I left, but not while I was there. Her stepfather let out a tirade about what a slut she was and how she'd gotten the death she deserved. He didn't seem too surprised." Tom sighed. "It was all I could do not to grab him by the scruff of his dirty shirt and explain he had never been a decent stepfather to her and he was a miserable excuse for a human being."

Wow. My brother didn't usually show his emotions, and after this tiny outburst, he fell silent. After all, Carolyn had spent whole days and nights at our house while we were growing up. Everyone knew she didn't get along with her stepfather, Will Downey.

"Of course, I couldn't touch him since I'm the detective on the case." Tom had gone to the police academy and worked his way up on the police force in Apple Grove.

He was still a street cop when Angie, Carolyn, and I were in high school. Always curious, he took the detective's exam after I left for Chicago. It was just before our parents died, although that horrible time and the different events blurred a bit in my memory. I knew he'd been called to Carolyn's house for domestic disturbances between husband and wife before he became a detective. He knew her stepfather.

"Also talked to Wyatt and his wife."

"Neal? Why?"

"She was babysitting for the Wyatt kids the night she disappeared. He and his wife had gone to a birthday party for the high school principal and had too much to drink. The punch packed a wallop, but they got home safely, and he offered Carolyn a ride home."

"Not a bright decision, was it? He'd have been fired for a DUI if he'd been stopped."

"True, but he was young and stupid and figured he wouldn't get caught. Carolyn told him she could walk home—it wasn't far. He agreed and figured, like everyone else, when she'd disappeared, she'd taken off with the theater guy she'd told him about. Said he'd stayed up till two grading test papers that night. His wife, Viv, corroborated his story. I believe he genuinely regretted his decision now that he knew she was murdered. He told me he wondered how life would have changed if only he'd taken her home that night. It's the 'what if' questions that give you such regret and sleepless nights."

Sounded like Mr. Wyatt. "Will there—will there be a funeral?"

"I imagine. The office in Bloomington will let me know today, and I can tell her parents Carolyn's body has been released."

"Tom."

"Yes?"

"Thanks. Thanks for being you. It can't be easy. Carolyn loved you like a brother, and I think she would have been happy to know you were on the trail of her killer. Angie and I are so angry—you must catch him, and he has to pay. I know I've grumbled and been angry about Mom's sculpture, but I think this is more important."

"Me too. Talk to you soon."

Once again, I considered how much I loved my family, and Carolyn was part of our extended circle. With that thought, I went next door to talk with Louise about the board agenda. She was checking inventory and invoices for the items we'd sold in our little store at the front of the building before we closed.

My own report for the board was finished, and it lay on my desk, waiting for the dreaded meeting. I took three deep breaths and blew them out slowly. I'd fight the good fight, but would I have a job tomorrow morning?

Chapter Twelve

Tuesday night. Ten o'clock. Louise was sprawled on the love seat in my office. We were both exhausted after the marathon board meeting. Usually these monthly meetings started at seven and went to eight-thirty. Not tonight.

Louise yawned and then managed to find her voice. "I counted nine out of fifteen on our side. The usual three were grumpy, including Ivan, and not at all pleased with us. It was unfortunate that several have moved into the grumpy group. Maybe I should update my resume."

"They couldn't find anything wrong with the work for the exhibit. We've checked off the list about the way we thought it would go. We're up to date." It's just a tiny matter of a burglary and a dead body in the basement. You know, only the usual little problems. Kind of hard to get by those. The wall clock made a convincing case for my exhaustion. "I know they weren't happy about the building renovation because we don't know enough about what will happen when we try to raise the floor from the new foundation beams in the basement. They'll have to be as patient as I am. I don't like it either. We'll see how the local exhibit goes. We're putting all our marbles on opening night as far as winning their confidence."

Louise sighed. "At least we have enough volunteers to help set up the opening night gala. By then, maybe we'll have the sculpture back and the murderer in jail. Four weeks. Plenty of time. We should see entries begin to arrive in another week."

"I hope so. I have no idea what to expect. It's as uncertain as the building renovation." I paused, my memories shifting to long ago. The problem with coming home again wasn't that you couldn't, but people who knew you "back when" still thought of you as a child. It was as if you were frozen in time, the immature teenager they remembered, but they had moved on with their own lives. Some of those naysayers were on the board, believing I would fail. I still could. I reminded myself I had supporters too. Then I realized Louise was still talking.

"Jill, you've worked hard. The information is out all over town, sponsors are committed, volunteers are on our list, and Jordan's social media work is fantastic. Have a little faith."

I nodded. "I'll try. You're right. I should listen to you. Why don't you head home? I'll close. Neal and Ivan are still in the boardroom talking to Seth Pillsbury about a line in the budget. I'll have to wait for them. See you tomorrow."

As Louise collected her purse and locked her office door, I began to stack the papers I'd been working on for a grant.

"What did you think about their idea to research a grant to put in security cameras?" Louise lingered in my doorway.

"It's a great suggestion. Also, an updated security system since we've seen how badly this one works. I've written it down, and it's now on my ever-growing list for tomorrow. I can understand their concern. See you in the morning."

Once she left, I sat at my desk and waited for Seth, Ivan, and Neal. All in all, it had gone better than I thought it might. The six dissenting votes on most items were people I'd expected. Despite Ivan's blustery hot air about the break-in, the majority on the board was inclined to give me one pass for stupidity. When Ivan was voted down, his face got bright red and he sputtered like my parent's old coffee percolator. I was used to the "drive-by comments" he threw out under his breath. They were always about my incompetence or the staff's, meaning Louise's, ineffectiveness. If nothing else went wrong, and the exhibit happened as planned, I'd be in the clear. Dodged a bullet. All would have to go as scheduled, and it would have to be perfect. I was determined it would be. In the middle of these thoughts, I heard voices coming down the hallway. It was the man himself. He knocked loudly on the panel of my open office door.

"Well," Ivan's glasses were perched on the end of his nose like two round ship portals with uber-thick glass. "I have serious doubts about your administrative mistakes, Ms. Madison. I will wait and watch. You'll err again. I'll be there. Soon. I'm sure." He sniffed loudly and turned to leave. "Oh, and make sure you're on time for work. That Sandoval woman can only cover up for you so many times." He stuck two fingers up to his eyes, turned them toward me, and hissed, "I'm watching you," before he left.

What a petty little bureaucrat. Unfortunately, that opinion didn't overcome my anxiety. The door to the boardroom opened, and Neal and Seth walked toward me.

"Thanks, Neal, for explaining the change of lines in the report for my notes. It makes a lot more sense."

"No problem. Anytime."

Seth walked past my office. "'Night, Jill. Keep up the great work."

"Thanks, Seth." *One vote from the good guys.*

I began to lock my drawers and filing cabinets before I went home. Neal paused at my office door as if he had something to say.

"Thanks, Mr. Wyatt—uh, Neal, for being here tonight. It made all the difference in the financials. You speak their language."

"No problem. I enjoy learning how your nonprofit works. I haven't had this type of work for quite some time."

"While I'm thinking of it, thanks for the latch on the cabinet in Louise's office."

He smiled. "Easy. I had a lot of part-time work when I was a teacher to help pay the bills. Grocery stocker, house painter, hardware store clerk, carpenter, to name a few."

He checked his briefcase for all his papers, but it seemed to me he was looking for an excuse to hang around. I waited.

Finally, he stopped fidgeting and closed his briefcase. "I read the story in the newspaper. I know Carolyn was a friend of yours, and I imagine this is awful for you."

"Oh, yes. We were very close."

"I simply can't believe this whole situation."

Grabbing my sweater and purse, I walked toward the door to leave. "We were best friends."

"I remember she went out with Mitch Payson."

"Yes."

"I always thought he was kind of humdrum. Carolyn was much smarter."

"They dated a lot through high school."

Neal shook his head. "I don't know. He might be a possible suspect for Tom to check out. Carolyn used to say he had a temper."

"I'm sure Tom will figure it out. He's quite persistent."

"Good to hear. I told Tom she'd talked about a college guy too."

"Yeah. College guy's on his list." I hit the night-light switch and found my door key. "Thanks for your help tonight."

"Sure." And with that, he left me to close the building, but I remembered I needed to go back into my office.

Grabbing a couple of folders I wanted to take home, I locked my office door and heard Tom's ringtone. He asked how the meeting went, and I told him, relief evident in every word.

"I talked to the college guy today. His name is Evan Shaw."

"Carolyn's college guy?"

"Yes."

"Did you interview him on the phone?"

"No. Strangely, he lives in a house near Hamilton."

My turn to be surprised. "Wow! Twenty miles?"

"Close enough."

"How'd you find him?"

"College records. He was in this traveling acting group, and they rehearsed here in Apple Grove at the college for several weeks."

I thought about the mathematics for a moment. "Enough time for an eight-to-ten-week pregnancy?"

"Yes. My idea too. When he came to the door and I identified myself, he realized why I was there. I imagine he'd read the newspapers. His wife called out to him, but he told her I was a business contact. Then he moved us out to the yard."

"He's married."

"Yes, and has two kids. I gather he works in sales from home. Must do well. His attitude was confident, if not cocky."

"And what about Carolyn?"

"He said they'd had a brief fling—his words—for a couple months when he met her at a bar near the college."

"Probably the Rusty Nail."

"Uh huh. Described her as a groupie-type party animal looking for a good time."

My anger rose. "What? Are you kidding? Carolyn wasn't like that. She was kind, beautiful, and looking for a man she could fall in love with. Is there any way to find out if he was there the night she disappeared?"

"I'm thinking about that. Dan Gonzales has been the bartender at the Rusty Nail for, oh, twenty years or more. He has a memory for faces, names, and dates. I'll talk to him since he might remember. We'll see if he corroborates this cocky traveling salesman's story."

We signed off, and I picked up my purse. My anger about that guy's comment was still simmering. On my way home, I stopped for an ice cream cone since I deserved it after surviving the board meeting. I remembered a conversation Carolyn had with Angie and me in high school. Maybe it came back because I'd talked to Neal, our teacher.

It was our senior year, and she was dating a basketball player as far as the world was concerned. She'd also been seeing Mitch Payson quietly, and one night she made an offhand remark about how she'd probably end up with him. Mitch wanted to start an auto repair shop, and one of his relatives planned to help him financially. It was a vague memory. Maybe she meant she'd settle for him since they'd been friends clear back in early grade school. She wanted to have a little romance before she settled down. Maybe that wasn't Mitch's plan.

Chapter Thirteen

ngie and I showed up at Cindy Lanphere's house around five-thirty. It was Wednesday, traditionally a slow night at the bar, so Angie said she'd go to work once we interviewed Cindy. I didn't remember Cindy well from high school, but Angie remembered she'd been in choir with us and maybe in the group of majorettes who danced with batons at the half-time of the football and basketball games. After Carolyn moved out of her mom's house, they'd shared a place. Angie had been there once or twice to witness the dilapidated apartment.

Now, ten years later, Cindy lived in a modest two-story frame house on the east side of Apple Grove, nestled among other homes of middle-class people with families. I'd called her after Tom said we could help last Saturday. Angie and I figured it was a test to see how well we'd do as Tom's apprentices. Over the phone, Cindy told me she was married to a railroad engineer who was gone on his shift for the next week, and she worked as a dental hygienist. They had a couple of kids, a boy and a girl, but she'd shipped them off to her mother-in-law while we were there. Grandma always loved to have the kids. So, we'd made a date for the following Wednesday. Probably just as well the kids would be gone since we'd be talking about murder.

That was how we came to be drinking iced tea after work in her kitchen, a mixture of white cabinets, gray walls, black appliances, and red towels. The counters held a few appliances, which gleamed from repeated cleanings, and all was in its organized place. On the refrigerator door, I saw the traditional photos of kids and drawings from grade school. Cindy had been plain in high school, but now, slimmed down and with a flattering blond haircut, jeans, and white blouse, she had matured into a lovely woman and mom. After the preliminaries and catching up on old times, I took my notebook out of my purse, and we got down to business.

"I never knew anyone who died by violence before." Cindy's wide eyes tracked back and forth from Angie to me. "I mean, I grew up on a farm, and we shot deer and stuff, but this is horrific. I read the story in the *Ledger*, and I couldn't believe it."

Angie nodded her head with encouragement. "Right there with you."

"Yeah, you guys were, like, really good friends, weren't you? I mean, I seem to remember your connection from high school." Cindy paused. "Would either of you like lemon for your tea?"

I shook my head. "Nah. We're fine. To appease my curiosity, how did you two get together to share an apartment in the first place?"

"Oh. Well, let's see. I think Carolyn suggested it. I used to get lunch at the café where she worked, and we often struck up a conversation. My memory is she needed a place to live because she was old enough and she didn't want to live at home anymore." She took a sip of her tea and glanced at Angie. "I mean, later I found out there was a lot more to it than that." She looked down for a moment and hesitated. "I know she was a friend of yours, and I don't mean to speak ill of the dead, but I have to say I didn't realize she had such a social life. Dating."

Angie and I both laughed since we knew how Carolyn turned male heads. She visibly relaxed, encouraged by our laughter.

"You see, neither of us made much money. I worked as a clerk downtown and went to school a few nights a week to become a dental hygienist. Figured we'd throw our lots in together. We got along great, especially since she was often gone at night and I was kind of a homebody after work and school. We were compatible."

"Toward the end of the time you were together, did she talk about a guy or guys she was seeing?"

Cindy nodded. "Occasionally. Often, she said a few things that made me think she was dating this guy, Payson. I know he's still around town. It seemed to be on again, off again, and she was often upset with him. If I remember correctly, I don't think she was going out with him toward the end. He parked his old brown truck across the street and watched the house. I talked to her because it made me nervous, but she assured me he would never come near me. He didn't make her nervous at all. I thought stalking a person and parking outside her place was a little unnerving. You know, like normal people don't do that."

Angie set her glass of tea on the table. "I can understand your feelings. Maybe he was a little obsessed with her."

"Exactly. Before Carolyn left, she gave me two months' rent. She was leaving town with this guy and didn't know if it would work out, so she would give it time. After one month, if she wasn't back, I should go ahead and find another roommate to rent with me."

Angie leaned toward her. "Did she say who this guy was?"

Cindy shook her head. "No. No, she didn't. Carolyn could be…secretive. I know she was happy about it. I'd come home, and she'd be getting ready to go out. She hummed a song she'd heard, kind of gliding around the bedroom as she dressed." Cindy stared at both Angie and me. "Don't you see? It's why I was so shocked when I saw the newspaper story."

"Makes sense to me." I glanced at my notebook. "Her stuff. What happened to it?"

"I took it to her parents' house when it became clear she didn't plan to return. She'd boxed her things—wasn't much—and I took it to her mom. She also left her mom a note." For a moment, Cindy paused as if she wasn't sure she should say what she thought. Then her face looked like she'd decided. "I don't know if you knew her parents, her mother, Ruth, and her stepfather."

"Yes," came out automatically from both of us.

"I didn't want to be at their house if her stepfather was there, so I waited until he left before I took the things to her mom."

"Why was that?" I figured I knew the answer.

"I almost shot him once."

"What?" Angie and I both said, totally shocked. Not what we expected. Too bad she must have held herself back was my unstated thought.

"Yes. I knew she hated her stepfather, and once I met him, I could see why.

In fact, one day when I was gone, he came to the apartment to see her. I showed up in the middle of their argument. He was mean, and he didn't want her to get away from him, kind of like having power over her. She lived away from home and made her own decisions and, for the most part, she was happy. He hated that. Usually, she didn't talk to me about things, but this had shaken her."

I nodded. "Yeah, we know Will Downey. He's as stupid as he is mean."

She paused a moment, "Oh, yes. The gun. A few days later I was at the apartment, and Carolyn called to let me know he was following her home from work. I met them at the door and aimed my Smith and Wesson right at her stepfather. Explained I'd won all kinds of shooting prizes for accuracy and he was close enough I'd not miss. I said if he ever came near our apartment or Carolyn again, I wouldn't miss. Self-defense. No problem."

Angie smiled. "Oh, I wish you had a video of that scene. People would pay to watch Downey get what he deserved."

Cindy started laughing. "Yeah. Everyone thinks I'm kind of quiet and harmless, but my brothers taught me how to shoot, and my dad bought me a handgun when I moved out on my own." She stood for a moment, moved to the counter, and picked up the pitcher of tea to refill each of our glasses. "Then I persuaded her to take out a restraining order for harassment against him. She did."

"Cindy, you're wonderful. Thank you for keeping an eye on her." Angie pushed her glass toward Cindy.

"Don't thank me too much. The thing is, Carolyn's stepfather could easily have caught her away from the apartment. I doubt a restraining order would have mattered much to him. He's the first person I considered when I read the shocking story in the newspaper. She detested him, and he hated the idea she had gotten beyond his reach."

Angie glanced at me. "After she babysat that night, could he have caught up with her?"

"Wyatt said Carolyn left on her own, so it's possible her stepfather waited for a chance to confront her." I didn't want to think about it, but it was possible.

Cindy watched both of us, one at a time. "Mr. Wyatt, the teacher? I always liked him."

"Yes. She babysat for his kids the evening she disappeared. Angie and I are used to talking out loud about this case."

"Case?"

"Oh, we're not on the police force, but my brother Tom has a lot of people to interview, and he figured we could be helpful if we talked to you since we knew you in high school."

"Makes sense."

"Of course, Tom might have follow-up questions for you too. He knows how to contact you."

"Right."

We couldn't say anything about the pregnancy since Tom warned they wouldn't release that little bit of information. I glanced at Angie. It was time to wind up this interview.

I closed my notebook to put in my purse. We thanked her and left, climbing into Wiley's truck so Angie could drop me at home. After we closed the doors, we both simply sat for a moment, not bothering to put on our seat belts or start the engine. It was as if this interview made it official. That night, September 23, 2007, Carolyn had vanished into the darkness. Who waited for her with a reason to strangle her and bury her body? Mitch? Her stepfather? Evan? We both must have turned over the same questions in our minds because we took a deep breath at the same time, looked at each other, and shook our heads.

"You know, at times I think a murder investigation is a lot like painting."

"Oh. Why?"

"You step back ten or twelve paces, look at your work, and realize a different perspective helps. Now we know how Cindy understood Carolyn's behavior before her disappearance, and we heard our own thoughts about her stepfather corroborated. Whichever guy it was, we have to nail him."

Angie nodded. "I think you've got something there." Then she started the engine.

Chapter Fourteen

Angie and I parked across the street from Payson's body shop near a store that had been here for decades. It was Friday. I'd left work for a long lunch hour, and Angie had picked me up again in Wiley's truck. He'd had his custom-detailed truck for a month, and we figured no one would recognize it, so we were safe. Byler's was a women's clothing store on North Second Street, known for its great bargains, but more importantly to us, its location across the street from Mitch's place was perfect. Crowded displays filled Byler's square footage, and you had to paw through dress after dress to find an outfit you liked. Still. It was a satisfactory place to shop for low prices. I remembered we used to troop to Byler's with my mom each fall when it was time to go back to school.

Prom. The store had a special area for prom dresses, and I remembered fondly those shopping trips with my mom, Carolyn, Angie, and Angie's mom. My dad, of course, wanted nothing to do with it except to say "yes" or "no" to my prom dress, "no" predominating if it showed too much skin. He wasn't a compromise type of guy when it came to his daughter. I thought my parents shored up the payment for Carolyn's dress.

"Why are we watching Payson's place again?" whispered Angie.

"Because I haven't seen him for a long time, and I'm not sure I would know him if I saw him these days. It was dark the other night in your parking lot. I think Tom heard rumors Mitch's drinking was hurting his business. I remember him in high school. He was good-looking, quarterback of the football team, not the sharpest tool in the box, but he seemed like a decent guy."

"Gotta tell you, he drinks a lot at our bar. Wiley's occasionally had to cut him off and he's gotten belligerent."

I turned and stared past Angie and across the street into the picture window of the garage. It had old-fashioned gold letters that said, "Payson's Autobody." I remembered a trip there once when I was home from college. My dad's car had been fender-bendered by a truck driver in a parking lot at his office. Ironic. Dad sold insurance. If I remembered correctly, Payson's shop had all kinds of auto parts for purchase as well as an area where customers could sit and wait. My artist eyes found it cluttered. The cash register was near the front in the window. Behind the store was a parking lot and a huge shed where they worked on cars or painted them. An alley led back to the lot where his clients' cars would be off the street.

As I watched the front window, Mitch stood at the cash register talking to a customer. They both laughed. He put some money into the register, closed the drawer, and shook hands with the man.

Angie whispered and touched my arm. "Look. Your brother."

Sure enough, Tom got out of an unmarked car he'd parked on the street and glanced over in our direction. Instantly, both of us scrunched down in our seats.

"Do you think he saw us?"

"No. Does he know Wiley's truck?"

"I don't think so."

We peeked through the corners of the car windows as Tom talked with Mitch, who was still behind the cash register. Mitch talked to Tom, but I could tell from their body language their conversation was becoming heated.

I watched the window. "Wish we could hear what they're saying."

Finally, Tom left, and we stayed down in the seat. He didn't show up outside the truck window, and I could vaguely hear the car engine start, so we didn't move for several minutes to be sure.

Angie looked over at me. "Well, we know Mitch must be an official suspect or Tom wouldn't be asking him questions."

"I have a feeling he and the college guy are at the top of Tom's list of most likely murder suspects. Think it's safe to sit up again?"

Angie pursed her lips and wrinkled her nose. "Maybe."

I lifted my head an inch or two and saw Tom's car was gone. "Whew! Safe, Angie."

We both sat up as the door to Byler's opened. Several older ladies came out, carrying sacks, and we watched them make their way to an old sedan, their movements slow. Several walked with canes. "There we are, you and me in our eighties."

We turned back around, and Angie was about to start the truck when a face leaned in through her window.

OMG. Mitch Payson.

"Ladies. Afternoon, Angie."

We both looked at him, speechless.

Then Angie got her voice back. "What do you want? How did you know we were here?"

"Your old man's truck."

"You know Wiley's truck?"

"Make it my business to know. It's what I do. Work on cars and trucks." He leaned back and checked out the door. "This one's a beauty. What exactly do you want, parking across from my place while"—he pointed—"her brother is talking to me?"

"Uh, we stopped at Byler's to look for dresses." Angie managed to spit that lie out. She turned and looked at me with a what-do-I-do-now expression. Huge eyes, guilty expression, like we'd been caught with our hands in the cookie jar.

Mitch still had gorgeous skin and those dark eyes he had in high school, and his hair was almost black, its thickness abundant. No receding hairline. He was still handsome in a dissipated way. His eyes kind of twinkled, and he had a smile as if he was having fun with us. I'd always liked Mitch.

"Heard you were back in town, Jill, working at the art place. Your mom's name on it. Seems like the kind of thing you'd do."

I nodded. "You're welcome to come over and take a look any time."

"Ah, thanks, but all that stuff's not for me." He turned and looked back at his shop briefly. "Wish your brother would leave me alone. He's awfully stubborn and opinionated."

"Tom is a bulldog when he gets an idea in his mind."

"Yeah, well he's got the wrong idea this time. Nosing around here asking questions about Carolyn. I was as shocked as anyone when they found her buried at your place." He paused. "Look, I'm a peaceful kind of guy. Don't want no trouble. I told your brother I wasn't even seeing her when she disappeared. She was with someone else, I guarantee you. We had a huge go-around two weeks earlier. I swore her off forever, like I'd done so many times. She was two-timing me with somebody. I knew the signs."

I leaned over toward Angie to see his face better. "We heard Carolyn left town with a guy she met at the college. An actor."

He shook his head. "I don't know about that, but I know she was seeing somebody, some new guy. She was anxious and ignored me. It had gone on several weeks, and I told her I was done." He pulled back and looked at the curb. Then, as if he'd had an idea he'd forgotten, he looked back at us. "Talk to her stepfather. He's a person the police should have investigated, if you know what I mean."

He leaned in a little closer. "Look, I loved that woman. I wouldn't have killed her. We argued sometimes, and I could always tell when she was about to leave me again. But murder her? Not me. Never." He pulled back, checking out the street then leaned in again. "You guys know me. We were friends in high school. Seriously? No way I could have hurt her."

I smiled. "Yes, I remember good days and bad, Mitch. My brother's an honest man and a brilliant detective. If you're innocent, he'll know it."

"He sure didn't sound like he'd crossed me off the list."

"Have a little faith. Jill's brother will get to the bottom of it." Angie turned to me. "We gotta go." She started the engine, and Mitch leaned back, worry on his face. We took off.

"Did you believe him?"

"No. And he has stinky beer on his breath. Don't think I'm mentioning this to Wiley." Angie glanced at me. "Did you believe him?"

"I'm not sure." I looked in the rearview mirror as Mitch stood, solitary, in the street. "I haven't seen him in years. Remember how Carolyn ended yet another relationship with a guy and Mitch always took her back? I know she was our friend, but sometimes I felt sorry for Mitch. He wanted this car business, but she wanted to get out of town. Two ships passing…"

"Did you see those muscles in his arms? He could easily have strangled her, perhaps one-handed, without blinking an eye."

Chapter Fifteen

The end of the week at the art center was slow, and we slid into the weekend with enough time to talk about our list of projects. Then Saturday was so crazy I hardly had a moment for Louise or Jordan. At least five of my phone calls were inquiries about when our art classes would begin. We'd compared notes around ten about the upcoming week, but beyond that, we were swamped with visitors and paperwork. To my joy, a few entries for the Heartland exhibit trickled in. Three, to be exact. It was a start. *I will show them success.* We still had a little over three weeks before the show went up on the walls. I'd only had two memos this week from Ivan the Bean Counter. Louise and I smashed his objections into oblivion.

I put Mitch out of my mind, and my working hours helped that focus problem. Jordan's trips to place posters around town were paying off, and we received several phone inquiries about the art show. Radio spots were on the air several times a day, and we had a daily promotion in the newspaper under the Events Calendar. Louise fielded questions from artists, and I planned to meet early next week with the hospitality committee. The group would decide on a menu, wine, and volunteers to set up and tear down. My first big plan to bring in the town was through the volunteer program, and then classes would kick in.

Until now, I'd worried about a lack of entries to our call for artists. These arrivals told me I was wrong, and I assumed we would hear from more over the next three weeks. I knew most entries came in at the last minute from my gallery work in Chicago. In fact, eventually, Louise would have to say "no" to late entries.

Then came all the phone calls. I'd been on the phone throughout the day, and Tom called early in the morning. He yelled at me for being near Mitch. How did he always know what I did? He mentioned "witness tampering," and I backed down. I meekly told him I'd stay with my art center work for the foreseeable future. However, he had no idea how much Angie and I wanted to find who killed Carolyn and make sure he was punished.

"Jill, leave the actual interviews of the suspects with me. However, if you remember any details involving Payson and Carolyn, like maybe something she told you, get back to me. You did a great job on Cindy, but Mitch is another story. He may be more dangerous than you think. His alcohol problem began after she disappeared. Could be guilt."

"Mitch? Seriously? You think he was the murderer?"

"No telling what he might have done if she told him she was pregnant by some other guy. I know you like him, but he can get angry like anyone else. Jealousy is a common motive for murder."

"I've known Mitch since we were kids. I find it hard to believe he'd hurt Carolyn, let alone kill her." I clicked to the home screen on my computer and sat back. "Well, maybe you're right. Maybe he's changed. Guess we'll see. All right. I'll call you or text if I remember anything."

After I tapped off, I looked back at my computer, where I'd been researching the week Carolyn went missing. My screen revealed the archives of the *Apple Grove Ledger*. Hmmm. Kimberly Nelson. The name seemed familiar. Did I know her? Oh, yeah. She was in my class in high school but didn't graduate. I kinda remembered her. Blond, big-boned, and muscular, not in the same social circle as Angie, Carolyn, and me. Adding "stupid" might have been true, but also unkind.

There it was. She'd been arrested in a bar fight, and Carolyn was the victim she'd beaten up.

Immediately, I called Angie. "Do you remember a bar fight between Kim Nelson and Carolyn before Carolyn disappeared?"

"Vaguely."

"She had a run-in with Carolyn a few days before the murder."

"Now it sounds familiar. Yeah. Nelson. She was cavewoman mean. I do remember. Something about a boyfriend she was with at a bar, and she thought Carolyn was hitting on him, a veritable mountain of prison tattoos and mean looks. No one, I mean no one Carolyn would ever have glanced at twice. I can't remember what happened exactly beyond that."

"Kim was arrested for assault and destruction of property—chairs, bottles, and miscellaneous items at the Rusty Nail. The assault charge was levied against Kim because she started it. The story reads like Carolyn was defending herself. Anyway, Nelson was hauled away, and her case was on the court docket a month later. Meanwhile, she spent the night in jail before the tattooed mountain bailed her out. I don't know about you, Angie, but I know a lot of people who don't forget grudges."

"I think it's possible Kim is involved in this murder because she lost face in this dispute. Carolyn disrespected her, and she might have wanted to get her back. Maybe it was a plan that backfired. Perhaps Kim wanted to rough her up, not kill her. Now I remember. A week or so after that brawl, we stopped for a drink following the college play. When we walked in, I saw Kim there with two mean-looking guys. She glanced in our direction, I saw her eyes narrow, and she pointed Carolyn out to these guys. It was crowded, but I hustled us out the back door, and we took off. Tom would want to know about Kim's alibi for the night Carolyn was murdered, and if she's still the human mass of scariness I remember, the police should handle this. I love you, Jill, but I'd prefer to see you live."

"Mmm…I think this one might be better for Tom to tackle. I'll call him."

After Angie hung up, I sat for a long time and simply thought about Carolyn. She, Angie, and I had loved each other fiercely and had been together forever, from grade school on. I could name oodles of kind acts Carolyn had done for people, and we had had such fun growing up in this small town. We had the lake in the summer, my mom and dad's bicycle-built-for-two (but we managed three), hanging out at the root beer stand, and exchanging brags about the kissing bridge at the lake. When I considered our history, I marked the change in Carolyn around junior high or early high school. It was a while after her mother remarried. But I had to admit we had compiled an impressive list of people who might have had a reason to kill her, even if accidentally. There was Evan and now Kim. Tom would add Mitch. Maybe her stepfather. How did this girl we loved rack up so many people with grudges?

I stood, stretched, and walked out to the front of the gallery to change the direction of my brain. Strolling past the spot where my mother's sculpture of us had been, I was fearful Tom would never find it. Then there was Carolyn. I loved my brother and knew he was a smart, amazing detective, but I didn't think he had ever led a murder investigation.

Once back in my office, I'd almost figured out which column of figures I should check next when Angie's ringtone went off.

"Jill," she paused, "I need to share an idea because I can't hold it in any longer."

"Sure."

"I feel we should have done something."

I sighed and took a long breath. Gazing at the half-eaten cookie, I set it on my desk. "Yeah. I know what you mean. It makes me sad to think we didn't do more to help Carolyn get out of town like she always wanted to do."

"Me too. Since they found her body, I've felt so guilty. I'm not sure what we could have done, short of building a raft and floating her down the Mississippi away from Apple Grove."

"Amen."

"I keep thinking if—no, when—Tom finds her killer, I might be able to rest easier. You know, a little redemption. I just can't stop thinking about her. Strangling. Why weren't we there for her? Another thing. Carolyn's mom and stepdad have planned only a graveside ceremony for her on Monday morning at eleven."

"Well, all right. I wish they would have a service where her friends could say a few words. It isn't our decision to make, I guess. We'll be there."

"You're right. Talk to you later."

I ended the call and realized it was later than I thought. Although it was light outside since it was June, Tom had warned me about being here alone or leaving late by myself. I organized papers on my desk for tomorrow, pushed in my chair, and found my purse on the love seat. Next to my purse was the mail Louise had dropped off earlier in the day. I'd completely forgotten about it. She took care of incoming art entries but left the other mail for me to open.

Several bills were on top, and I laid them aside to put on Louise's desk in the morning. Next was useless junk, so I threw it in the circular file. On the bottom was a manila envelope addressed to me.

"Hmm. Wonder what this could be. Postmarked, but no return address."

I took my letter opener and slit it across the top. A group of photographs, five-by-sevens, fell out on the desk.

"What the heck?" I sat down, turned the desk lamp on, and examined them. My breath caught. I instantly realized what people meant when they described the hair on their necks standing up. Moving the first picture off the top of the stack, I scanned the others. My heartbeat raced, even though I was holding my breath. Someone had taken close-up photos of me in front of the art center as I was walking in or at lunch with Angie, opening the door to my house, sitting with Angie at her bar while Andy and Lance played in the background, and even at the ballpark on the bleachers next to Tom and Mary. I put my hand to my mouth and tried to catch my breath. Why would someone do this? How could he or she get so close to me? What did this mean? I stuck my head out the doorway of my office as if someone was watching my discovery, but I was alone.

Despite my determination to find out who killed Carolyn, I wasn't totally reckless. I opened my purse, pulled out my phone, and speed-dialed Tom.

Chapter Sixteen

Standing next to Angie at the Restful Home Cemetery Monday morning, my thoughts were far from Carolyn's service. Mindful of Tom's words on Friday, I had spent the weekend at home, and if I had to leave the house, I called Andy or Lance. I locked the doors and windows, didn't leave the art center after dark, and noticed a police car circling my block several times.

"Whoever did this knows everything about your locations. The photos are digital, so it could have been anyone. He's stalking you. These photos say he's dangerous and isn't fooling around. They're a warning." Tom had put his hand on my shoulder. "This is serious, Jill. Someone thinks you're snooping into Carolyn's death. I think you should move in with Mary and me until we catch him."

I talked him out of his suggestion with promises. Since the original envelope that came to the art center, I hadn't received any more photos at home, and my phone calls came from legitimate contacts...except for the robocall that wanted to sell me a "very special" miracle pet groomer.

Andy said the photos were from a distance with a close-up lens. No fingerprints showed up on the envelope or photos except mine, but the more I thought about it, the more I figured it didn't seem like Kim's style. Photos were too civilized and, besides, she'd never send me photographs. She'd just come over and knock me dead with one blow. Subtle wasn't her style. Subtle took intelligence. On the other hand, Evan Shaw might be intelligent, and we knew he could take photographs.

Back to the present. I scanned the cemetery. No Mitch. No Evan. No

Kim. It was a peaceful place, gorgeous colors of viridian green in the noon sunlight. The grave markers weren't stones but engraved metal rectangles, black trimmed in gold, laid flat on a cement base. I imagined they would have to have Carolyn's made since it wasn't in place yet. All around us were vases with flowers next to various markers, and I could imagine coming here occasionally, having a talk with Carolyn, and bringing her flowers. Purple irises. Those were her favorites. A bit humid for June in the Midwest, the weather had turned out beautiful for such a sad day. It was only fair. I kept my head down and considered all she'd meant to me. Then I looked up and studied the mourners.

Carolyn's mom, Ruth, stood closest to the open grave, her face stoic, her gaze down. She was in a black dress with a jacket over the fitted top. Someone had handed her a bouquet of daisies, and she held it on the side away from her husband. I thought she looked much older than her sixty-some years. She appeared to have aged considerably since I'd seen her. Carolyn's stepfather—he whom Angie and I called Stupid—stood silently in his out-of-date suit, his tie hastily knotted, his stomach rolling over his belt. Ugly toad. From a distance, he didn't seem as terrifying as I remembered, but I'd grown up. My life had been fuller, and I'd seen more of the world now. He would be forever trapped in his small house with his silent wife, without children, step- or otherwise. They stood facing us, Carolyn's only family, on the other side of the grave, with the minister at the end of the deep, dark hole my eyes avoided. From one burial ground to another.

On "our" side of the grave were Angie and me, hanging on for dear life. Angie's parents, Tom, Mary, and Andy were in our group, along with a couple of women our age I vaguely remembered from high school. Cindy, her arms across her chest, listened to the clergyman. She glanced up, and I nodded toward her. I scanned the crowd for anyone with a camera. Nothing.

"I am the resurrection..." the minister read from a well-worn Bible.

Angie squeezed my hand. I could imagine Apple Grove without Carolyn because she'd not been here alive for eleven years, but I'd always been sure she was out there somewhere. In true Carolyn style, I figured she'd turn up when we least expected it with a husband and family. This time I was wrong.

Wiping my face, I tried to listen to the minister's words as he droned on. It was obvious he never really knew her. He relied on a few scriptures and talked about resurrection once or twice. I concentrated on a lovely shade of gold made of white and cadmium yellow light. Feeling calmer, I studied Carolyn's parents, her mother's head bowed, her stepfather expressionless—no compassion, no recognition of her relationship with his wife. My eyes hardened as I saw him stand on the edge of her grave without a concern in the world, his secrets buried.

The benediction. People began to move restlessly around me, and Carolyn's life on this earth was now at an official end. Angie and I looked at each other, both with the same expression.

Angie spoke first. "We should speak to her mother. You know, say something."

"What?"

"We're sorry. Or we wish we'd watched her daughter better. We were careless."

"How about 'we hope your husband burns in hell for how mean he was.'"

Angie's face told me "inappropriate." Another hand squeeze. I was an expert at interpreting their meanings.

In the end, we said all the right words. Carolyn's stepfather kept hold of his wife's arm, and she lowered her gaze, never once acknowledging us, other than a murmured "Thank you." Despite my sense her stepfather was a strong man and obviously controlled Carolyn's mom, I looked at his face and saw his total disregard for Angie, me, or his stepdaughter. We were nothing.

And that was the moment my own eyes narrowed, my grip on Angie tightened, and my resolve hardened even more to find out the identity of Carolyn's killer. Her real family didn't care, so that left Angie and me, her family who loved her.

I stopped at home and ate a quick sandwich then headed back to work. Every so often I swore, thinking of the ugly toad, the uncouth man who stood over our Carolyn's grave.

Chapter Seventeen

The last couple days, while sitting in my chair at the art center or lying on the sofa at home, I couldn't get Carolyn's funeral or the names of the suspects out of my mind. Couldn't concentrate. Louise wondered what was in my head. She stared at me with an odd look and asked questions to see if I was myself and not a clone from another universe.

Mitch flitted through my mind. I had to remind myself I hadn't been here for years or seen Mitch during that time. I kept picturing him as our teenage friend, but Tom was investigating him as the murderer. Maybe he was right. Perhaps Mitch found out about Carolyn's pregnancy and, angered because he'd waited for her to come back and marry him, he'd killed her. Another man's baby was the final straw. He was certainly strong enough. He could've followed her home, strangled her, wrapped her up, carried her to his truck, and stashed her till he could find a place to bury her. Why the Lowry Building, and how did he get in? It would explain why Cindy believed he stalked Carolyn.

He wasn't at the graveside service, and I doubt he was big into photography as a new hobby. Maybe if I talked to him, he'd tell me what he knew. Oh sure, he'd spill his guts. I checked my watch. A little too late for him to be at work, but it was worth a drive past his garage. Making sure the front door of the art center was locked, I went out by way of the alley to my car in the back.

Starting the engine, a sense of guilt nagged at me. Tom told me not to talk to Mitch because it would be like witness tampering since he was a prime suspect. If he'd murdered Carolyn, he was a dangerous man. I considered

Tom's warning. Having grown up around Mitch and gone through all the school grades with him, I found it difficult to believe he was a killer. Of course, he was a kid and a teenager back then. Was he so different as an adult? Tom said he drank more and more now than when I knew him. He'd heard rumors around town Mitch needed cash because alcohol was hurting his business. My gut instinct simply told me he couldn't have done this. If Tom was right, I had to find out for myself, and if I talked with him, maybe I could confirm Tom's suspicions or my belief in his innocence.

Mitch had been the All-American football quarterback in high school, the homecoming king, and a guy who was never without friends. He ruled the high school hallways, but he wasn't smart enough to go to college, even if his poor family had had the money to send him. Still, he was a good mechanic, and one of his uncles had staked him in the autobody shop after high school.

He and Carolyn dated off and on all through school, having met in elementary school and sworn in junior high to love each other forever. She was his first love. Ah, the love-for-eternity promises we made with such ardor at fourteen. He was always there for her, but after junior high she began a pattern of dating other guys. Then she'd return to Mitch. He was a patient man. He'd ask her to marry him, she'd refuse, and then he'd wait for another opportunity. Angie said their fighting had escalated before Carolyn disappeared. Once she supposedly left town, Angie and I figured he'd get over her and find another love.

Evidently, he hadn't.

His autobody shop was about ten blocks from the art center in an area of businesses and warehouses which dealt with trucks, cars, and transportation. I drove by his business slowly and noticed a nightlight in the back of the store. After circling the block, I ventured down an alley, parking behind the store in a lot where he had his paint and repair warehouse. Somewhere I heard a dog bark and wondered if Mitch had a killer watchdog on the premises, but the barking wasn't close by, and the property wasn't fenced.

Crickets made their usual night noises, the dog barked in the distance, and an air force of moths flew around the one halo of light over on the other side of the building lot. The loud hum of a rickety old air-conditioner was the only noise to compete with the crickets. Seeing a light in the back of the body shop, I walked over to the door, intent on figuring out if he was still around.

A deep voice came out of the darkness behind me. "Something I can help you with, Jill?"

Once I started breathing again, I turned around and faced Mitch, dressed in coveralls liberally splotched with oil and paint stains. The colors blended rather nicely, a pleasing palette to my eyes. Under the coveralls was a sleeveless T-shirt, which displayed tattoos on the shoulder of each muscled arm. Alcohol fumes swirled around us, and, combined with paint chemicals, they made my nose itch.

"Mitch. It was good to see you the other day after so long. Thought I'd stop over and ask how you are since we've both suffered quite a loss with Carolyn's passing." Once again, I noticed how handsome he still was, but alcohol had taken its toll, and dark circles under his eyes testified to sleepless nights.

He looked at me, puzzled, and reached around to open the door to the body shop. "Come on in. You can join me in a late afternoon glass of whiskey. We'll drink to Carolyn."

As I walked in, I considered what I should ask him.

He hit a light switch as he crossed the threshold. Finally, in an uncertain tone, he muttered, "I guess I expected it."

I turned around. "What?"

He plodded past me to an area with a small table and three chairs. A half-empty whiskey bottle and a dirty coffee cup sat on the table, evidence he had started without me. He gestured to one of the chairs, and I sat. "She ran with the college crowd." Leaning his elbow on the table, he put his other hand around the cup and stared at the whiskey. "You know Carolyn. Guys fell for her in no time." He shook his head. "In the end, I always thought she'd come back to me, of course, but...it didn't happen."

Pouring more whiskey in the cup with a shaky hand, he took a deep swallow. "You know, I always liked you, Jill. You were all right." He pushed his chair back and stood. Then he walked into a small office and returned with a glass thick with dust and fingerprints. Pouring a couple of fingers into his cup and two into my greasy, fingerprinty glass, he clicked my glass with his cup. "To Carolyn."

Reluctantly, I downed the whiskey while I watched him drink his what—fifth or sixth glass of the night?

I let out my breath and decided I'd start with an ancillary question to get things warmed up. I lowered my voice to a steady pitch. "Mitch, do you remember Kim Nelson from high school?"

He hesitated for a moment as if working to bring her picture to mind. "Kinda. Blond?"

"That's the one. I found information that she and Carolyn didn't like each other. You know, bad blood. I have a feeling she might know something about Carolyn's murder."

"Carolyn was afraid of her. That I know. We ran into her and her band of tattooed maniacs in a bar one time. Nelson tried to start an argument with Carolyn by calling her names and such. I backed her out of there, and we left. Her whole body shook once I got her in my truck." He stared right into my eyes, his jaw clenched. "You think she murdered Carolyn?"

"I don't know, but she's on my list of suspects."

"She'd had a run-in with Carolyn one time and attacked her at the Rusty Nail. You know, she should have kept her mouth shut and her gaze off other guys." His eyes narrowed to a hard look.

"Did you see Kim there often? At the Rusty Nail?"

"Now that you mention it, yeah. She had a boyfriend with prison tats and another guy of equal ugliness. Don't think even I'd want to mess with them."

He paused for a moment, staring at the whiskey in his coffee cup. "Where am I?"

"What do you mean?"

"On your list. Your list of suspects."

"Depends. Do you have an alibi for the night Carolyn disappeared?" He didn't answer me, so I reframed my question. "Did you see her that night?"

Again, no answer, but instead, he went off into a whiskey-haze land of his own. "I couldn't go to her funeral. Couldn't think of her buried there. I loved her, Jill. Never loved anyone else." He slowly shook his head. "I don't know. Never understood her. When we were at Tyler Elementary and later at the junior high, she was the kindest, sweetest…Well, you remember."

"Absolutely." I waited to see what he'd say next. Nothing. "And you never married in all these years?"

He took a deep breath. "I happen to believe you have only one real love in this world, and she was mine. After that, nothing else matters."

"She didn't always treat you well."

He took another swallow from his coffee cup and set it down hard. "She changed. Never could understand. It was because she ran with the college crowd." His eyes narrowed. "Suppose she thought she could keep up with them, even though they called her a 'townie' and laughed behind her back. Then the latest guy would end it, and she'd come back to good old Mitch. That was why I watched out for her, you know. Some nights I sat outside her apartment to make sure she was all right."

Now tears filled the corners of his eyes, and I realized he was becoming maudlin.

"Angie and I hoped she'd end up with you, and she'd settle down."

"Wasn't gonna happen." He reached for the whiskey bottle again. "She wanted more than I could give her, wanted to go off somewhere else. You know, the adage nice guys finish last."

He slurred his words and repeated himself. He also hadn't told me where he was that night. "I'll never understand…never."

Tears trickled over his cheeks in an unending stream, and I felt sad for him, but I tried to give him the benefit of the doubt. Maybe seeing me, Carolyn's friend, had made matters worse.

He poured more whiskey in his coffee cup, but I put my hand over my glass. Once was enough. I'd already considered the various forms of bacteria I'd swallowed from this glass, but maybe the alcohol would kill them. I looked directly at him and he wiped the tears from his cheeks with the back of his arm. Quiet for a moment, I considered what to say next.

His face had turned red in a dramatic twist of emotions, and he pounded his hand on the table. "I was too easy…carried the torch for her and always took her back. Then she'd get restless with ordinary, boring old Mitch and dump me. I will say one thing. That girl could make me so angry. It was back and forth. Eventually, I'd had it. She drove me to drink, and when I fell deep in the bottle, I blacked out and couldn't remember what I'd done. Then she was gone. When I heard the news of her death, I couldn't believe it." He stared at his glass. "Made sense in a way since I didn't think she'd just disappear."

Despite Tom's warning, the words came out of my mouth all by themselves. "Did you know she was pregnant?"

He stared at me as if I'd said the Pope was my brother. "Pregnant?"

I couldn't decide if he was a good actor or honestly shocked. Tom thought he knew it. Why would Mitch lie, at least by omission? "I think not far along, maybe two months. Could the baby have been yours?"

He looked at me, and his eyes darkened. A scowl on his face indicated I'd asked the wrong question.

"No, not mine. Never forgot to carry protection. Do you think I'd put her in such a position? You know, small town, gossip, her reputation."

Here he was defending her. I couldn't help myself. I liked Mitch, and Carolyn certainly hadn't treated him well.

As he poured yet another cup of whiskey, I began to worry about alcohol poisoning. It was as if I wasn't even in the room. His eyes looked past me, his lips pressed into an angry slash.

"Mitch?"

"Yeah."

"You all right?"

His eyes were glazed, and his hands, now in his lap, were wound into tight fists.

"Mitch?"

Slowly he focused on me, his eyes moving from anger to determination. "I remembered something. I think I know. I'll take care of it. I'll deal with it."

"Deal with what? Who?" I asked softly, thinking he'd say either Kim or the college guy.

"That's for me to know and you to find out."

"If you know a secret about Carolyn's death, please, tell me."

"Something I remembered...about that night."

"What? "

"I'll take care of it. You don't have to worry."

I couldn't decide if I should take Mitch off my list of suspects. Tom figured he knew she was pregnant and, because he realized he'd never have her, killed her in a fit of rage. On the other hand, what if he was telling the truth? Tom could be wrong. He knew something. I didn't know what. My gut instinct said he didn't kill Carolyn, but maybe he knew who did.

Chapter Eighteen

Thursday afternoon found me sitting in my office talking with Jordan about nonprofits. I struggled to focus because Mitch constantly crept into my thoughts. I'd spent yesterday considering what he'd told me about his breakup with Carolyn and his knowledge of someone else in her life. Eight to ten weeks. He could have been the father, despite his concerns about her honor.

Jordan had worked out quite well after a suggestion or two about approaching visitors who came into the art center. Since she'd mastered every job I'd given her, I decided I'd take more of her time from Louise to instruct her in the various jobs she'd have to do if she ran a nonprofit. This morning it was time to update her on the board's hospitality committee.

"See this list, Jordan?"

"Yes. More volunteers?"

"In a way, but it also illustrates an important job for a director of a nonprofit. Our upcoming Heartland exhibit needs donations to help pay for the opening night reception. Part of your job as head of a nonprofit will be to raise money. You put together sponsors, volunteers, and membership drives."

"How do you figure out who to ask?"

"Great question. You need to get a feel for the community first. I am lucky since I grew up here and my parents knew area people in the arts. Programs help bring out volunteers too. You'll notice I'm gone occasionally to meet with possible sponsors. The promotion of the art center goes hand in hand with the board, as well as the various committees of board members, like the hospitality committee."

"It's all intertwined, so to speak?"

"Yes. I recently added Neal, who'll be able to explain the accounts each month and answer questions. Hospitality falls under public relations, and they met yesterday evening to decide on the menu, wines, and decorations for the Heartland exhibit."

"I love to talk about food and decorations. Sounds like fun."

"You may come to our next meeting, if you'd like."

"Tell me when and I'm there."

"I will. The hospitality committee decided some time ago that the theme for the opening night of the Heartland exhibit will be a summer picnic. This means we'll have red-and-white checkered tablecloths and centerpieces of wildflowers in Mason jars. You may have noticed the poster for the exhibit has a picnic table and hamper with wildflowers and food."

"I like the way you coordinated every aspect."

I looked at her and smiled. "That's my job, communication and coordination so the art center programs go smoothly. My friend Angie owns a bar, and she knows all about various types of alcohol. She suggested sangria made from moscato and a variety of red wines for the beverages. Of course, we'll have lemonade since it's a picnic, and because we need a non-alcoholic alternative."

"What's on the menu, and who brings the food?"

"The hospitality committee makes and carries in the food, along with a few other volunteers. That's why it's important to have responsible, enthusiastic people."

"I understand. Do you buy local food?"

"You betcha. We'll have small bite-sized sandwiches, cheese balls and crackers, bite-sized cookies, cut veggies, mini-toasted corn dogs, and lemon bars. It's a perfect picnic for our opening reception in July. Many of the ingredients come from the farmers market downtown."

"One question. Summer picnic won't always be the theme, will it?" asked Jordan.

"No. Every exhibit will be different. I've already begun to think about the theme for our first national juried exhibit. When you're in charge of an art center, you must think ahead. Always be on your toes."

"I've been thinking about a question I meant to ask you, but I kept forgetting."

"Fire away."

"Why an art center? Why not simply an art gallery?"

I considered for a moment. *How to explain?* "I guess because I didn't have many opportunities to learn about art when I was growing up, except through my mother. I was lucky. The public school had a lightweight program, and the Y occasionally had craft days, but those were the only programs available. I went back to school after college, got an Arts Management degree, and took on this building. It appears much of the town, including a few faint hearts on my board, thought this was foolish. I hope to prove them wrong."

"Now I see why you're in and out all the time and busy while you're here. It's your passion. You bring lots of people together. Lots of multi-tasking."

I pointed over to my wall. "See that whiteboard? It's the only thing that keeps me sane. It's my brain. I think I may need to buy a second whiteboard or get a larger one. The longer the center is open, the more directions I go."

"I can see you would have to be highly organized."

I sighed. "My office doesn't look it, does it?" I gazed around at all the piles of objects on the tables, shelves, desk, and love seat. At least ten new memos crowded my pointy-headed Ivan spindle. "Well, it's four-thirty, and you need to go. I haven't forgotten you're off to a reunion with your family tomorrow. Have a good time. On Monday, I think I'll have you work on a new area. Membership."

"Thanks. I've learned more from you than during a whole semester at school. See you Monday."

Louise had left around two because she had a dentist appointment.

I'd asked her, "Who's your dentist?"

"Fred Novinger. He's in Edgington. Gives me a family discount because he was married to my cousin's mother, but now they're divorced. Of course, the restraining order makes it a little awkward."

"A restraining order? Against him? Doesn't that worry you?"

"Nah. It's her he hates, not me. Me, he likes."

This meant I was left to finish up. I still needed to work on membership and the grant application for the security cameras. I went to the storeroom to check on today's entries. Counting, I reached fifteen. While it wasn't a lot, it was a start. We still had two weeks before we installed the exhibit.

I studied several of the entries, and it wasn't hard to pick out the ones I liked the best. Two photos of Midwest windmills and barns, a mixed-media collage of wildflowers, a couple of chalk renderings of unusual faces, and quite a few watercolors. My favorites of all, of course, were the oil paintings. I pulled one out from the others and studied the brush strokes and the colors. I took in a water mill, the wheel turning over above a lazy stream. A field of wildflowers was in the distance, and the color of the sky was white with a mix of permanent blue and cerulean blue, one of my favorite hues.

I began longing for a paintbrush. Almost smelling the oil paints, the solvents, the gesso, I felt the brush in my hand, my fingers with the right amount of pressure, the possibilities in my head as I leaned toward the new canvas on the easel. I had ordered several new tubes of paint. They were stored in the family room, ready to go. I simply had to get my courage up and unpack the boxes.

I set the painting down and left the storeroom, closing the door. When I looked out the front window, I realized it was almost dark. Where had the time gone? When I worked, the hours flew by because I loved every minute of what I did. It had been fun to explain my responsibilities to Jordan, especially since I was feeling my way along.

Grabbing my tote, I locked my office, turned off the lights, set the alarm, and went out the alley door, locking it before I started through the alley to the sidewalk west of the building. I had my tote over my shoulder, wondering if it had bricks in it. I was so tired. The sidewalk behind the next four buildings took me to the corner, where I crossed the street and walked the first block. Ignoring where I was going because my feet recognized the familiar path, I ticked off in my head what I needed to do tomorrow.

Our old neighbors' yards came into view and, out of habit, I took the shortcut through the backyards to get to my house faster. A line of tall bushes separated the Crocketts' yard from that of the Blankenships. A break in the line of bushes would give me entry into the Blankenship yard, and I noticed the familiar dirt track in the grass where we kids used to run through the bushes. The present-day children must do the same. I stopped to hoist my tote strap on my shoulder. Twigs broke in the dark behind me. I turned to look, holding my breath, but I didn't see anyone.

I hurried a little faster through the Blankenships' yard, walking down a small hill to reach the Colliers', where they had a swing set I didn't see and almost tripped over. It was even darker now than when I'd left the center, and I heard my brother's voice. "Don't go out alone. Don't be by yourself after dark. This guy means business." We had huge trees all through the neighborhood, and if anyone were to follow me, he would have lots of cover and shadows to hide in. I walked as fast as I could, my breath coming heavily, my heart pounding in my ears.

Besides the thump-thump of my heartbeat, I was sure I heard footsteps behind me. Had I imagined them? I couldn't stop to check it out, so I moved as fast as I could. I was into the Wendovers' yard, and once I cleared the house, I took a tiny glance back. Was that a shadow moving on the side of their garage? Up to the Palmers' house, the last yard with trees scattered throughout before our block. Even a huge weeping willow. Looking quickly over my shoulder, I saw a shadow move near the old oak in the Palmers' yard.

That was when I began to run.

I sprinted across Mary Street, its one meager streetlight down the block shining on the asphalt. Racing across the smooth surface, I had two more neighborhood yards to go. Looking back, a dark figure, a black shadow, moved along near the Palmers' trees on an exact line with me. Into Driscolls' yard, running, running, with another swing set and a round umbrella table, and an above-ground pool affording me a little cover. Out of the Driscolls' yard and into ours, running as fast as I could go now, my breath coming out in spurts, my legs exhausted, especially since I'd worn heels to work. Thank God I hadn't twisted an ankle.

My red silk neck scarf came loose from my neck and fell off behind me, but instead of stopping to retrieve it, I pulled my tote from my elbow, where it had slipped, and my fingers rifled through lipstick, wallet, tissues, pens, receipts, lip balm, and, finally, thank God, found keys. Grasping them, my fingers sorted around until I found the familiar house key. Up the steps to the back deck. Opening the screen door, I pushed the key home, pulled it out, stumbled over the threshold, dropped my tote, locked the screen and the inside door, and collapsed into a kitchen chair, totally out of breath and shaking. I hadn't turned on a light. I simply sat in the dark, while my chest heaved up and down, up and down. I stretched my legs out to stop their shaking.

I wasn't sure how long I sat there, quivering in the dark. Had I imagined someone? I'd heard twigs break, but couldn't it have been squirrels or neighborhood cats or other nocturnal creatures? The shadows—trees? I was used to studying shadows since they were an integral part of painting, but right now my terror seemed to conflict with my vision. I took deep smooth breaths, laid my head back, and listened to the quiet. Wasn't gonna tell Tom. He'd kill me. He'd lock me in their house until I was forty.

Finally, I rose, kicked off my shoes, almost stumbled over my tote, and carried it out to the dining room, still not turning on a light. I walked through the hallway to the front door and made sure it was locked. It was. Thinking about it for a moment, I decided to turn on the front porch light, in case anyone was sneaking around outside or trying to look in the windows. Windows. I began to systematically pull shades and curtains on the first floor. My anxiety level was still high, my heart slower but still pounding in my head.

There. Home at last. Doors locked. All was well. I walked back out to the kitchen and considered whether to turn on the light. No, I'd switch on the light out on the back pole at the far end of the yard near the shed, plus the one on the deck. I clicked the switches by the back door, pulled open the window curtains a narrow slit, and peeked out into the now well-lit yard. No one lurked anywhere.

Before pulling the curtains shut again, I gasped, my face flushed and tingly.

Hanging from the handrail on the deck, tied with a knot, was my red silk scarf.

Chapter Nineteen

Everything was dark. I wasn't quite sure where I was until I realized I had a blanket over my face. Peeling it off, I discovered the night had become morning. I was on the sofa in the living room of my house, fully clothed. My shoulders ached from tension and the way I'd slept. I remembered last night, the dark shadow following me and my decision to sleep downstairs in the living room instead of upstairs. Somehow it had seemed safer. Staring across the room at the bookshelf, I saw by the clock it was six forty-five in the morning. What day was it? Oh, Friday. Work at ten.

I punched in a text to Angie. **CODE RED My house**

Code red was from our teenage years. It might mean "danger" or "hot guy in vicinity." Usually we could tell which.

A pause ensued. I watched my phone screen. Nothing…Nothing…Come on, Angie.

Her text flew back: **What? This early? Code Red? Hot Guy?????????**
On 2nd thot, bring muffins
Seriously? What about Code Red?
Banana Muffins. Then Code Red.
Coming 10 min. Dress. Muffins. Drive to yr house

I started the coffee and went upstairs to shower and change clothes. By the time I returned to the kitchen, I heard the key in the front door. An undetermined number of people had a key to my house. You'd have thought the sister of a detective wouldn't have this problem, especially when he always said, "I don't care if it is a small town, lock the doors."

Coffee, two muffins apiece, twenty minutes later, and a description of my harrowing night, complete with a bit of shaking and nerves.

"Don't you remember Tom saying, 'Don't go anywhere alone, and definitely not at night'?"

I heaved a deep sigh. "Nothing has happened, so I figured it was safe."

"Until last night. I don't want to be the last of the three musketeers alive." She took a big bite of muffin and mumbled through a mouthful of bread, "But if I am, can I have your mom's sculpture if Tom finds it?"

"Very funny. Maybe. If I don't decide to have it buried with me." I drained the last of my second cup of coffee. "We need to think this through."

"Which 'this'?"

"'This,' meaning who killed Carolyn. Whoever stalked me and tried to scare me must know I'm asking questions."

Angie nodded her head, took a last bite of her banana muffin, and brushed off her hands. "Ready."

"Let's consider the suspects. First, Mitch. He was candid when he wasn't sober. He might have been jealous since she broke up with him, and he figured she had someone else. But he seemed genuinely shocked about her pregnancy. He knows something. If not Mitch, then who?"

"We should mention Kimberly. Can't count her out."

"I thought about her. We don't know much yet about the Kim connection, and how could she get into the Lowry Building? We need to get on that." I stood and cleaned the crumbs from the kitchen table.

"Can do."

I thought again. "Mitch said Carolyn had broken up with him weeks earlier and she acted like she had somebody else in her life. It might have been Evan. We need to find out when he arrived and if the baby could have been his. I'll check the internet for the college news back then." I put the coffee cups in the dishwasher and sat on the chair across from Angie. "And we know how she was at times, kind of coy and flirty." I pictured Carolyn for a moment. "Maybe it is even a suspect we don't know other than Mitch or Evan."

Angie looked at me, disappointment painted all over her face. "Yet another guy she was seeing? This was eleven years ago. How are we supposed to find out? A Ouija board?"

"Do you have one?"

She tilted her head, with a skeptical expression. "I think your mom outlawed that since the great Ouija board disaster of ninety-six."

"Oh, yeah. Forgot that."

"I don't think we should make this any more complicated than it is. Kim or Evan, or maybe Mitch. I think we should concentrate on Mitch, Evan. Start there."

I sat back, my shoulders slumped in temporary defeat. I hit my forehead with the heel of my hand. "Think, Jill." I considered this complicated mess. "We need to put ourselves back then. How do we find out what was happening with Carolyn about the time she disappeared?"

"Not to change the subject, but have you told your brother, the detective, about your stalker last night?"

"Are you crazy?"

"Have you told him about the drinks with Mitch?"

"Not that one either."

Angie walked over to the kitchen door, pushing the curtains aside so she could peruse the deck.

"What are you doing?"

"Checking for your red silk scarf. I don't see it."

I walked over to the door and looked out. No scarf hanging on the railing.

"I know it was there last night. I saw it."

"Are you sure?"

"I'm sure. The deck light is still on, and I didn't dream I saw it in the light."

Angie unlocked the door. "I'll go check the yard. Maybe it blew off during the night."

She walked around the yard, inspecting closely the area around the bottom of the deck. No scarf.

"No scarf." She repeated my thoughts on her way back up the deck stairs. "Now what?"

"We should watch people in town and see if it's around anyone's neck."

"You think some guy would wear your red silk scarf around his neck?"

I shrugged my shoulders. "Do you have a better plan?"

A worried look came across Angie's face. "What if he kills somebody else with your scarf? You could be arrested."

"You think my scarf is a murder weapon? Seriously? If that happens, you've never seen my scarf before, got it?"

"Right."

And that's why I loved her...loyal to a fault. "We should make a timetable of Carolyn's last day before she disappeared."

"I'm in."

"So far, I think our number one suspect is Evan, although Tom likes Mitch for it. I think Mitch knows who did it, meaning not Mitch. We only have him and Evan as possible candidates for fatherhood. Can't count Kim out as a killer. Or her scary friends. Could be the pregnancy had nothing to do with it. If Mitch knows who killed Carolyn, it means he didn't, and maybe I can worm it out of him."

"Are you crazy? You plan to talk to him again?"

"Remind me to drink milk and eat food before I go over there this time. If I can catch him in a somewhat-clear mind, maybe I can get him to fill in the details of Carolyn's last day...if he knows them. First, I have to get organized and go to work."

"Let me make sure I'm straight on this. You'll talk to Mitch, even though Tom told you to leave him alone."

"Correct. Tom's wrong this time. I'm not afraid of him. He won't hurt me."

Angie began picking up her car keys and purse. "I think I'll go home and add to my four-and-a-half hours of sleep. I'll probably dream of stalkers in red scarves."

Chapter Twenty

Talking to Mitch was pushed to the back of my mind while I worked at the art center. I was cleaning up details for the exhibit when Neal stopped in with financial questions. Feeling ecstatic because five more entries had come in yesterday and today, I grabbed a cup of coffee for each of us while we studied the figures. It was late Saturday afternoon, and the week was winding down. Neal did a super job for us. The spreadsheets he'd developed gave us a roadmap for our financial future.

"I like the way you arranged these columns. It makes each area much easier to understand."

"Thought that might be the case. I emailed these to you as attachments, which means you'll have all the information on your laptop."

As I looked across at him my unfiltered mouth showed up. "A small stain—could be soup or spaghetti—right there on your tie." I leaned over, pointing to it.

Neal glanced at his tie and started laughing. "Yeah, I forgot. From lunch."

I pulled a laundry stain remover stick out of the many problem solutions in my desk drawer. I was prepared for anything. "Here. Use this on it."

"Thanks. You take the cap off and rub the stick on the stain like this?"

"Exactly."

"It was tomato soup. Luckily, I don't have more than a small spot. I volunteer at the homeless shelter down on Sycamore Street once a week. In the summer, my kids come along too, since I think it's important for them to know about volunteering. You know, helping people."

I nodded. "Great idea."

"My family's been blessed, and I never take those blessings for granted. I loved teaching, but it didn't pay enough to support a wife and two kids." He took another sip of coffee. "Viv, my wife, has a full-time job now, but she stayed home until the kids were in school. I went to night school, summer school, we scrimped, we saved, and I finished my CPA. I've done better financially each year. We were even able to afford a cabin out at the lake, and we'll spend time there once softball is over. The lake house belonged to the Shusters who were anxious to sell, which meant we bought it for a song. Anyway, I still think it's valuable that Bree—you know her from Emily's softball team—and Drew spend time in the summer helping. It's why I take them on my volunteer job."

"I'd say you have a smart idea to get a lake cabin. I remember the Shusters' place at the east end of the lake. Your kids will love it. When they were little, Carolyn babysat for them on occasion. I stopped in to get her car keys one night when she was watching them. They were still in the footed-pajama stage then."

"Boy, that's been a long time."

I looked at the spreadsheets again, thinking about Carolyn. "You know, I was gone when Carolyn disappeared. By then, I was at college. Now, Angie and I are doing our own investigation."

"You are? Helping your brother?"

"Well, you know, because she was our friend. We've constructed a timeline of her activities the day she disappeared. Take a stab. When did she leave your house?"

"Tom asked me that too. I guess it might have been around eleven. Of course, it's been years ago. I think eleven sounds about right. Yeah, around eleven."

"By the way, I have another person to ask you about. Do you remember a girl in school with us named Kimberly Nelson?"

A look of alarm crossed his face. "Hard girl to forget. Sure. She was in trouble most of her time in high school. Why?"

"I've heard mention of her involvement in an altercation with Carolyn prior to Carolyn's death. I wondered if you might remember anything about her."

"I seem to associate her name with suspensions. She was in a class I taught for kids who were, well, 'math-challenged,' I think is the term. Not easy to deal with, she often picked arguments. I think she was suspended more than once for fights. Hmm. Scary girl to cross. Don't think she ever graduated." He began picking up papers to leave. "I remember I read in the newspaper, oh, years ago, she'd been found guilty of something. Might have been assault. If she's still in the area, I haven't seen her lately. Of course, I might not recognize her now."

I stood and thanked him again for helping us before he took off. I needed to leave too. Jail time. Kim might have been given jail time in the altercation with Carolyn, but Carolyn wouldn't have been there. She'd already disappeared. Her absence would have been a real advantage to Kim. No victim to testify.

Earlier in the day, I'd checked the internet to see when Mitch's garage closed. It was open tonight until 8. I called and left a message on his answering machine saying I'd be over around closing. Angie would have gone with me, but it was Saturday night, and she couldn't be away from the bar. I suspected, based on Mitch's reactions and words, he might know who the father of Carolyn's baby was, or who the killer might be. I needed to ask him about the night she disappeared. It would only take a brief stop at his garage, and his answers would help construct our timeline.

I wanted to ask him for a name to go with his suspicions about Carolyn seeing someone else. Maybe he told me the truth when he said he was keeping an eye on Carolyn to monitor her safety. Since I knew for sure she'd left Neal's at eleven, I wanted to know where Mitch was at eleven. I'd written the questions on a notepad, and now I stuffed it in my tote. I figured I'd stop by the post office and the grocery store before I saw him.

First, however, I'd call Angie. Glancing at the spindle on my desk, I smiled at the fifteen or twenty memos from Ivan. Hardly any had arrived in recent days. He was losing his touch. Louise had offered to bring in a dartboard and put his photo on it, but, since his recent absence of hostilities, a soft spot had developed in my Ivan thoughts. Careful. He was still out there lurking, waiting to strike.

When Angie answered, I heard lots of bar noise in the background, and I told her my route.

"Can you think of anything else we should ask him?"

"Yeah. Who else did she date during the all-important eight to ten weeks before her death?"

I looked at my watch. "It's six-thirty. If I take the groceries home and put them away after driving by the post office to drop the bills in the dropbox, I should be just about right to see Mitch."

"Be careful. Remember, CODE RED."

"Got it. Talk to you later or tomorrow morning, depending on what I find out."

By the time I'd driven to the post office, the grocery store, and my house, I was eager to go to Payson's. I'd eaten a container of yogurt, drank plenty of water, and found my second wind. I hoped this would keep me sober, despite Mitch's whiskey, especially since I didn't plan to stay long.

It was dark by the time I pulled into his parking lot. I'd left a message hours earlier to tell him I'd meet him back at the warehouse where he worked on the cars. That way, if Tom happened to drive by, he wouldn't see me in the window of the store. Sound plan. I parked my car, locked it, and walked over to the warehouse. No lights were on, not even the nightlight. I looked all around. Strange.

I checked my phone. Eight oh five. Only a few minutes late. Well, maybe he'd been held up with a late customer. Pushing open the door, I was surprised it wasn't locked.

"Mitch."

No one answered. I literally jumped when the air-conditioning unit kicked on. Remembering he had an area in the back with chairs and a table, I figured I'd head over there and wait for him. Perhaps I'd find a light switch. I could see the car hulks loom, so my eyes had become accustomed to the dark. The smell of paint, engine oil, and gas fumes was everywhere. It hadn't been long since they'd knocked off work.

"Mitch," I called again. Nothing.

Maybe I should try him on my phone to see if he forgot. Could be he didn't want to talk to me. He might even be home by now. Why would he leave the door unlocked? I dropped my tote on a chair and, holding up my phone, I checked for his number. As I walked toward the back, my feet slammed against something solid, causing me to dive headfirst on top of a pile of rags or maybe a roll of drop cloths. My phone rocketed to the floor with a crunching sound, but the pile of stuff saved me from crashing on the cement. It was a shock to suddenly be on my stomach on top of a hill of rags or blankets, but I had pulled out my phone and it distracted me. Whatever had they left out in the middle of the room? At least it was a soft landing.

Then I touched something wet and sticky. Oh, yuk. Oil.

I reached over on the floor and was able to use my hand to locate my phone, aided by grabbing a handle that stuck up in the pile of drop cloths. Thank God the phone was still in one piece. Hitting the home button, I turned on the flashlight app.

Oh, my God! My mouth was wide open, my breath shuddered to a stop, and I almost dropped the phone. I was on top of Mitch. He was hard to identify on his stomach, his face skewed to the side. Blood all over his face, blood on the floor, blood on his clothes. Blood everywhere. He had a knife sticking out of his back which I'd, unfortunately, grabbed when I reached for my phone. His hair was all matted down with blood, and his mouth was wide open in a silent scream. The flashlight on my phone revealed his open eyes staring at nothing.

I think I heard sirens in the distance.

CODE RED! Oh, definitely CODE RED.

Chapter Twenty-One

In the unforgiving fluorescent light of the police station, my clothes were horrifying. A stain stick wouldn't do the trick this time. My white summer capris and pink linen blouse were stained brown and dark red, while my hands and arms were covered with dried blood. I couldn't even bring myself to study the color patterns. By now, I'd had several hours to get over the horror of Mitch's blood all over me, but his eyes, staring into nothingness, continued to float through my head. Just seeing those eyes made my breath come out with a ragged sound. I looked at my hands on my lap, brushing them back and forth across each other. Lady Macbeth in the Apple Grove Police Station. Only, I wasn't sure I'd ever get out all these "damned spots."

I didn't have my cell phone, so I sat and slowly breathed in and out. Waiting. The clock over the front desk said two a.m. Sunday. Wish I were in bed. Breathe in. Breathe out. How long would they keep me here? Jake Singleton, who had gone to high school with me, manned the front desk. He'd brought me coffee an hour ago and looked at my appearance with charitable eyes. Now he left the desk, returning with a ham sandwich and glass of milk, which he brought over to me on the bench.

"Don't have any napkins. You can use the cellophane wrap to hold this. Here are some tissues. Sorry you can't wash your hands, but I don't know exactly what Tom will want as far as evidence."

Unexpectedly, my eyes filled with tears because I was exhausted, and Jake had been kind. The last thing I'd eaten was yogurt after work.

"Will it be much longer?"

"Tom called in about a half-hour ago and said they'd be on their way soon. They have to clear the scene and make sure they've collected everything they need."

I nodded. "I understand."

Poor Jake. He regarded me with sympathetic eyes because I looked like I'd been hit by a runaway train. Hmm. He knew my "by the book" brother and felt sorry for me.

I watched him turn and stroll back to his desk. It had been hours since I'd left the art center. I wolfed down the sandwich, working hard not to look at my hands, and was almost done with the milk when a door opened and Tom, Ned Fisher, and Chief Wilcox appeared in the back hallway. Only Tom came out to the front where we were. About the same time, I glanced over at the front door and saw Mary, an angel of mercy in our midst, carrying a few of my clothes over her arm.

Tears filled my eyes and overflowed, and droplets of pink fell on my already blood-spattered pants. I didn't even want to think about what my face must look like with rivulets of tears striping my cheeks. And why was I still crying? This wasn't like me.

My brother had an angry look, followed by an equally angry, "Well, what do you have to say for yourself after I told you to stay away from the suspects?"

Mary walked over to him, patted his arm, and whispered. "Tom, stop it! Can't you see she's covered in blood and scared? You don't need to bully her."

He looked at the ceiling, bit his lip, and sighed deeply. I couldn't look at his face because I could see his disappointment in me throughout his body language.

"I told Mary to bring you clean clothes. We'll have you change and clean up in the bathroom, but we'll need your current clothes for evidence."

"What? My clothes will be in an evidence box in the basement of the police station?"

"Exactly." His eyes said, "And if you know what's good for you, you'll stop arguing in front of the policemen, stop embarrassing me, and do as you're told."

I followed Mary meekly down the hallway to a restroom. She helped me wash with paper towels, not the equivalent of the two-hour shower I planned to have the minute I walked in the door at home. Once I changed, she took my clothes out at arm's length, handing them to one of the policemen who dropped them in an evidence bag. I probably couldn't have washed the stains out anyway. I loved that blouse.

Walking back down the hallway, I asked Tom, "What next?"

"Since you're now the star witness in Mitch's murder, we're going to one of the interrogation rooms, and you'll tell me everything again, maybe several times."

Mary turned to him, a curious look on her face. "Shouldn't she have a lawyer?"

"You, too?"

"Well, I thought—"

He looked at both of us. "She doesn't need a lawyer because she's not being charged with a crime." The exasperation in his voice was a product of his anger with me, plus the late hour. "Despite her inability to listen to my advice and leave the suspect interviews to me, she's now a witness. Would you like to come back and join us while I record her story?"

Mary examined his face. "No. I'll go ahead and go home, dear." She turned to me and gave me a hug.

"Thanks, Mary, for bringing my clothes. I'll be fine now that I know I'm not being arrested and thrown in jail." I considered adding "by my angry brother," but I was too thankful he was here.

Nodding, she turned and left, while Tom took me to an interview room at the back of the police station. Ned joined us as a witness to my humiliation. Considering our history, I guessed it was only fair. After we sat, Tom set a small recorder on the table, pushed a button, and began to ask me questions. I told him what had happened from the time I left the message on the machine at Payson's to the moment I fell over his dead body.

"Think back to what you've told me. Close your eyes and look all around his garage. What else did you see?"

"Not much because it was dark. Oh, the door was unlocked, which I thought was strange. I wouldn't have known it was his body with a—a knife in it if I hadn't had my cell phone. Oh, yeah. My cell. Can I have it back?"

"I'll see you get it once we sort through the evidence. Focus, Jill. Think back and tell me what you saw."

"Uh, before I focus, I need to know if you can keep me out of this. If the board finds out I've found another body, I'm not sure I can explain my way out of this one. Dumb luck? Bad luck? My job depends on this. I'm sure Ivan Truelove will declare a holiday."

"Maybe you should have considered that. What did you see?"

I closed my eyes and tried to put the picture into a frame with nine sections, the way painters did. Usually the important forms and objects came at the intersections of each corner. This wasn't a painting. Nothing. It was too dark in the garage. "Sorry. It was awful dark there."

"Now tell me again why you went over to Mitch's."

I took a deep breath, realizing how exhausted I was, and remembered my phone again. Oh, no. I hoped Tom wouldn't see the text messages between Angie and me on my phone. I memorized a note to myself to be more discreet in the future, especially if I stumbled over a body. "He had intimated he knew Carolyn was seeing someone, and I figured I'd go back and question him about that person. We needed information for Angie's and my timeline, like when Mitch had stopped seeing Carolyn, so we could clear him from fatherhood or not."

"You and Angie have a timeline?"

"Yes. The timeline is important. Haven't I always heard you say crimes have a great deal to do with timelines, motives, alibis, means, and methods? You believed Mitch murdered Carolyn, but I couldn't imagine that. If he wouldn't tell you who she was seeing, I thought he might tell me."

My brother stared at me as if he were tongue-tied.

"I worked hard to drink nasty whiskey with him from a glass that probably added horrifying bacteria to my bloodstream that will kill me soon. I did it so I could build an interrogator-witness relationship. So he'd talk. I'm not stupid, you know."

He shook his head slowly. "No, you're not stupid. That's one of the reasons it's hard to keep you alive." He pressed the button, turning off the recorder. "Ned. Go tell the chief I'm taking my sister home." As the door closed, Tom said, "And since you're not stupid, I will tell you a few things that stay in this room."

Despite my exhaustion, this was a new angle. I sat up, my eyes feeling the strain of too many hours awake.

"How do you think we got to Payson's so quickly after you found the body?"

I narrowed my eyes and pursed my lips, trying my best to think of the answer to this one. "Telepathy? A really big hunch?"

"Uh, no. We had an anonymous tip from a burner phone."

"A burner phone?"

"Untraceable. Male voice. Gruff. Uneducated. And, by the way, did you notice the hilt on the knife?"

"No. You mean in the dark, as I was lying on a dead body, probably in shock, and covered with blood?"

He ignored my flippancy, a scowl on his face. "It came from the shed in the backyard at our house. It was always out there on that shelf full of tangled junk and paraphernalia. Remember, Dad used to use it to clean sweet corn in the summers."

I squinted. "Hmm. Now that you mention it, I do seem to remember, but lots of people have those knives."

"Dad's is missing." He sat back and folded his arms. "Now, what do these two pieces of evidence tell you?"

I thought for a long moment, focusing. I was exhausted. "Someone is trying to blame me for all of this?"

"Yes."

"Well, I guess I should tell you about the guy who stalked me when I walked home from the art center Friday night."

He sat up suddenly. "The what?" Boy, was he angry with me now.

"I know, I know. I should've listened to you. He never came close to me or tried to hurt me, but he scared me. And he took my red neck scarf." I paused, considering that. "I loved that scarf." Then another idea grabbed me.

"Maybe it was to be planted at the scene of a murder. Did Mitch have a red scarf with him?"

Tom looked at the table for a long time. I could see it in his eyes. He thought if he strangled me, Mary would never forgive him. Finally, he started talking again. "We have a lot of question marks in this case. How can Mitch's death be connected to Carolyn's? Or is it? Was he killed because he knew a man Carolyn dated back then might have been her killer? Or he saw Carolyn with someone? Did that someone murder him before Mitch could either talk to us or blackmail him?"

I watched the wheels go around in Tom's head and considered the tangle of questions that led me to wonder why anyone would become a police detective. "My sculpture. Does its theft have anything to do with all this?"

"I think it might in the sense it hasn't shown up with my usual contacts, and that leads me to believe it's still in town. The broken window at the front door of the art center was smashed to make us think kids had been messing around. Kids wouldn't want your sculpture. In fact, they wouldn't know what to do with it. By the way, the window was broken from the inside."

"The inside?"

"Yes. A clumsy attempt to make it look like a break-in. Instead, they mistakenly broke it from the inside." He paused and picked up a pencil to twist around in his fingers. "That reminds me. I need to ask you a question. Did you change the locks when you moved into the Lowry Building?"

"No. I guess I figured since the building had been empty for so long, it didn't matter."

"We'll get them changed in the morning."

"I still don't understand why this burglar took my sculpture, especially since it hasn't shown up like anyone wants to sell it."

"I think it goes along with the possibility this suspect doesn't want you to succeed in that building. It might have been because the killer knew about the body in the basement. The sooner you failed and left, the safer the killer was. You didn't fail. You found the body, and he switched tactics, trying to blame you for Mitch's death."

"Oh. I never thought of it that way."

He closed his notebook. "I need to think about this. In the meantime, take a break from helping me on this case, and I don't want you to be alone until we catch this maniac. Andy, Angie, and Lance should be able to stay with you in shifts. I don't want you at the house alone. Can I trust Angie, or will you lead her into temptation?"

I looked at him with wide eyes. "Temptation?"

"Exactly. You know what I mean."

I yawned, and my eyes hurt. "No, we'll be good."

Tom looked at me skeptically, and I tried so hard to keep my face straight, but all the while I was considering our timeline and filling in more details.

"Ned will increase patrols in the neighborhood. The autopsy will be Tuesday because of the Fourth of July holiday. Meanwhile, I'll sit down with you and come up with a plan, one to keep you safe and find the killer or killers."

"Can I go home now?"

"Tonight I'll take you to my house until I can put oversight into place."

"All right." I was too tired to argue, and when I thought about it, I was thankful I wouldn't have to go home alone.

Chapter Twenty-Two

"I asked Angie to come over so we could put our heads together." Tom looked at us both. "You two already know a great deal about this case and you're familiar with the victims. I'll talk to Andy and Lance about my plan to keep you safe and never alone. However, they're not in on what I'll tell you now."

Sunday morning. They'd let me sleep till ten, and then we'd had breakfast out on the deck. Flowers of every hue were in full bloom in the backyard. I thought of it as "Mary's backyard" because she was the one with the green thumb. Day lilies, coneflowers, petunias, daisies, and some purple flowers with huge petals I didn't recognize filled the flowerbeds. Another reminder, of course, that my small Illinois town was beautiful in June and July. After we ate, Mary left for the grocery store to refill the Madison coffers. Being here where I knew I was safe made me more relaxed.

Angie took a sip of coffee and reached for a muffin. "I noticed Jill wasn't mentioned in the newspaper story this morning in the *Ledger*. It said an anonymous call tipped off the police to the murder."

"Oh, thank goodness," I raised my arms in thankful praise. "This is exactly what Ivan could use to fire me. Now that I'm not named, that's perfect. Not sure he'd believe my tendency to find bodies."

Tom smiled. "On occasion, the police department gets a break if they want to withhold important evidence that implicates possible suspects. We also get cooperation when we want to protect witnesses. We don't need a stampede of reporters showing up at the art center." He cleared his throat. "So, let's put our brains together. What we say remains in this place. Clear?"

We nodded.

"This whole case is deadly serious," he looked at me, "and I don't mean it in a funny way. Now we have two bodies—one recent—and the cases are related. Jill, your instincts are spot on. That's why I'm talking to you about this. You were right about Mitch. Angie, you know many of the suspects in this case. I'm including you because you were there years ago when this happened."

I watched Tom's serious demeanor, and I was sure he was trying to get us to see this was no longer fun, like we were amateur detectives. I couldn't help but feel a bit of pride that he felt we could help.

"I talked with Jill the morning after the stalker followed her home and scared her half to death. The stalker must have wanted her to stop her questions."

I broke into this one-sided conversation. "I'm here. Just sayin'."

"I know you are, girlfriend, but you haven't always shared with the law."

"Turncoat."

Tom was attempting to hide a smile at this rift between Angie and me.

"We'll turn over a new page in this story, and from now on we'll not have Jill running around trying to interview people who might kill her. She needs to have someone with her all the time. I'm not worried about when she's at the art center, but once she leaves is when she gets into trouble."

Trouble? Did he think I'd asked for all this? I raised my hand. "Once again, I'm right here, front and center."

"The killer's plan is to scare you. You've had those photographs Andy said were taken from a distance, and you've been stalked on the way home. In both situations, this person watched you. Whoever is doing this has been throwing you off your game at the art center, making you anxious and worried by his actions. Then he tried to put you in the middle of a murder scene with your own knife. It's as if he watches you from afar but takes any opportunity to scare you, to get you to stop asking questions. You knew Carolyn well. You might pick up a clue missed by others." He swatted a mosquito on his arm and brushed the remains away.

"What does all this mean? He wants me to be worried? He puts me at a murder scene? Well, he has my attention."

"I figure it's one of two things. Either he knows you're investigating because you've made no secret of it. Witnessed you and Angie sitting in Wiley's truck in front of Payson's." Here Tom shook his head. "Perhaps he wants to scare you away. Or, it's possible the killer thinks you know something about Carolyn's murder, but you don't realize you know it. Maybe he thinks Payson told you who he suspected."

Angie leaned in toward Tom. "Where do you think we should start?"

"I'm curious about Carolyn's life before her disappearance."

Angie and I both sat up. "Exactly what we thought," we said, almost in unison.

"I agree." He looked at our beaming faces. "She disappeared September twenty-third, two thousand seven. We know she was seeing someone, but we don't know who. According to Payson, she'd broken off her relationship with him."

I nodded. "He implied he knew who she was seeing and said he'd 'take care of him.' That someone got to him first."

Angie raised her hand like we were in school. "I think we should check out her horrifying stepfather. He's at the top of my list. How many times did we have to take her in after a huge fight with him? Maybe on the night she disappeared he lost his temper and strangled her."

"William Downey. Already checked his record. He's had a few misde-meanors and several domestic calls, but his wife never pressed charges. He's looking like a better suspect now that Payson's out of the picture." Tom looked at me pointedly.

No time like the present to spring my suggestion. "I have a job for Andy and me. I haven't been up in the attic at the house since I moved back, but maybe we could go check for Carolyn's letters. Before, I figured the letters weren't much more than gossip or day-to-day details of her life. Now, however, I think I could have missed some subtle clues since we know she didn't write them. Supposedly, Carolyn mailed postcards to both Angie and me. I remember, at the time, I recognized her handwriting. Now, I don't know how that could have been the case."

Angie shivered. "I can help with those. That is creepy. The killer must have sent them."

I nodded. "I'm not sure I kept the postcards or letters, but if I did, Mom would have put them in the attic." I thought for a moment. "I can't remember the date of the last letter. I think she might have mentioned a guy she was seeing. Now that we know someone—" I paused, unable to say it right away—"murdered her, those letters might read a bit differently."

Angie looked at each of us. "I know I didn't keep my postcards."

"Tomorrow is the Fourth of July, and Andy and Lance do inventory on the Fourth every year. I bet Andy would be glad to help me look for those letters and postcards. Mom saved everything. It wouldn't take long, and then he could get back to the store."

Tom's gaze scanned each of us, one at a time, and he nodded his approval that we had devised our own plan to spread out the chores and move us forward. We were working together as a team.

"I'm going to Payson's garage and do a more thorough search. We'll check his financials and take another look around his house."

"And I hope you remember, in the middle of all this, I'm supposed to put on an art exhibit in a little over two weeks. We'll have to juggle, balance, multi-task. Right?"

Angie stretched and turned to me. "Why not check the attic now? We may have the answer to her murder."

I put my hand on my forehead and sighed. "You haven't seen our attic, Angie. It may take all day tomorrow, and I'll need to pry Andy away from the store."

We looked at each other and moaned. No Fourth of July for me.

"Payson's autopsy is on Tuesday, and we'll know more after it's over. The important takeaway is we need to be with Jill one hundred percent of the time. We'll get the locks changed at the art center first thing Tuesday."

"You know, we might want to change the locks at my house too, because I have no way of knowing who has keys to the house. I had forgotten Angie had one."

"You gave a spare house key to me when we were in high school. It came in handy from time to time." She winked at me.

"Ah, yes," I looked up. "I hope, Mom and Dad, you don't know everything."

Tom rose and headed for the kitchen. "I'll call Andy and send him to your house so you aren't alone tonight. Then I'll drop you off there. If you and Andy find those letters tomorrow, text me."

"Me too," Angie chimed in.

I grimaced and looked at them. "I feel like I'm on house arrest."

My brother stuck his head around the kitchen doorway. "You keep thinking that. Remember, Jill, never alone."

Chapter Twenty-Three

July Fourth, and Angie and I should have been out on beach towels at the lake, playing volleyball in the sand, and eating hot dogs. Instead, I was standing in the doorway to the attic of my house with my brother Andy looking at a mountain of boxes, and it must have been at least a hundred degrees with the tiny attic windows painted shut. While Lance worked in the storeroom at the gift shop, Andy, ever ready to get out of work, volunteered to be my protection and helper.

"If we find those letters and postcards, we're taking them downstairs. It's like a sauna in this attic." Sweat streamed down Andy's forehead. "And it's only morning. If this search goes past noon, we may die up here."

"Since when does the bodyguard get to call the shots?"

"Since I don't want to pass out and leave you unprotected. I promised Tom I'd stay conscious."

I stared at the daunting room, all wood—rafters, floor, walls, and support beams. No, the chimney was brick, its crimson and white color faded over the years. Gazing at the rafters, I saw the repair of where lightning had blasted through one night after Dad trudged up the stairs to see if we'd been hit. It was the second blast that almost killed him. It streaked right through the same gable. "Who says lightning doesn't strike twice in the same place?" he'd said. He was deaf for the next week.

I looked across the attic. "Man, what a fire hazard."

"What do you expect? House was built in nineteen oh five."

Neither of us moved from the doorway. It was as if the full impact of sorting through dozens of boxes had come home to us.

"Do you think I should go downstairs and get a fan? I could stand in the doorway and hold it while you investigate." He turned his eyes toward me with one of those pleading looks only Andy could execute.

I gave him my evil stare, not bothering to answer. Instead, I looked around the room, noticing the window where the attic fan used to be. My mom suspected the bats were getting in around the fan, so Dad had removed it.

"Remember the night the bat got in and Tom had his first taste of being in charge?"

I could hear Andy laugh from behind a stack of boxes. "Hard to forget."

"Why wasn't Dad home that night?"

"As I remember, he was at an insurance meeting and Mom was at some event at the college. As the oldest, Tom got to be in charge, and oh, he loved to boss us around. I think we exchanged a few blows."

"I must have been five. I remember screaming because this bird swooped over my head in the living room, at least I thought it was a bird."

"Ha! So did Tom. Remember, he grabbed a broom from the downstairs closet and tried to knock it down, smashing two vases, a pot of ivy, and five or six other objects in his path. Oh, and one was a sculpture of Mom's. Looked like a tornado had swept through the entire downstairs. Sheer carnage."

"When I eventually came out from behind the sofa, I couldn't believe the potting soil on the carpet and pieces of glass everywhere. I remember thinking, Uh oh."

"I can still see this bird fly up the stairway in the living room, Tom marching up the stairs humming the theme from *Rocky*. Big hero stuff."

"I was behind the sofa, shaking, with a blanket over my head, but I remember he called down with a trembling voice to ask you if birds had ears."

"You never saw it because you were hiding behind the sofa, but the bat stared at him from a perch over my bedroom door." Andy chuckled.

"Oh, yes I did. I went up and watched as he swatted it down, put it in a box, and carried it outside. My hero."

"Too bad about the timing. There was debris everywhere when Mom walked in. Remember the look on her face? I don't recall what privileges

Tom lost, but, despite the bat, I know he loved being in charge. Just think. We can take credit because we gave him a taste of power and he went into law enforcement. I'd like to think we were responsible."

"And I'd like to think mutiny would have been better."

We were both silent for a few moments.

"Do you think he'll ever find out who murdered Carolyn?"

"I don't know. I hope so."

"We're not getting anything done. Where should we start?"

Andy turned more boxes around. "Some of them are marked with their contents. Looks like Mom's writing. Maybe we should check first for envelopes with your name on them or 'college' or something."

"I'll start over on this side, and you work over there. If in doubt, open the box and see what's in it. I brought packing tape, so we can always seal it back up."

We worked, grunted, and wiped sweat from our foreheads for the first half-hour. By then, deodorant was useless. Looking over at Andy, I saw he, too, had gone through a bottle of water, and his clothes were as drenched as mine. Man, it was hot in this attic. Outside, I heard firecrackers pop. After all, it was the Fourth, and kids in the neighborhood always shot off random firecrackers.

My phone dinged. An email. Pulling it out of my pocket, I glanced at the sender. "Why? Why even on the Fourth? Does the man have no life?"

"Who is it?"

"Ivan the Terrible. 'Suggestions' for me even on the Fourth."

"What now?"

"He reminds me we have no money to put a handrail on the basement stairs. We're fully insured with medical, however."

"Seriously?"

"I think when he isn't counting his nickels and dimes for his company, he looks at his list of a thousand annoying messages, picks one, and texts me."

"Want me to take him out?"

I sighed. It was a possibility. "Probably not. He'd only come back and haunt me. Maybe we could find his darkest secrets to blackmail him with."

"The man has no secrets. Look at him."

"Well, maybe you're right. Besides, if you snuffed him out, I'd undoubtedly be the one to stumble over his body, and he'd open his eyes and say, with his last breath, 'I should have expected you to show up first. It's a habit of yours—finding dead people.'" I shoved my phone in my pocket and kept up my search for a solid ten minutes. Then I just had to talk. "Remember when we used to go out to the lake on the Fourth, back when Dad was still working?"

"Sure." Andy overturned a box.

"What a great memory. Mom cooked for days, and we loaded up the car with blankets, tablecloths, and mountains of food to take out to the lake. My favorite part was the movie on the big screen after dark and the gorgeous, but explosively loud, fireworks."

"Swimming and playing tennis. Me. Remember when Dad finally beat me at tennis? He crowed about it for weeks afterward. Imagine my total disgrace."

I sat back for a moment, my back against the wall. "You know what my favorite memory is?"

"I can about imagine. I'll bet it involves you, Angie, and Carolyn hiding booze in the bushes and sneaking drinks during the movie."

I laughed. "Close." If I closed my eyes, I could see it again, even though I'd forgotten so much of my childhood. "I came back from a walk with Carolyn, and Angie was watching the movie. So were Mom and Dad. He sat with his arm around her, talked in quiet whispers, and at times laughed at whatever one of them had said." The picture began to dissolve in front of my eyes.

Andy was unusually quiet.

After a few moments, he broke the silence with a soft "Yeah."

"I wish they were still here."

"Me too."

"Everything changed after the accident. Everything."

Andy coughed and cleared his throat. "Time to get back to this. We have to find those letters before I can't breathe."

"Oh, here's a box with my name on it. Let's see. Darn! Only clothes. Why did Mom keep all these clothes? I'll never wear these again." My hand felt something hard and not clothes-y, and I pulled out a framed photograph. Oh, the three musketeers. Angie, Carolyn, and me in about our junior year in high school. Carolyn worked at the root beer stand downtown, and Angie and I made nightly trips since she snuck us extra fries.

It would have been thirteen years ago. Angie looked so tiny in her skinny, crotch-hugging jeans with a western shirt—the blue one I loved—and a trucker hat. Her blond hair hung down her shoulders, the green having finally grown out from our failed hair-coloring experiment. She had her arm around my shoulders, and we stood on a picnic table outside the root beer stand. I, of course, hadn't straightened my hair yet. That happened in Chicago. I wore those skinny jeans then, too, and topped mine with a T-shirt featuring Destiny's Child. Carolyn wore a D.A.R.E. T-shirt, gray cargo pants with zip-off legs, and her favorite Uggs. The camera had captured a moment in time. I smiled at our naivete. We thought we were so sophisticated. I checked the photo more closely, squinting at the three of us. We were shouting something. I shook my head. So long ago...maybe 2003 or 2004. I was brought out of my reverie by Andy's voice.

"Okay, wait a minute. Hold on. This could be college notebooks. Or high school."

"Let me see, Andy." I put down the photograph and walked over to where he sat with an open box next to him. Leaning over, I rifled through it. "Yes! This is it. Look, under the notebooks. A couple of bundles of letters." I pulled them out, a pink ribbon tied around them. My address was on the front of the envelopes in Carolyn's handwriting. "Faradin Hall. Ah, I remember it well. My sophomore year. Had a weird roommate." I pulled out the two bundles and checked the postmarks. "One bundle is from two thousand six, one from two thousand seven."

Andy took back the box and rummaged through it. Suddenly he began digging at a manic pace and pulled out a bunch of paper.

"Hey, postcards, Jill. This could be it!" He waved his find in the air.

"Let me see." He handed me one, and I recognized her writing immediately. I gasped. The postmark on the top card was later in 2007, after her death.

My blessed mother had saved them. These could give us clues to her killer.

"Fantastic! Oh, Andy. This is amazing. Text Tom and Angie. This is exactly what we've been looking for. Clues to Carolyn's thinking back then and postcards from her killer."

"Does this mean we can go back downstairs to the air-conditioning?" asked Andy.

"Yes. Thank you, Bro. I think I'd better look through these before Tom sees them. A bit of discreet redacting may be in order."

We closed the attic door, me grabbing the photo of the three musketeers, and headed downstairs to the kitchen, the first stop for more water and ice.

Andy looked at the kitchen clock. "Can't believe how long we were in the attic. Remind me to volunteer Lance next time. I'm watching the rest of the ballgame while we wait for Tom and Angie. Tom threatened me if I left you for one minute."

"I'll take a quick shower before they come." I walked up the stairs. "Love the way you're all coordinated to be my bodyguards. Oh, and don't sit on the furniture while you're all sweaty. Find some towels if you must. Seriously, if a murderer came in the house to kill me, could you stop him?"

We yelled to each other, him downstairs and me on the upper landing.

"Of course. I'd take one of Mom's sculptures and hit them over the head."

"Make sure it's one of the less expensive ones, please."

"How do I tell?"

"When you pick it up, if I scream, you'll know you should set it back down."

"Oh, you're no fun."

"And stay out of the letters while I take my shower."

"Of course. Watching the ballgame."

A moment later, suspicion crossed my mind. I tiptoed back down a few steps and peeked through the stair railing and into the living room. Andy sat on the sofa, a beer on the coffee table, and my letters in his sweaty hands.

"What did I say about the letters?" I called from the stairs.

"Not guilty. Watching the ballgame."

Once I'd taken my shower and dressed, I went back downstairs, tiptoeing into the living room.

"You can't sneak up on me. I know you're there. Man, I can't believe what's in these letters. The things you got away with." He looked up. "Hear that, Mom and Dad? I wasn't the only crazy one in the family. I just got caught more often. Carolyn had a full dance card."

"Yeah? And I'm sure it got her killed."

Chapter Twenty-Four

Tom lay on the sofa in my living room, a floor lamp near his head, glasses resting on the end of his nose, reading letters from Carolyn. Angie sat in an armchair, her legs dangling over the side, reading the letters after Tom finished them. I was on the floor reading Carolyn's letters as Angie dropped them down to me. On the coffee table was a big cardboard box with the remains of a pizza in it and three beer bottles, their contents in various stages between full and empty. It was silent in the living room, except for the quiet announcements of a baseball game on television. Tom had turned the sound low, but he felt he must keep an eye on the score. Every so often he sighed or mumbled when he happened to glance at the screen.

They'd come immediately after Andy texted, and we'd examined Carolyn's letters for the past hour, reading mainly ones from 2007. Tom thought it might be better to read the letters from the spring of that year too, so we'd know how things had changed by the time she reached September. I'd finished my second year and was starting my third at Patterson State, a small liberal arts college in northern Iowa. Staying at the college that summer, I'd worked on the campus and painted, but a few weekends I'd made it home. Carolyn still wrote. She told me it helped her sort out her thoughts.

Tom began our letter discussion. "Time to put our heads together. What can we make of this?"

"I feel guilty because Jill left town, and once I met Wiley, I didn't spend as much time with Carolyn."

I had conflicting feelings between guilt and why fight the inevitable. "It's understandable. We had to realize everything would change after high school."

"For the better for you and me. Not for Carolyn."

Tom roused himself and sat up. "I'm interested in what she wrote about the stepfather. They didn't get along, and Carolyn worked like the devil to make enough money to get out of Will Downey's house. He's become more and more interesting as her possible murderer."

Strangely, I found myself defending Mitch. "I think he tried to keep her clear of her stepfather. Carolyn and her stepfather always fought, and Mitch knew she was afraid of the old toad."

"Mitch. You were right, Jill. Someone killed him to shut him up. What did he know? I thought he was the right suspect for Carolyn's murder, but I was wrong."

I glanced at Tom and Angie. "He gave me the impression he knew who the father of Carolyn's baby might be. Remember Cindy saying he watched their apartment, Angie? He told me he was trying to protect her rather than stalk her."

Angie thumbed through several of the letters that had ended their journeys on the coffee table. "Listen to this last letter, which was mid-September. She knew she was pregnant by then. She wrote, 'I've met someone, Jill, someone who's everything to me. And he loves me too. I think he's the one—you know—the one who was meant for me. He's handsome, fearless, and kind like Sir Lancelot. I knew he'd come along, fall in love with me, and treat me like a princess. We'll go away together and start a new life. We have a problem or two to deal with, a few difficulties in the way of our being together, but I hope, by the time you get home, we'll have decided how to solve those. I'll get away from my stepfather. This guy is wonderful, Jill. I must count and figure out the solution to a problem I have. We can talk about it when you get home on fall break unless we run away before then.'"

Tom stirred. "Counting, huh? That must refer to the baby, as the 'problem' she mentions. Could she be talking about Evan?"

In my own mind, I didn't see Mitch as someone to run away with, so it must have been this Evan guy. "Angie, did she say anything to you about these guys she's referred to? Did you see her with anyone or meet anyone she was dating?"

Angie shook her head. "Only Evan briefly. I thought he seemed self-centered, but he was nice-looking and quite presentable. Like I said, we kinda lost touch that summer and fall because Wiley and I were into the serious stage. You know how it is…you work and see the guy whenever you can. I hardly saw Carolyn. Her description of this mystery guy sounds like it could be Evan. You know Carolyn. She could be naïve about guys, and I believe often beautiful women attract men they shouldn't trust. At least that's my theory."

Tom took his glasses off, waving them through the air. "Her murderer might not have been the man she was planning to leave with. I'm thinking more and more about her stepfather. I checked on Downey. Married Carolyn's mother when she was a widow and Carolyn was twelve. The three of us know how badly he treated Carolyn since she ended up with us so often. Downey had no children of his own, but maybe he saw Carolyn as an annoyance and her presence only multiplied his anger as time went by. I found out an interesting piece of information, however. He worked for a cleaning service as a janitor for several downtown buildings and doctors' offices in the early nineteen nineties. This meant he had keys to those places. One of them was the Lowry Building until it closed."

I gasped out loud. "The Lowry Building? That means he would have had access to it, not only to dig the grave, assuming he killed Carolyn, but he's had access to it since we've started the art center."

"I can't get a warrant to search his property for the key. Not enough legal cause."

He didn't understand that was why Angie and I were so helpful. We didn't work for the law.

"The other direction leads to whoever filled her head with leaving town. That wasn't the stepfather. Evan, most likely. Somehow Mitch's murder is connected to Carolyn's. It may be he knew a piece of information the killer didn't want out, or Mitch knew who he or she was."

Tom looked at both of us seriously. "I'm talking only to you two about this because you were right about Mitch. I was sure he was the one. This talk goes no further than this room."

Angie and I looked at each other and back at Tom, nodding.

"I know more about Kim and her groupies." A look of distaste appeared for a fleeting moment on Tom's face.

And now Angie chimed in. "I hope you took several of the deputies with you."

He nodded. "She's a piece of work. IQ of a rock, but sly."

"Does she have an alibi for the night Carolyn disappeared?"

Tom slid his glasses back up from the end of his nose and looked over at me, his eyes thoughtful. "Not quite. She claims she and Carolyn had settled their differences. Somehow, I doubt it's true. The night Carolyn disappeared, Kim says she was at the Rusty Nail with her boyfriend, Jack Rensler, who, by the way, has a prison record that goes back a couple decades."

"I knew he was scary." Angie looked at me with concern. "How do you find out if it's true? The alibi?"

"The bartender's still around. He remembered he saw them the night Carolyn disappeared, along with Evan and his college friends. He believes he saw Evan leave around eleven-thirty with a dark-haired woman, and Kim, Jack, and another unsavory individual named Eli Heslen left maybe ten minutes later. He couldn't be certain it was Carolyn who left with Evan. The bartender was on a break near the front door, smoking weed at the time. The reason he remembers was because he was aware of the fight between Kim and Carolyn a week or two earlier. It might have been Carolyn with Evan. He wasn't sure. Since they were leaving, he would've seen her back."

"That means Evan might've been lying when he said she never showed up." Inside, I fumed about people who couldn't seem to give us definite information.

"Yes."

Angie set her beer on the table, a curious look on her face. "The bartender never actually saw Kim and Carolyn together?"

"Correct. However, Nelson's case was pending for assaulting Carolyn. When she disappeared, no victim was there to testify, only witnesses from that night. Kim got off with payment for the property damage. Seems pretty lucky for her, doesn't it?" Tom's question hung in the air.

I considered other possibilities. What if Mitch realized it was Kim and her posse who killed Carolyn? The motive might not have been the baby. It could have been revenge. I looked at Tom. "What were these scum from the underbelly of town doing the night he was murdered?"

"Perhaps he put two and two together and blackmailed Nelson or confronted her. She and Rensler were supposedly together at her apartment on North Street the night Payson died, and Heslen was in prison for assault with a deadly weapon. Nelson and Rensler could have killed him together. He put up a fight."

Poor Mitch. He said even he wouldn't have taken on Kim and her cronies. I thought about their alibi for a moment. "What can you do to check?"

"For now, we're planning to compare her prints and Rensler's against prints from Payson's shop. We'll see what develops. I'm not optimistic. The anonymous tip that night fingering you was male, gruff, uneducated. It could have been Rensler." Tom cleared his throat. "The letters tell us she was leaving with a guy. It wasn't Payson or she wouldn't have said she'd tell you about him."

"True. I already knew Mitch."

Angie sat up and put her feet on the floor, leaning toward us. "She was afraid of her stepfather and of Kim and Jack. This Evan sounds like the guy she described. Who else could it be?"

"She told Evan she was pregnant and he didn't want to stay with her or he doubted the paternity of the child. Maybe she insisted, and they had a fight."

"You've met him, Tom. Did you think he could be a killer?"

"Hard to say. Ten years later he's married and has kids. He was anxious when I talked to him." Tom pointed to the coffee table. "Grab those postcards. Let's see if we can glean anything from them about the killer."

"Right." Angie hesitated before picking up the postcards. "Should I have gloves or something?"

Tom smiled. "I wish. Andy and Jill have both handled them, and they also went through the post office. Here. Split them up and let's see what we think."

Silence for ten minutes as we each read and reread the postcards. "This seems spooky to think her killer wrote these."

Tom turned to me. "Spooky but true. What can we tell?"

"I'll go first. Whoever he is, he's educated. Educated lets Kim out. He uses long words like 'meander' and 'economic depression.' Carolyn would've done that." Angie stacked her postcards back together.

Tom nodded his head. "Makes sense."

"The handwriting is Carolyn's when you compare it to her letters, but every so often he makes a mistake. Look at the capital A's in this one, and look at them in this letter," I pointed. "We'd never have noticed back then. But now…"

Tom examined the postcard and handed it to Angie. "Note the date. It's one of the last ones postmarked. New York City. Maybe he was tired of the charade. It's brief."

"Does anything suggest clues as to his identity? They seem rather innocuous. Things Carolyn might say about landmarks. Like this one." I handed it to Tom. "She mentions typical tourist destinations like the Empire State Building in New York City. Or they took a ferry out to the Statue of Liberty. That tells us nothing. Nothing personal in any of these cards. Carolyn would have been more thrilled, and she would have written these expressly for me. He also continually writes 'we.' She would have written about herself."

Angie stretched her arms out and yawned. "This is so frustrating."

"Oh, my God. Listen to this. 'In San Francisco. Ate in Chinatown.' Impossible."

Tom perked up. "Why?"

"Carolyn didn't eat Chinese cuisine. She was overly sensitive to MSG." I shook my head. "Funny, I didn't even think of it at the time. It didn't register. I probably skimmed through her short message and threw it on a table."

Angie broke in with, "Here she says 'we took lots of photographs. Can't wait for you to see them.' Your stalker took photos."

"So did Evan for the repertory group."

Tom pulled several of the cards and put them in order. "Whoever it was, he's clever. If you look at the postmarks and dates, you can see a travel pattern across the country that makes sense. San Francisco to Los Angeles to San Diego. Then a week later they're in Salt Lake City. Three days later, Denver. Then south to Santa Fe. If you stack them by dates, and he wrote ten more after Santa Fe, the distance and planning makes sense."

"Could your itinerary be checked against the tour company Evan was in?"

"It could. The dates and stops were listed in a story in the newspaper. Anyone could have seen it."

Angie picked up a card and stared at it. "Do you think the killer actually went to those places?"

"A prime question. I think he must be someone who either went there, say, like the traveling acting company of Shaw's, or he had other people post them with a story that made sense. If it was Shaw, how did he get Carolyn's handwriting samples?"

"Maybe she wrote him notes, you know, little love letters." I began to feel we should give up. "Imagine the planning all of this would take."

Tom sighed. "Either a clever person with lots of contacts or a desperate one. Maybe both."

"It means we're looking for someone clever, desperate, and able to copy handwriting. Seems to me Evan could fit the educated, postcards, and motive, as in no baby. Downey is still in play to be a killer, but he's not intelligent. His motive was anger management and anger at Carolyn with a life of her own. Jealousy, maybe. Kim and Jack could do both murders, but how would they do the postcards? Their motive was revenge and removing the witness for Kim's court hearing."

Angie looked at me. "I wouldn't downplay Downey about the intelligence. He may be stupid, or he could be clever like a fox. He's certainly mean enough."

"The biggest problem with a cold case like this is you have difficulty finding actual evidence. You have the body, which indicates a few things, several possible suspects, these letters and postcards, and a second death. Beyond that, we're at a dead end. Carolyn's death was ten years ago. Solid evidence is difficult to find in a case that long ago."

It was so frustrating. What if we were at a stop and couldn't find out anything else? How would we ever put Carolyn's murderer in prison? I looked at Tom. "We can't let this killer get away. He must pay for killing Carolyn. What do you do with a case like this? How do you solve it?"

"Such a question, my dear sister, is what divides the first-rate detective from the merely mundane one. I think. A lot. Then I go back over my interviews. Maybe I missed something. Who else could we interrogate? I think I'll give Evan a second opportunity to tell me the truth and check on William Downey. And I'll think about 'stuff.' By that, I mean actual pieces of evidence that provide a trail, like these postcards. Lots of thinking. Despite the firecracker screaming and popping, I need to sleep on this." He looked at me. "And you, art curator, have an exhibit to get ready. You both have helped a lot here. Thank you."

We called it a night, and Angie stayed with me on the night shift. Opening more beers, we watched a movie and tried not to think of the case. We were both disappointed and depressed about how little progress we'd made. I'd hit a wall both in the case and in my energy. "I'm not sure my brain has any more power tonight to figure this out. It's all mixed up in my head."

"Sorting everything out is what sleep is for. Besides, it's like when you're *not* trying to think of pink elephants. They sneak into your brain when you're relaxed and not expecting them."

Chapter Twenty-Five

Andy stayed at my house the following night, and he followed me to work on Wednesday morning. This constant guard business was getting quite old, and no other people had stalked me lately, so I figured it was increasingly unnecessary. However, I was willing to play along if it kept me free to stay at my house for another day.

"When we started raising the floor, it was sagging six inches."

Matthew and I were starting the day by checking the second floor, which he'd been raising a fraction of an inch at a time.

"I know. My trusty marble used to roll from the edge of the room to the middle like the devil was chasing it. You could see how the middle sagged."

"Try it now."

I set a marble down at the west wall on the second floor and, instead of rolling into the middle, the marble leisurely meandered a few inches then stopped. I considered marbles for a painting. A still life. "This is fantastic, Matthew. It worked."

"We're really close. Maybe another quarter inch of moving it up. I told you it would take quite a while since we'd have to move it very cautiously."

Weeks ago, he'd explained how they'd reinforce the building starting from the basement. At first, I thought it was the weirdest plan I'd imagined for making the building safe. A few people on my board figured we were crazy, but I was willing to give this a try, and it had paid off. The Lowry Building had been designed with three foundational support beams way back when, plus metal plates to reinforce the first-floor ceiling, the second-level floor, as well as the roof. Matthew's crew had reinforced the beams and floors with new metal plating and new wood, lifting the floors and ceilings by means of pulleys, a tiny bit at a time each day.

"This is exciting." I practically jumped up and down.

"Oh, don't." He put his hands on my shoulders. "No jumping. Let's not tempt fate. It's taken weeks to get these floors to where they should be. Softly. Softly."

Walking downstairs, I was in heaven. For the first time in weeks, I was humming a happy tune. What news I'd have for the board when they asked about the progress on the building and the success of the Heartland exhibit. No matter that a crazy murderer was stalking me or sending me photographs. So what if I had the Tom FBI guarding me constantly because of veiled threats. My building was finally level for the first time in decades, and I'd been part of the process.

For weeks we'd worked around contractors and construction people, us swearing a lot and hoping they didn't find some horrible situation, like termites, where the building might collapse around us. Despite my stupidity with alarms and the theft of my mother's priceless sculpture, which I knew Tom would find, I was doing something right. Apple Grove would have an arts center we could be proud of, with Mom's name on it.

The rest of the morning, Louise, Jordan, and I still heard the noise from the work in the basement, but now we were beginning to see the light. They'd be done with this phase before the Heartland exhibit, and it was full speed ahead for us. We'd have to teach the August classes in the downstairs gallery while they were building classrooms on the upper floor. Several artists brought their work in during the morning for the exhibit, wrapped up, wrapped up more, boxed, and taped to the extreme. We set everything in the storeroom to keep it together. The pressure was on.

The morning flew by, as it often did when I was working on a job I loved. Jordan had been in and out of our offices showing us new social media ads and greeting people who came to see my mother's sculptures. I'd talked with her about membership drives, the engines that kept nonprofits going.

Now it was time to take Louise upstairs while Jordan kept an eye out for visitors.

Louise was surprised. "You told me this looked very level, and now I see what you mean compared to the sagging middle we had before."

"Yes. Matthew estimates maybe another quarter inch, and all will be perfect. So, I thought this should be the time to consider what we'll put up here."

"What do you have in mind? I know we're putting the weaving group downstairs under this southwest corner."

"Yes. The west end on this second floor will have a small classroom over the weaver's area, and a fairly large storage space opposite with a hallway ending at the elevator."

"So the east classroom wall will be right next to the stairs?"

I looked at the area. "Yes. Then on the other side of the stairs, I picture a larger classroom, where we can also have board meetings. The weavers are going to take over the downstairs space where we've currently been meeting."

Louise nodded her head. "They'll be so excited. Two of them have already been in to look at that space. So, what are we doing with the rest of this huge area?" She pointed to the northeast side that extended clear back to the storage space.

"That will be a workshop. We can do all kinds of things in a space that size."

"Such as?"

"I would love to have plays and readers' theater in the gallery downstairs, you know, for special events. They could practice up here so they'd be out of the way during the day."

Louise looked around. "Then there's the southeast area that's left next to the classroom."

"Another storage closet. As time goes by, if we need more classroom space, we can move things into this smaller closet and turn the other storage space into a classroom. What do you think?"

"I think you've thought of everything. I can't tell you how excited people are to come to our classes in August. We've not only filled up the first class on watercolors, but the second and third classes are in good shape too. I've no doubt we'll fill them before the Heartland exhibit is ready."

"The timing is perfect. We'll start the classes once we have a successful opening to the exhibit. The weavers will move in during that time also, and I have a few other tricks up my sleeve. I'm really interested in pulling in some seniors, and I'm thinking about how we'll do that."

"Okay, Boss. Onward and upward."

By noon, I was starving, and an equally hungry Angie arrived to take me to lunch.

We drove to a new restaurant with a Midwestern theme, the Golden Spike, built recently near the Amtrak station. The décor had railroads, factories, Chicago, pioneers, and murals of various historical events in Illinois. It was quite a clever idea, and we ordered from a menu with cute names for Lincoln's Illinois, like "The Wood Splitter's lunch" which involved a pulled pork sandwich and fries.

"I can't believe I have a whole day off from the bar." Amusement twinkled in Angie's eyes. "Lunch with you, a little shopping for me, and maybe a movie. Like reliving my adolescence."

"Me too. Feeling extremely optimistic."

"And your optimism is because—"

I told her about the building report this morning, their encouraging news about the floors, ceilings, and roof, and the entries for the Heartland exhibit, which were now coming in like Christmas presents from UPS. "I think we're turning a corner, and everything is going well. New locks on the doors, safe floors to walk on, our team working like a well-oiled machine. Jordan is handling the publicity for us like a pro. I'm beginning to believe Mom must be watching over us."

My phone vibrated, and since it was Tom calling, I figured I should take it. Once I hung up, I relayed the news to Angie. "The autopsy exonerates me since Mitch died between five and seven. My cell phone pinged from a tower near the art center several times during that period. His system had alcohol in it, but a drug screen won't be done for a few weeks. He also said the murderer is left-handed, shorter than Payson, and quite strong."

"The positive news keeps piling up. However, that only narrows the killer to left-handed short people."

"For sure."

The waitress brought our food, and we spent the next few minutes dealing with silverware, napkins, and water refills. Lunch conversation was about clothes and music videos, but not murder.

As we were leaving the restaurant, we stopped to look at the photos on the wall and the artifacts under glass in exhibit cases.

"Look, Jill. These dress patterns from the late eighteen hundreds are amazing."

I walked to the table and looked at the various objects. Hats and photos of stern-looking women in corsets, plain blouses, and long skirts. I turned as Angie pointed to something under the glass. Children's early toys, school readers, a few farm tools, and back to early books, some propped open, others set so you could see the spines with their titles.

Angie looked at me, her eyes wide open.

"Are you thinking what I'm thinking?"

Angie smiled and nodded. Pointing at the slender book, she read the title. "Diary." She turned to me, her look skeptical. "I don't remember her ever mentioning a diary."

"I had one. Didn't you?"

"Yeah, but I burned mine. Better Wiley doesn't know everything about my lurid past."

"Could be a long shot, but what else do we have? Even Tom said he's down to his thoughts. If Carolyn had a diary, it might provide us with written evidence."

We hurried out of the restaurant, not speaking until we were in Angie's car.

"Jill, if Carolyn had a diary, it would be better than those letters."

"At this point, anything we find that's more personal might give us the evidence Tom needs. Oh, Angie. What an amazing idea! Start the car and let's talk about it on the way back to the center."

Chapter Twenty-Six

"We need to come up with a plan. Some way to get into the Downey house. Carolyn's diary has to be there."

We evaluated what we'd found at the restaurant on the way back to the art center.

"I can see it now. We drive to the Downey residence and knock on the door. Her horrifying stepfather answers the door, we ask if Carolyn had a diary, and he slams the door in our faces. Or threatens us. Is that the way you see it?"

"Better plan." I looked around and lowered my voice. "We stake out the place, wait till Downey leaves, and knock on the door, fully expecting her mother to answer. When she does, we ask her if Carolyn had a diary."

"And if she says, 'Yes, but it contains my daughter's private thoughts and I'll keep it,' then what do we do? Knock her over and take it?"

"We'll cross that bridge when we get there. Seriously, Angie, do you realize what this means? If Carolyn had a diary, she might've written about the person who killed her. She could've named names. Tom will have his evidence, and we'll have helped find her killer. This is exactly what we've been talking about."

"All right, girlfriend." Angie waved her bracelet at me. "I'm all in."

She dropped me off at the art center, and Louise left for lunch while I finished a pile of paperwork. When she returned, we looked through the entries for the art exhibit, unwrapped and unpackaged everything, and checked to see if they met the requirements in our prospectus. So far, so good. Five more entries arrived, two by hand and three by various delivery services. We added those to the quickly growing pile in the storeroom, and Jordan took a photo to put on our social media pages. How exciting! Just like Christmas.

Before we closed for the night, Louise checked the mail. We'd been so busy we hadn't thought about it. No photographs. No warnings. However, a letter addressed to me from the board treasurer, Ron Spivey, caught my eye.

"Wonder what this is?" I picked up my letter opener, slit the envelope, and eased the letter out. It was an announcement informing me of an emergency meeting Friday night with the board of the Adele Marsden Art Center. This couldn't be good.

I tried to keep the board meeting tomorrow night off my mind while we drove to Carolyn's house Thursday evening. While I still had Downey on my list of suspects, I realized that just because Carolyn hated him didn't make him a murderer.

My phone rang, the ringtone signaling it was Tom.

Angie chuckled. "Aren't you tired of his *Law and Order* ringtone?"

"Kinda, but it is so my brother." I punched the accept button and put it on speaker. "Hi, Tom."

"Hi, Jill. Angie with you, and that's why I'm on speaker?"

"Of course."

"I had another talk with Shaw today after speaking with Dan Gonzalez, the bartender at the Rusty Nail."

"And?"

"Evan's story changed a bit after I explained I had a witness who placed him at the Rusty Nail, leaving with a woman. He said, 'Not Carolyn.'"

"This means to check his alibi you have to find the woman."

"I did. He was able to give me her name, and I tracked her down through the college alumni records. Lives in California now but remembered leaving the Rusty Nail with him because he'd been celebrating their departure the next day. They spent the night together in his room. Oh, and she is a brunette, like Carolyn."

"I guess that means Evan's off the hook."

"Here's more. Evan admitted the story wasn't quite complete when he spoke with me the first time. He went to Wyatt's that night because Carolyn had told him she'd be there, babysitting. She believed they were leaving town together, but Evan had no such plans. Then the braggart came out and said he'd lied to her and told her he was engaged. 'You know women,' he bragged to me. 'They'll try anything to get you hooked. She was a two-bit groupie looking for a way out of town. It wasn't me.'"

I fumed at the description of my childhood friend. "Despite that, he invited her to stop at the Rusty Nail and have a drink to let bygones be bygones?"

"Shaw said exactly that. He also said she never showed at the bar."

I scoffed. "What a jerk! 'Sorry, my love, but I have another woman, and you're out of the picture. But hey, let's go have a drink.' And then when she didn't show, he took another woman home. I thought if he could take photographs, possibly father a baby, and pick locks, he'd be a great suspect. Now, with an alibi, I guess not."

"True. Sometimes you think about a case and go over and over the details and you can still be wrong. I figured he looked good for this, at least for a while. Evan was a little more believable when he gave up, reluctantly, the name of the brunette."

"Then Carolyn must have been picked up by Downey, who strangled her. He also had a key to the Lowry Building. Or maybe it was Kim and Jack, who found her walking home and killed her. Jack could undoubtedly pick a lock. Thanks, Tom. Angie and I both appreciate that you keep us in the loop."

"And I'm happy to hear you've finally taken my advice and that Angie's with you. Don't let down your guard. Whoever this killer is, he's dangerous."

He hung up and I turned to Angie. "Imagine how excited he'll be if we get Carolyn's diary from Mrs. Downey."

"...or finds us tied up in Downey's basement after he calls Tom to come get us for trespassing. I'm sure he'd press charges. Wonder what Tom would do to us."

I thought about that grim prospect for five seconds and decided to plow on. "Come on, Angie. This will be a challenge. We could find her killer." I'd rather face the scary stepfather than my angry brother.

We pulled up to the Downey house, a dingy two-story place near a corner of Trinity Street, a bit nicer than a few houses on the block, but not much. The once-white boards of the siding needed paint, many were splintered, and most should have been replaced. Their screen door had several areas of torn, hanging screen, and quite a few spindles in the porch railing were missing. It hadn't had much love in all the years we'd known Carolyn, but now it was a dismal dump. I checked for the Downey truck in the driveway. It was an old Ford with lots of rust over the wheel wells and around the doors. No truck. This was perfect because we planned for him to be gone. Angie drove by and parked on the back side of the block, where Wiley's truck wouldn't be seen from the house. Since Mitch knew Wiley's truck, we figured everyone else in town did too. Maybe even Downey.

I looked at Angie. "Ready?"

"Let's go." She opened the door, and we trudged around the block to the home where we used to pick up Carolyn in better days. The neighborhood was more run-down than I remembered, but I'd been away for years. I'd had no reason to drive over here since I'd returned home.

We climbed the porch steps, hoping they were solid, and knocked on the front door. No dog barked—a reassuring sign. Knowing Carolyn's stepfather, if he had a dog, it would be the mutt from hell. No one came to the door. We knocked again.

Finally, Ruth Downey answered our knock, peering out through a narrow slit. A chain hung between the door and the frame, indicating she took no chances.

"Hi, Mrs. Downey. It's Jill. Jill Madison and Angie Emerson."

"Oh, Carolyn's friends. Yes?" She didn't remove the chain or open the door any wider.

"We wondered if we could come in briefly and talk with you."

Ruth looked past us. I figured her anxious eyes scanned the street for her husband's truck.

She stared at both of us again. "Well, 'spose it's better than standing on the porch having the neighbors wonder. But not long."

After she shut the door, we heard the safety chain slide from its bracket. The door opened, we walked in, and she quickly closed it behind us.

"Mrs. Downey, we're terribly sorry about Carolyn. We saw you at the funeral and wanted to extend our condolences once again." Watching her face, I wondered if she understood what I'd said.

She looked at me with a vague stare.

Angie picked up in the silence from the poor, beaten-down woman. "Mrs. Downey, we figure you have Carolyn's things packed away, but we wondered if she kept a diary, you know, a record of her life?"

"Why would you want her diary?"

"Angie and I didn't see her much over the last years before she…she passed away. We hoped her diary could fill us in on her life."

I wasn't sure what was happening, but Ruth's face said she was listening for a familiar sound and abruptly she told us we had to leave. She opened the door, and we heard the truck long before we saw the lights.

"Mrs. Downey." Angie spoke quietly, right into her ear. "We can help you leave. You don't have to stay here with…with him."

"No, go." She almost shoved us out the doorway, her eyes wide with terror, and waited for her husband.

We walked down the steps right about the time Will Downey pulled into the driveway.

He opened the truck door and climbed out, swaggering over toward us, with a nasty grin. "Well, if it ain't the two do-gooders, former friends of my stepdaughter. What the hell ya doin' on my property? Carolyn ain't here no more, or haven't you heard?"

"We're quite aware. We stopped to pay our respects to Carolyn's mother." I watched his face and arms, thinking if he made a move toward us, we could run.

"She ain't here cause she's dead in her grave. Don't surprise me one bit." He spat on the ground near our feet and watched us.

I turned and looked at Ruth, and I saw a glimmer of hatred toward this man who'd disrespected her daughter.

Before I could add my angry retort, Angie took over. "We're leaving, Mr.

Downey. Bye."

She grabbed my arm and turned me around. We both took off, hoping he wasn't behind us, not exactly at a run, but speed walking toward Wylie's truck. Within seconds, we heard Downey's truck door slam, and I glanced over my shoulder to see if he got into his truck to run us down or went in the house to the poor, hapless mother of our friend. It must have been the latter.

"I don't think I want to go back there," Angie muttered as we rounded the corner, where Wiley's truck came into view.

"We have to. Didn't you hear what she said? 'Why would you want her diary?' She must've had one, Angie. This means it's still in her house. We need to wait until Stupid's gone, then climb in through Carolyn's bedroom window. This could mean the difference between finding her killer or letting him get away with murder."

"Why, oh why do I let you drag me into these situations?"

"Me? You're the one who usually pulls me into something that will get me into trouble with Tom." Then I reconsidered. "Cause I'm your best friend and we want to find out who killed Carolyn. Every time I think of her and the life she could've had, I get so angry. Whoever killed her has had a life. This might be our last chance to get our hands on her diary. Tom's already done his search through her stuff, but you and I knew she'd have a diary. Come on, start the truck for now, and we'll pick a night when Stupid isn't here. We can do this, Angie."

"As long as you crawl in to do the search and I play lookout. I don't want to be in the house if that psychopath shows up."

"We'll figure it out and make a plan. Now, we should go back to my house since I need my protection squad for the night. Right?"

Angie pushed the truck starter. "I'm afraid Wiley may have to hire more help at the bar if this protection brigade doesn't end soon."

By ten that night we were eating pizza and pleasantly blitzed on a second bottle of Chablis. It was the slightly hazy time of night where you weren't quite sure you'd remember it in the morning, but you didn't care. You should probably go to bed, but it was too much effort. The board meeting tomorrow night didn't even bother me since I was happily anesthetized. Angie was in her favorite chair, legs over the side, while I was on the sofa, trying to stay awake. We had a dumb movie on, the sound set low. Neither of us watched it.

After several glasses of wine and a discussion of the general state of the world, my mood turned back to men.

"It's a good thing you saw Wiley first, or we'd be married, and you'd be single." When it brought no response, I looked over at my friend, and she was sound asleep. "Wake up, Angie."

"What? Who?" Angie's eyes blinked open and she sat straight up in her chair, looking around frantically. "Are you okay? Is someone trying to break in?"

"No. No one. I just needed an awake person to listen. I wish I could find a guy. You know, someone to go out with occasionally."

"I think you said that already. Several times. Tonight." She began to slouch down again, but not before saying, "Give it time."

"Time? Are you kidding? I'm thirty." I took another sip of our most marvelous Chablis. "When my mother was thirty, she had Tom. That puts me behind already."

"You'll catch up," she murmured.

"Catch up?" I sat up on the sofa and stared at her. "How can I? I'd have to have a baby this year. It's already July. How many months are left? Let's see...August, September...not enough, Angie."

"Oh."

"Did I ever tell you about the night I came home from a date in high school and saw my parents—"

Suddenly Angie's eyes opened, and she sat up straight. "Oh, my God. You didn't."

"—dancing in the living room. Percy Sledge's 'When a Man Loves a Woman' was on the turntable. They danced slowly, very slowly, with the lights down low. Her head was on his shoulder. Every so often he kissed her. Most romantic scene I'd ever seen. Of course, back then I thought it was corny. Very corny. Now, I think it would be wonderful, but I'm still behind, timewise. I think I need someone to dance with me."

"I think you've had too much wine, BFF."

"Prob'ly right. Bed calls. I made Andy's for you."

"Might want to take one of these bottles upstairs with us just in case we have an intruder and have to use it as a weapon. Bring the empty one. See, still on my protection detail even after way too much Chablis."

Chapter Twenty-Seven

Friday was a nerve-racking day. Tonight might be the end of the road, or at least a horrible scolding if the board kept me on. I tried to stay busy all day with work on the exhibit. Jordan and Louise were quiet around me, probably not quite knowing what to say. Everyone kept at their jobs, but I sat in my office for a while and thought about what I should say tonight, that was, if I had a chance to talk. My stomach did a perfect rendition of a rolling sea, making me think I might lose my breakfast. I'd talked with Andy last night, and he was very encouraging. Told me to give them hell.

"Jill," Louise called from my doorway. When she said nothing else, I turned around.

Jordan stood beside Louise with a small, polka-dotted flowerpot in her hand. "We decided we should make a little gift to cheer you up." The flowers were made with construction paper, the small pot filled with the green paper grass people used in Easter baskets. They both tiptoed into my office and placed it on my desk.

"Figured you could use some rally-around-the-boss cheer."

After Louise set it on my desk, I couldn't help but smile. "It's perfect."

Jordan added, "Turn it around."

I leaned over the desk, turning the little flowerpot around. On the back of the pot's rim was a message. "Give 'em hell, Boss." Now, that made me laugh out loud. "If only."

Jordan smiled. "Is there any way we could go in, talk to them, and tell them how amazing you are?"

I shook my head. "Don't think so. It's time to take my medicine."

"It isn't your fault Carolyn turned up in the basement or you fell over another body during your investigation. It isn't fair." Indignation sounded from every syllable of Louise's voice.

"I probably shouldn't have been investigating Mitch. As Tom's warned me quite often, he wasn't a guy I should've questioned. Tom knew, of course, but I was more naïve. I set myself up for that one, and the killer took advantage of my gung-ho investigator curiosity. I do have to agree I couldn't have anticipated one of m—my best friends would be buried in the basement of a building I now manage. What are the odds?"

"Exactly what we mean," chimed in Jordan. "You didn't have anything to do with it."

"It remains quite clear I left the alarm off, resulting in the theft of a bit of change and a priceless sculpture."

Louise had a more pragmatic theory. "But you owned your mother's sculpture. The loss is yours."

"The insurance company won't see it that way. They'll raise their rates on the art center, and other artists may not be eager to leave us in charge of their work."

"It hasn't happened so far with the Heartland exhibit. We have over sixty pieces in the storeroom now, with more on the way."

"Nevertheless, I'm not quite sure the board will agree. They must have confidence in me. A board of oversight is essential for a nonprofit agency. I could throw myself on their mercy, but the politics of the situation were already a little shaky after the burglary. We'll see. I have no way to know how the evening will turn out. What I do know is I'll fight for my job."

Both stood inside the doorway, apparently not quite knowing what to say.

"Look. I love the way you two are loyal and helpful. For now, I still have my job, so back to work. We should examine the pieces and make sure they don't need to be fixed, rewired, or re-glued. Louise, it would be great if you could check each of them to make sure the artists followed the rules."

"I will. We had several come in today, but they're still packaged. I'll get them open and check everything."

"Perfect. We have six days until we install them for the exhibit. This means whether I'm here or not, by the good graces of the board, someone will have to make sure the exhibit is ready. Jordan, I need your sense of style to double-check how to show the various pieces together. We should think about their size, color, and medium. It isn't too early to consider where they'll go, what they have in common, or how we should group them for the best effect." I glanced at the calendar over my desk. "Tomorrow's the deadline. Jordan, send out an email blast today to the artists on our membership list to remind them we can't take any more entries after tomorrow at five."

"Will do." Jordan left.

Tom texted to say he'd had no luck with Kim's or Jack's fingerprints at Payson's garage. If they were the killers, they left no prints.

Louise and I were busy pulling pieces from the storeroom. Once we unwrapped them, Jordan set them in various parts of the gallery, thinking about how they would look their best. We checked them for any necessary repairs, especially those that had been shipped.

Unpacking the various entries was a labor of love, and I marveled at the oil paintings, generously lent to us in hope of positive reviews. I sat on the floor and considered why I was an oil painter, not a watercolorist or an acrylic painter. Acrylics dried too fast, and watercolors were not easily controllable. But oils, well, they allowed me to be creative, and if I screwed up or changed my mind, I could correct it. Why, art curators were even finding corrections in the *Mona Lisa* since they now had the technology to examine the various layers of paint. The board would see my errors as I went along, and I didn't think they would be as forgiving as layers of oil paint.

At various points in the afternoon, I checked with the workers in the basement. They would be done on Monday or Tuesday. We'd discussed the timing because, once the exhibit went up, they couldn't work. I had a feeling they'd remember this project for the rest of their lives. It wasn't every day you worked on a building foundation and found a murder victim. Or at least I hoped not!

I recalled the construction crew's intricate, time-consuming plan and early-bird work involving precise tension to lift the floors while the rest of the world was waking up. Even if I got fired tonight, I had done an amazing job on this building. No one figured a thirty-year-old, who had never done a building renovation, let alone on an 1870 building, could possibly know how to do this, but this thirty-year-old did.

At various points in the afternoon, I got texts from my adoring supporters.

Tom: **Hope things go well 4 u 2night**

Andy: **Want me 2 come over 2night and knock some heads 2gether?**

Lance: **If you need a character witness, text me, not Andy**

Angie: **Can bring wine-large amts-2 soften them up. Worth a try?**

Mary: **If they're smart, they'll recognize yr worth and keep u**

Family. What could you do without them? I came home with the idea I could find a place for myself here, a whole new audience where I could provide programs I'd never had as a child. Was I kidding myself? I'd sure screwed things up.

I glanced at the time on my phone—4:30. Louise and Jordan would leave shortly. Time was such an odd concept. Only a few more hours and I'd know whether I still had a job.

At seven on the dot, Ivan cleared his throat to begin the board meeting in what would later become the weaver's area for the art center. True to form, Ivan sported a navy polka-dotted bowtie. Judge Ronald Spivey was the board treasurer, and he had been solidly on my side. The judge had been a friend of my parents. While I knew he had confidence in me, I wasn't sure what would happen tonight. I scanned the other fourteen faces around the table. Some looked skeptical, others smiled, and the remainder appeared neutral. A few couldn't look me in the eyes. In the artist's picture frame of my mind, they were arranged in a semicircle from supporters to skeptics.

Pointy-headed Ivan started the proceedings. "We all know we're gathered tonight because a number of you have expressed concerns about the burglary at the art center, as have I, and the negative publicity Jill and the art center have received in recent days."

I swallowed hard, wondering if he would list my transgressions. At least they'd given me a chair to sit on rather than made me stand like a penitent while they stared up at me from comfortable chairs.

The judge spoke up. "I believe the best way to deal with this is to have you express your concerns to Jill in the form of questions. We'll give her time to answer. Then we'll close the session and discuss our ideas while she waits in her office. Is that agreeable to everyone?"

Several of them nodded their assents, and Ivan looked annoyed. The judge was stealing his position.

"Jill? Does it seem like an acceptable idea to you?"

I nodded. "Sure."

"Let's begin with you, Jim." The judge referred to Jim Thomas, college professor.

"I hope you understand, Jill, we've all been rooting for you and have been quite pleased with most of the actions you've taken here at the art center. We understand your passion for this project. However, many of us have wondered about your age and inexperience. Do you have any explanation for why the alarm wasn't set at the center, leaving your mother's sculptures unprotected, her masterpiece stolen, and the art center completely accessible?"

I took a deep breath before I answered. "No, Dr. Thomas. That was my fault. I could blame my brutal work hours, but it would only be an excuse. The alarm was a mistake. My fault. It hasn't happened again, and I'm already on the search for grant money to put in a safer system."

"This is exactly the lack of responsibility I've seen in you, Ms. Madison." That was pointy-head.

After his comment, a collective silence lasted for a long minute as if they were deciding who might excoriate me next.

Finally, Annette Lashly, mother of six, spoke. "I know, Jill, the body of Carolyn Anders found in the basement had nothing to do with you, and we all express our sympathy because we understand she was a friend of yours. This wasn't your fault. Its resulting publicity, as well as the rumor in town you were found at the murder scene of that Payson man, makes us wonder if you're a magnet for all this drama. Would you be able to stick with your job here, leaving the detective work to the police department?"

I took a deep breath. "I agree, Ms. Lashly. My brother, Tom, is a fully capable detective. I shouldn't have stuck my nose in where it didn't belong. I had a need to help find the killer of my friend, Carolyn. She meant the world to me. Loyalty is one of the character traits I prize, along with justice. I can't promise I won't dig for the truth about her death, but I can promise you I'll be more thoughtful about situations and their possible outcomes. No more negative publicity. I'll be more circumspect."

At this point, Ivan the Terrible snorted.

Again, it was quiet. The tension radiated because some of them didn't like my answer. I couldn't help it. If investigating my friend's murder meant I might lose this dream job, I had to let the decision rest in their hands. I'd said my piece, and that was all I could do. A few other board members asked questions I could answer with ease.

The judge spoke up. "How is the Home in the Heartland exhibit coming along?"

He'd thrown me a creampuff question. I knew the judge was on my side, a valuable supporter.

I visibly brightened my facial expression and tried to appear positive in every way. Out of the corner of my eye, I saw Ivan roll his eyes dramatically. "We have over sixty pieces today, and tomorrow at five is the deadline. I'm quite encouraged by the quality of the work and the assortment of various mediums. Today, we checked them for any damage during their transport and for their adherence to the rules of the exhibit." I warmed to the task, my adrenaline kicking in.

"Our intern, Jordan Grant, is doing a sensational job on social media, and Louise Sandoval, our office manager, has worked side-by-side with me to decide the best way to present each piece." I paused for a moment, considering what else to say. "They'll be ready to install the artwork on the twelfth, and we have a juror lined up for the next day, as you know. All is well. Smooth."

I tried to make eye contact with each of the board members as I gave this statement, and some met my look, while others examined their notes. I could almost count who was with me and who was against. It wasn't a pretty picture. Desperate, I decided to make my final plea. This had been on my mind all afternoon.

"Recently, I've considered several ideas I'd like to mention." I took a deep breath. "I knew when I moved back here to my hometown to envision and manage an art center, a dream I'd nurtured ever since my early years in Apple Grove, it wouldn't be easy. Many of you think I'm too young. I don't have enough experience to be able to take an old, nineteenth-century building and remake it into a modern art center where children in our town will receive what I didn't—a nurturing environment for arts education. Sure, I was fortunate. I had parents who supported my artistic talent. Not everyone has such an advantage. The fact you're on this board demonstrates your interest in the arts. I am thankful, indeed.

"It's true I didn't know much about the renovation of old buildings. However, I did my research, read and read, visited the sites of other updated buildings, and worked with a professional architect. We had no plans, no blueprints, no papers that indicated how this building had been assembled in the first place. Our architect can tell you we were working blind, and occasionally we were hit, as you know, by events we hadn't expected.

"Our construction workers will be done on Monday or Tuesday, ON schedule, and UNDER budget. Despite the publicity about the burglary and murder victim, I must say we've done a terrific job. We made this happen. It wasn't by accident, and I'm not being arrogant, because I can't begin to count the number of nights when I didn't sleep thinking about what might go wrong next."

My emotions rose to the surface and I struggled to keep them in check. "The bottom line is we've done it. It's amazing. We couldn't have made this happen without your knowledge, advice, and support. I'll admit to the error of the alarm disaster, and I've paid a huge price already. My mother's sculpture. Sadly, I hate to think the other events were simply a distraction from our goal here. I hope you'll find it in your hearts to decide I'm still the one to keep this art center alive."

I looked at their faces. Maybe I'd picked up a few more votes. I couldn't do anymore, and my mantra pounded through my head. *I will show them success.*

Ivan the Terrible asked for an immediate vote on my job status, but the judge spoke up.

"Now, Ivan. I think the board needs to discuss this. If you'll step out to your office, Jill, we'll talk among ourselves. Thank you."

Instead of slinking away to my office, I walked out into the hallway with my head high. Over the past week, when events began to go south, I'd thought a great deal about my recent life, my non-painting, and this art center. Moving out to the front window, I looked out at the old-fashioned lights on the public square. When I lived in Chicago, I spent months after my parents' deaths where I could hardly get out of bed. My friends in the art community got me on my feet and to a psychiatrist. I was different, despite the help. My creative spark wasn't there. For the last two years in Chicago, I'd worked to pay my bills, but the stack of unfinished canvases sat in the corner of my apartment and accumulated dust and self-pity.

When Tom and Mary suggested I come home because of the money in my parents' trust fund for an art center, at first, I refused. My self-confidence was at its lowest ebb, and I hadn't even let them know I hadn't painted in forever.

One day on a lunch break in Chicago, I took the time to wander through an art gallery near the one where I worked. I often did that. My eyes could still appreciate art even if my brain and fingers couldn't create it. There, in a sculpture exhibit, was a piece my mother had made years earlier. It was an imaginative and humorous depiction of a squirrel, peeking out from her nest. I smiled as I remembered Mom's phone call in which she'd described this latest work. I loved my mother for her nurturing, her beauty, her artistic talent, and her love for all of us. I thought about her for days after I saw her sculpture. Maybe it was a sign.

I called Tom and discussed the art center. I guessed I might try it. The worst I could do was fail, and I had already done that in Chicago. I threw out the half-finished, desperate-attempt canvases, packed what I wanted to keep, gave the keys to the landlord, and hauled myself home. My emotional connection to the creative world was missing. Apple Grove and the art center had begun to return my creative self, full circle.

In recent days, I noticed Lance's hands around a cup of coffee. His long fingers reminded me of a pianist's, long, slender, and able to span an octave plus. The lines and contours were smooth and perfect. It was slow at first. I'd always noticed colors, but now my eyes began to take in shapes, shadows, and light once more.

After the exhibit was up, I might try to hold a brush again. I'd brought home my paints, which were still usable. Then I'd ordered additional paint tubes because I hoped I might be able to get over this hurdle. If the board decided to let me go, I wasn't sure I'd ever paint again. Painting took belief in myself. If they gave me a second chance, my slowly recovered emotional life would be in every stroke of my brush. I stopped gazing out the window at the streetlights and wondered if the board was almost done.

Walking back to my office, I realized if I lost this job, I might have to clear all my personal items out tomorrow. In the distance, raised voices but muffled came through the vents.

I looked at my parents' faces in the wall photograph. They had overcome mountains compared to problems in my life. An interracial couple wasn't as common as today, and they'd met in Chicago. Finding an apartment was a nightmare. They would rent to my Caucasian father, but Mom insisted on confronting the situation. While they were never told, "We don't rent to mixed couples," they were often told the apartments were already rented. Or there was a problem, and they were taking the apartment off the market. That was simply code for 'we don't want you here.' Compared to their stories I heard growing up, my life in this small town was a breeze. I should never complain.

It was the longest hour of my life before the board members filed out past my office, their faces downturned, revealing little about my sentence. Ivan gave me a scowl. That might be good.

Judge Spivey stopped in my doorway, a half-smile on his face. "You've been given a reprieve, but only temporary one. I believe in you, Jill. Several others, well, they were hesitant after this unfortunate publicity. Your best bet is to have this exhibit go well. No problems. No bumps in the road. If you can pull that off, I think you're home free."

"Thank you, Judge. I appreciate your help and support."

"You're welcome. Keep up the stellar work but set your focus on the exhibit. I know you're already planning for classes and workshops and special events that aren't far behind."

After he walked out at the end of the group, I grabbed my purse, stood up on rubbery legs, and headed out of my office to check all the locks on the doors and set the alarm. Tom could still count on my help. I'd have to be careful. No more walking into dark places where I might stumble over dead bodies. This was my last opportunity to make the art center happen. I could not blow this.

I was back home later that night when my best friend and partner-in-sleuthing, Angie, called.

Chapter Twenty-Eight

"Did you mean it when you told the board you wouldn't stop trying to find justice for Carolyn?"

"Absolutely. Wouldn't you do the same thing if I were found murdered? After all, this crazy person is still out there."

Angie was silent for a moment.

"Angie...of course you would, right? Angie?"

"I have something to tell you. I hesitate because you said the board warned you not to get any more bad publicity and to stay away from police detection."

"What?"

"You know I hear things at the bar when people are a little loose with their thoughts?"

"Yeah. What did you hear? Was it about Carolyn?"

"Not exactly."

"Angie, spit it out."

"I'm not like you and Tom. I think her psychopathic stepfather killed Carolyn. I've always believed that."

"So?" Sometimes Angie could take forever to get to the point.

"I heard from a couple of guys, well, overheard, that Stupid plans to be in a poker game with them Monday night."

"And this information is important because—"

"The diary. Remember when you said we should check her bedroom for the diary?"

I considered her idea. She was right. We still had no evidence Tom could use for an arrest. On the other hand, if I got arrested for breaking and entering, my job would be toast, and I'd be in jail. I couldn't afford to lose all my plans for the art center.

"Nah, I can't take the chance. This art center is the best thing that's ever happened to me. I can't risk losing it. Can you imagine what the board would do if I were arrested?"

Again, silence on the phone. Then a sigh.

"Angie, I know what I said about loyalty. We both loved Carolyn, but I can't lose this job. I gotta stay away from Downey's house. Do what Tom says. I can't get into any trouble."

"Yeah. I understand. Guess you're right. Okay, good night, Jill."

"What's the plan once you're inside?"

I had caved. Despite my good intentions, Carolyn's diary might be the key to finding her killer. Memories of Carolyn pulled me back. I'd spent the weekend in restless sleep, and now it was Monday, the night Stupid was supposed to be gone.

We sat in Angie's car, a small, nondescript Honda, about a block from the Downey residence. Perfect for a stakeout. Much less obvious than Wiley's truck.

"We don't even know if I can get in the window. If I can, I'll tiptoe around, check out the closet, look for the diary, find it, tiptoe back out, and possibly jump instead of trying to use the drainpipe. Should take five minutes, tops. I remember the layout of her room."

"If I see Stupid's truck coming, I text you, right?"

"Right. I'll turn off the sound in case you have to text. I'll have it on vibrate." Before I could shut it down, however, my ringtone went off with the theme from "Law and Order." Tom. Why was his timing always superb? Here I was doing exactly what I shouldn't do. Even so, guilt reared its ugly head with my anxious breathing. I'd better answer the phone or he'd wonder why I didn't. I accepted the call and put it on speaker.

"Hi, Tom." I tried to sound normal, as if I weren't planning a high-stakes burglary with a psychopath who could come home any minute and legally kill me for breaking into his house.

"Jill. I have a bit of information for you."

"Angie's here with me, so I put you on speaker."

"Good. I talked with Downey who said he was away from home until late the night Carolyn disappeared. He didn't even know she'd disappeared since she wasn't living at home anymore. His story is he'd been out of town in his tow truck but returned home around eleven-thirty that night."

"He had a tow truck?"

"Yeah. For a brief time, he had a towing business. Said he stopped to help a woman with a flat tire."

"Can we find her?"

"Probably not. It's the beauty of his alibi. She had an out-of-state license, paid with cash, and, as you might imagine, he didn't keep careful records for the IRS."

"What a shock." Angie made a silly face at me after her cynical comment.

"When he got home that night, he had mud all over his pants and shoes. He said his wife will attest to his description. Checked the weather, and it did rain. Could be the dirt came from burying a body or fixing a tire."

Angie jumped in. "Or both."

"No way to check his alibi other than his mousy wife, who'd say anything he told her to," I added.

"I'm still connecting the dots."

"Think away, Detective." I looked at Angie and crossed my fingers where she could see them. "Angie's keeping an eye on me. You don't have to worry."

"I'm sure you took to heart our little discussion about the need to stay out of any more trouble. You must keep the confidence of your art center board." He took a breath and I imagined him folding his notebook, figuring I was in for the night. "I'll call you if anything else comes up. Good night."

My guilty conscience kicked in because I'd deceived Tom, and what a price I'd pay if we were caught. It was only a little lie of omission. I punched the disconnect on my phone and turned to Angie. "Well, I didn't exactly lie. We are together. He didn't ask me where. Besides, when we find this diary, he'll be so excited."

"I agree. Carolyn's diary might incriminate Stupid. We're almost out of suspects."

"We know Tom got stuff from her house, but no diary. It must be a sign, Angie. Either her mom or Stupid knows something incriminating is in her diary."

"Maybe they destroyed it."

I looked at her thoughtfully. "It's possible but remember her mom's face when she mentioned Carolyn's diary? If anyone knows where it is, she does. She might be protecting Stupid by keeping it."

"Or she might feel guilty about looking the other way if he hit her daughter."

"Either way, I'd like to see if we can find it."

"Sure. I'm in."

"I hope the window to Carolyn's room isn't locked."

"I wouldn't exactly say their house is an ad for A to Z Home Security, and I doubt it's in the best of repair. We'll see." Angie grabbed her keys from the ignition.

"Got the flashlight?"

"Yes. It'll fit in your pocket. Here."

"All right. Let's do this." I was confident in the knowledge Stupid's truck hadn't been there when we went by the residence in our perfect getaway car. I hoped he'd play poker well so he wouldn't have to cash out early.

We crossed through several backyards and prayed not to fall over anything. The coast was clear. No clotheslines, no toys in the yards, no dogs to worry about. Luck was on our side. We reached Carolyn's backyard, figuring we'd camp behind a sizable thicket of bushes a few yards from the house. An old sandbox I remembered was still there, off to the side of the yard. Near it was a shed with all manner of junk.

Carolyn's bedroom was on the south end of the downstairs. A downspout hung right next to it with a drainpipe we could use to stand on so we could sneak in or out of the window. She'd made sure the downspout was securely attached to the house in case she had to grab it, but that was years ago. A dim light shone in the north end, where the kitchen was. Upstairs, the lights were on in Ruth's bedroom, a certain sign she was out of the way. I glanced at Angie and she took my hand, giving it a squeeze for good luck.

I tiptoed over to the downspout, keeping an eye on the window. When I put my hand on the pipe, it practically fell off the wall. My quick reflexes helped me save it, but my heart pounded. So much for Stupid as a proud homeowner. Waving to Angie to come over, I watched her look all around and tiptoe to the back of the house. I motioned she should put her hands together to give me a lift, as if I were getting on a horse. Figuring I could grab the windowsill and pull myself up, I thought I needed a little boost to make it that far. We searched all around, but it was pitch black with only the sound of crickets for company.

I whispered, "on three," and she boosted me up to the window on the first try, but I hadn't considered how to get it open with both hands on the sill. This wouldn't work. I dropped back to the ground.

"We have to find a solid object I can stand on so I can get the window open," I whispered. "Let's look around, see if we can find a helpful stepstool. I won't turn on the flashlight since a neighbor might see the light and call the police. Don't think I want Tom to take me to the station again. Once was bad enough."

By now our eyes were accustomed to the dark, and we carefully walked around, ending our investigation over by the shed. Right next to it, abandoned in the sandbox, was a metal washtub, the kind my grandmother used to use on the farm. I picked it up and dumped a pile of moldy leaves out of it. Motioning to Angie to follow, I carried it to the house.

Placing the washtub carefully on the ground, I stepped on top of it, making sure it would hold me. It did. Angie went back to the bushes to keep an eye out for Stupid's truck. I reached up to the window and checked to see if it would open or if it was locked. It opened. Fantastic! It was as if Carolyn was with us on this adventure. She would have loved the intrigue. Slowly, I pushed up the window, occasionally shoving a little harder when it stuck. After each push, I waited a few seconds to make sure no one had heard me. Once I had it high enough, I motioned to Angie to come give me a boost.

Grabbing the edge of the sill, I pulled myself up with her help, until I had one knee on the ledge. Again, I stopped to see if anyone heard us. Nothing. I pushed myself onto the window ledge until I sat, hunched over, then ducked my head and swiveled, dropping my feet on the floor. I was in. Giving Angie a thumbs-up, I dropped into Carolyn's bedroom.

Looking around, I checked my bearings. They must have been using Carolyn's room for a storage area since boxes with odds and ends cluttered her bed. Dust was everywhere. I held my nose once when I felt a sneeze, then I muffled it with my arm. Where to start? I didn't see a diary on her bed. Too obvious. Ruth intimated Carolyn had a diary, so it must be here.

The closet. I tiptoed slowly, waiting for a noise, even though the room was carpeted. I counted my footsteps. Five, six steps to the closet. Just as I reached it, I heard footsteps on the floor above me. I froze. The footsteps stopped, and it was quiet again.

The closet door was closed. Once I could breathe, I took my time turning the doorknob. After a few excruciating seconds, it clicked softly, and I was in. Closing the door behind me to keep the flashlight from bleeding light, I felt my way around, pulled the small flashlight out of my pants pocket, and waved it around the closet. Several shelves held Carolyn's belongings from high school. Yearbooks, a few novels she'd maybe read, a jewelry box, and several little figurines of princesses I recognized from when she was little. No diary in sight. On the floor, under the shelves, were sealed cartons. A larger carton was in the middle of the closet, one I'd almost fallen over when I crept in. These might have been the boxes Tom had examined.

I knelt, checking to see if they had any writing on them. It would be nice if Ruth had written the contents of the box on the outside, like CAROLYN'S DIARY, but no. I gingerly pulled a flap of the box open when my cell phone vibrated in my pocket. I couldn't believe it. Angie texted me.

CODE RED In driveway

Shoot! Stupid was back, and I'd have to get out of here while he was still around the front of the house. I shut off the flashlight, shoving it into my pocket, and dropped the cell phone in my other pocket. Opening the door a little less slowly than before, I was about to tiptoe to the window when I heard Carolyn's stepfather open the front door. I froze. Other sounds followed I didn't recognize, but so far, he hadn't come near her room. Should I try to leave or wait in the closet until he went to bed? Maybe cowardice was the better choice. I should get out through the window and live to fight another day. I couldn't afford to get caught.

I held my breath, listening as his footsteps came through the hallway past the door. I was so intent on listening to his footfalls I didn't see a box on the floor, and I stumbled over it, knocking it into a table. Back to the closet.

No sooner had I closed the closet door than I heard the door to the bedroom swing open. Oh, no, I gasped with my hand over my mouth. I'd left the window up. He was sure to see it, and this closet was the first place he'd check for a prowler. Holding my breath, I closed my eyes, expecting him to open the closet door at any second. Silence. Nothing. I listened. *Please, God, don't let him open this door.*

He swore and I caught the word "Ruth." Then the window slammed down hard, and the lock was turned into the slot. He swore a few more times, and then silence again. Was he looking around the room? Had I left anything? Thank God the room was carpeted, or he would've seen my footprints in the dust. My eyes were tightly shut, and prayers ran through my head as never before. Actually, God probably wasn't with me on this one since I figured theft was one of those ten rules that began with "Thou shalt not." I didn't remember breaking and entering on His list, only Tom's.

That was when I had an unusual moment of clarity. It was time to grow up and make intelligent decisions. This was stupid. Here I was, risking everything with this foolish, teenage behavior. Angie and me, we were playing rogue warriors again, but now we were older, and it wasn't a game. It was dangerous. If we got out of here without getting caught, I'd get back to my job. Period. I loved Carolyn, but this wasn't worth everything I'd worked for. I should have listened to Tom.

After what seemed like an hour, I heard footsteps go back out the bedroom door. He shut it and walked down the hallway. I waited. He climbed the stairs slowly, and I could hear each step. I counted to forty. Upstairs, a lot of yelling said he was taking this out on his wife. I felt guilty when I heard Ruth cry out once.

Under cover of the chaos upstairs, I crept out of the closet, unlocked the window quietly, opened it, and slid out. Turning, I lowered myself onto the washtub and hoped it would stay still. Of course, it didn't. I lost my balance, the washtub fell against the downspout with a loud noise, and I literally crawled behind the thicket of bushes knocking Angie over. With a "whumpf" she fell to the ground on top of me, and we both lay there, me holding my breath, Angie trying hard not to laugh.

Gazing up through the thicket, we saw the light go on in Carolyn's bedroom. Silhouetted in the light was her stepfather with a shotgun. This time, Angie and I both held our breath and hoped he couldn't see us and wouldn't fire or come out to investigate. Finally, when the light went out, we slunk across the backyards as quickly as we could. We hit the street and ran to Angie's car.

Sliding into the Honda, we crouched low, Angie turned the key and started what seemed like a catastrophically loud engine that drowned out the crickets. Then she moved down the street at a crawl with the lights off. After two blocks with no one behind us, she turned on the lights and began the drive home.

"Terrifying. He gets my vote as murderer of Carolyn."

I took a deep breath and let it out. "You may be right that we should move him up higher on our list. He's an animal. It was worth a try, even though my instincts said I was taking a foolish chance. I can't afford to lose my job. Her diary exists, but we're at a dead end."

"I say we keep thinking. Remember, pink elephant. When all looks bleak, think of something else, and a plan will come to you. You're right it would have to be less risky, although I'd visit you in jail."

Chapter Twenty-Nine

I sat in my office and pondered last night. We hadn't found the diary, but we hadn't been shot by Stupid either. We were one for two. I guessed that was a positive. I didn't know how we'd find that diary.

"Jill?"

I turned around. Jordan was in the doorway.

"Yes."

"It's ten."

Oops. I'd forgotten I'd asked Jordan and Louise to stop in at ten so we could talk about the details for the installation of the Home in the Heartland exhibit. I studied the calendar. It was Tuesday, July twelfth, and we would hang the pieces on the fourteenth. Friday we'd have the judging, and a day later, the opening. Thank goodness our plans were moving right along.

"Come on in." I pointed to the love seat, as they both arrived with notebooks and pens.

"First, the juror, Debra, will come on Friday, the fifteenth. We must have identifying tags ready to go up on the pieces after she's judged them and awarded prizes."

Jordan looked up from her notes. "Tags?"

Louise took over. "Tags are pieces of paper with the title of the piece, the name of the artist, and the price. We'll put them up next to each entry after the judging and before the opening."

"We don't put those up on the fourteenth?"

"No. It's a blind competition. We don't want the judge to know whose work she's judging. Once she awards the prizes, we can put up the tags.

Louise, you start on those tags today. Since we're past the deadline for entries, anyone who calls or stops in with a last-minute, late entry is out of luck. You can handle it."

"I will, even if I have to stand at the door and bar their entrance."

Jordan and I both laughed at that mental picture. I was glad I had Louise to deflect problems because it meant I could take care of other business.

"Jordan, I need to have you use whatever time you have today to clean the entire art center so it's shiny and bright for the public." I picked up a stapled set of papers. "Then I'll call the volunteers who said they'd help hang the exhibit and remind them of the time we'll start on the fourteenth. Once we finish those items, we only worry about the opening." I glanced at the list on my whiteboard. "We still have lots of advertising, thanks to Jordan, and the newspaper has already interviewed me for a story prior to the opening. The *Ledger* photographer will be back to take photos of a few of the entries once they're up. The other point I want to emphasize is we each will have the information about who won the prizes, information we will see but not show to anyone. Those prizes are awarded at the opening. Right?"

"Right," they said in unison.

"We're in super shape, team. We'll meet again to go over the details for the opening once we make it through the exhibit installation and have Debra make her decisions on Friday."

Jordan got up to leave. "Once we begin installing this exhibit, the following two days keep rolling with no stopping."

Louise nodded and pulled a packet out of a folder. "The printer delivered the exhibit catalogs an hour ago. I have them in my office. I opened the first stack and looked at one to make sure it was correct. It was perfect. Here's the first one, Jill, and here's one for you, Jordan."

I studied the catalog cover, a modern rendition of a country picnic in a field of green grass with wildflowers in the background, and the title "Home in the Heartland." The Adele Marsden Center for the Arts.

Looking at it, a deep sense of satisfaction went through me, and I grinned uncontrollably. "I have a strong feeling about this. The board will be pleased. Nothing else will go wrong, so it appears we're in shape. Execution is the last concern left."

"All right, Boss. Ready to go." Louise left for her office, and Jordan went in search of the vacuum.

Five minutes later, I had to use Jordan's phone to text Angie. My intern was now used to my inability to keep track of my cell phone. This time it was near the street behind the building. All right, maybe a few glitches.

Thirty minutes later, I was halfway through my volunteer calls when I heard the bell from the front door. I knew either Jordan or Louise would check to see who was there and give them information on my mother's sculptures and the art center. Louise knocked on my door.

"Package." She held up a small manila package with my name on it but no postage.

"We're done with entries. Too late. Deadline." I folded my arms.

"It has your name on it and the address of the art center."

I reached for the package, wondering for a brief second if I should put it in the middle of the floor until Tom could call a disaster unit with cute robots to check it out for scary chemical powder. After the last few weeks, I was a bit paranoid. Louise wasn't showing any signs of trying to catch her breath or turning blue, so I took the package with shaky hands and set it on my desk.

"How was it delivered?"

"You know the woman who works over at Byler's?"

"Byler's? The clothing store? The saleswoman? Sure. Can't remember her name. She delivered it? Weird."

"She said it was left in a dressing room. Since she assumed it was meant for you, she brought it over."

I glanced at it then back at Louise. "All right. I'll take care of it. Thanks."

For a while, I stared at the package. My name was on it in spidery handwriting. Was the sender attempting to disguise his or her identity? No address label processed through a computer. No stamp. Hand-delivered. Why was it left in a clothing store dressing room with my name on it? It appeared to be about six by nine inches and not very deep. It didn't move but also didn't tick. I figured those were positive signs.

Curiosity got the better of me. I didn't have any rubber gloves, like Tom, but I tried hard to touch only the corner, opening it with a letter opener. Out fell a book whose faded, cream-colored cover said "Diary." I gasped. Gingerly, I opened the cover with a ruler and immediately recognized Carolyn's handwriting. Letting the cover fall closed, I sat back and held my breath. *Who?*

Ruth Downey. I had misjudged her. Shame on me. She must have loved her daughter to turn over this diary without her husband's knowledge. Carolyn's mother left this for me at one of the few places she could go without her husband figuring out what she was doing. He wouldn't have followed her into the dressing room, maybe not even into the store. Perhaps his actions after Angie and I left their house convinced her to help us. She must have spirited this into the store, maybe in her purse or under a sweater. I took a deep breath and tried to decide whether I could bear to read Carolyn's words, knowing what happened to her.

Another idea struck me. We could have the answer about the paternity of Carolyn's baby or the identity of her murderer in this diary. Maybe the father and killer were one and the same person. I stared at the diary, thinking I should hold it for Tom. I should call him immediately. He'd expect me to, and he'd be right.

What a stupid idea. It landed right here on my desk addressed to me. *Open that sucker and see what she wrote.* Fingerprints were no longer an issue. First, I'd call Angie. No, I'd text her.

I skimmed through the pages, searching for names, my eyes darting back and forth. The earlier entries of Carolyn's diary were filled with the minutiae of life. Who was dating whom, places we'd gone around town, slightly illegal actions Tom would chastise me for, as well as thoughts about her mother and stepfather. Maybe I could redact information before I gave it to Tom, kind of like the government did. I toyed with the idea of pulling out the pages Tom shouldn't see, but I remembered I'd be tampering with evidence. I touched the letters on a page and whispered, "Carolyn's hand wrote these words." Taking a deep breath, I tried to control my feelings. *Oh, Carolyn,* and a tear trickled down my cheek.

Guilt rose in my chest as I read her belief that Angie and I had abandoned her, Angie to Wiley, me to college. Then she cheered up and decided she needed to make her own way and figure her life out. Mostly these outbursts involved getting out of town. My eyes narrowed at a passage about her stepfather.

My chest hurt, thinking about Carolyn having to deal with him. A particularly troublesome passage when she was sixteen led me to my worst fears. "My stepfather came home drunk from a poker game with his equally idiotic friends. I was studying in my room when he came in and picked up my books and papers and slammed them against the wall. Grabbing my wrist, he shoved me into the wall and claimed I was 'Miss Know-It-All' and didn't I know books were worthless? Then he declared 'my schooling' wouldn't get me anywhere but stuck in Apple Grove with him and my 'stupid mother.' My hands shook, and I tried to keep my head down...not look at him. When he's drunk like this, the violence in his eyes is frightful. He finally stormed out of my room, heading toward my mother, and I knew she would feel his wrath next."

I sat back and thought about how terrifying this was. Angie and I had both wondered about her stepfather from hints and ideas she'd dropped in our laps, but neither of us could imagine a parent hitting a child. Over the later years in high school, we worried he might be doing just that. Why didn't she tell us? I took a deep breath. She must have been too embarrassed. Too ashamed. Her home life was nothing like ours. Tom wasn't a cop until a couple years later. We could have told him. *Oh, Carolyn.*

If I had thought Downey was simply a doddering old man with a shotgun to wave about, acting like a big deal, my ideas about him were shattered by a later entry.

"I figured if I lived with Cindy it would solve my problems. I am an adult now, saving my money, keeping it in a safe place where he can't find it. One day, at work at the restaurant, he showed up drunk and made a scene. Embarrassed once again, I cajoled him to follow me out the back door. He was out of control, making crazy threats and telling me I had to move back home. I said I'd never live there again. Threatening to kill me and hide my body where no one can ever find me, his words convinced me I must get away from Apple Grove. But how? His rages have become worse, and his drinking has escalated.

"Cindy urged me to take out an order of protection, and I did. My stepfather was undoubtedly stewing and angry he couldn't control my life anymore. I worry about my mother and what he might do to her with his anger. He can be scary when anyone crosses him. Who will protect me when I'm alone and he shows up? Mitch. Sweet Mitch. I'll have to make it important for him to be with me so he'll keep my stepfather away. I feel guilty using him, but what else can I do?

"At least if Mitch gets angry, I can calm him down. A week ago, I had a run-in with a scarier person than my stepfather. Kim Nelson from high school. She accused me of hitting on her ugly, scary, tattooed boyfriend, Jack Rensler. NEVER!!! We got into a huge fight, me defending myself. She was the one arrested. She won't forget that. I'm trying to stay away from them. They hang out near the college dives, unfortunately, the places where I see my boyfriend. I need eyes in the back of my head. They could kill me and deep six my body."

"Jill." Angie's voice came from behind me in the doorway.

I looked at her, an angry expression on my face, and held up the diary. "It's Will Downey, her stepfather. It must be. Downey's the killer. He couldn't stand to see her have a job and a life of her own…couldn't make her decisions anymore and keep her in Apple Grove. Mitch reminded me she'd changed when he became her stepfather. It's so much worse than we imagined."

"Oh, my! The diary." Dropping onto the love seat, she put her bag on the floor and handed me a bottle of water. "Brought this because I figured you could use it. I couldn't think of anything else I could do to help."

I gave her the diary. While she opened the cover, I grabbed the bottle and took several gulps of the cold water. "I've read some of it, and it's awful. Oh, Angie, it's horrible. You read it and tell me what you think." I couldn't take much more, figuring we could share the darkness together.

She made herself comfortable and began to read while I went back to my list of volunteer calls. It took my mind away from the diary. An hour went by. I heard her sigh and close the book.

"Could you imagine it was much worse than we thought?"

"No. By the end, before it all stopped, Mitch was watching possessively, her stepfather was always lurking nearby, and she was planning to leave town with a guy she didn't name. Each page was more desperate. And add Kim and her henchmen too. Oh, Jill. She was scared out of her mind. She never let on to me when we went to the play at the college."

"If her killer is Downey, it was Evan, with the acting group, who was supposed to take her away. He's why Cindy saw her dance around. We know now she didn't leave, and he didn't plan to take her with him. She always believed what guys told her, and he gave her a fairy tale."

"Carolyn must have believed he'd take her with the acting troupe all over the country." Angie turned back quite a few pages and read, "'I've met someone new, and he's wonderful. He treats me so well, and he tells me all the amazing places we'll go. I'll get away from here, from Mitch, Kim, and my stepfather. He loves me.'"

I turned over all these new revelations. "She's writing about Evan. She must be, and her killer must be Downey. He's the key suspect. We need to turn this over to Tom." I paused and considered a plan. "I'd like to finish reading it first in small, unhysterical doses."

My phone rang. It was Tom. Did he have mental telepathy? I considered not answering it, but then I figured I should. I hit the "Accept" button.

"What the hell were you and Angie doing breaking into Will Downey's house?"

I gritted my teeth, mouthing "Tom" to Angie, but she nodded because she could probably hear him across the room.

"Uh, we thought we might find incriminating evidence?"

"The next time he'll fill your rear ends with buckshot, and he'll be within his rights. You hear me?" He slammed down the receiver.

"Yes, Tom." I looked at Angie, and she gave me a quizzical stare. "He's really mad. Downey must have recognized me. I didn't even have a minute to mention the diary. Oh, Angie, why did we leave her? We could have kept her alive."

Angie's eyes glistened. "She didn't have a chance, coming from the Downey home, but I'd like to think we could have saved her if we'd known."

Angie stood and stretched her legs while I made an unhappy face. "She always wanted to be with a man like Evan, someone who would take her away from Apple Grove." She sat back down and opened the diary. "I think this passage caps all she was feeling because it seems like her lowest point. It's from the afternoon before she disappeared. 'I want to leave town and start a new life. Perhaps he can make it possible before this little child growing in my belly makes his existence obvious. How can I stay here? My baby will be doomed to this same lonely place, just like me.

'The other day I thought about Angie, Jill, and me in our senior literature class at high school. It seems like years ago now without them around. Life was much better in high school. We read this beautiful poem called *Idylls of the King* about the Lady of Shalott. I love poetry and can remember it, every detail. I didn't understand it then. Now I think I do.

'This is what I remember. A beautiful lady lived on the Island of Shalott, where lilies bloomed, and she wore a snowy white robe. Everything around her was pale—white lilies, pale yellow woods, ivory willows. From her window, she could see spectacular knights pass by on magnificent steeds. It was then she realized what a sad and lonely existence she had in her tower. One of the knights, Lancelot, was especially handsome, but, despite her beauty, she knew he could never be hers.

'The Lady of Shalott had a curse on her which said if she left the tower, she would die. A life without love or friends wasn't worth living, so she left her tower and floated in a barge down the river to Camelot, dying, her beauty frozen in a pale whiteness...floating toward the love and life she could never have. How lovely she was in death, *a pale, pale corpse*, and how ironically Lancelot remarked upon her beauty. What longing she'd had, this Lady of Shalott. She could only live in the shadows, but life went on beyond her ability to be part of it. If Jill were to paint a picture of her, she would call it *Death in a Pale Hue*. In many ways, it would be like me, longing for a love I can't have and a life beyond this miserable place.'"

Chapter Thirty

T hursday morning I practically leapt out of bed, started the shower, and laid out my clothes. This was the day we would install our first exhibit. What beautiful words: our first exhibit. I couldn't think dark ideas about Carolyn's death today. I hadn't finished reading her diary, but I'd get it to Tom tonight after work.

On the other hand, I was excited! Jordan, Louise, and I had worked for hours on the various pieces to make sure they were in perfect shape. Before we left the center last night, all the entries, which weren't free-standing, sat against the walls or on tables, ready to be hung.

I hummed Pharrell Williams's old song "Happy" in the shower as I considered how this would redeem my reputation with the art center board. I knew a few of the board members might still grumble, especially Ivan Truelove. How did he ever get that name? They'd have to admit, thirty years old or not, I'd done my research, hired the right people, and finished the renovation under budget and on time. This was my new mantra: *Under budget, on time.*

Once I made it down to the kitchen at eight forty-five, I realized the volunteers were due at nine. I'd planned to stop and buy donuts on the way to the center, and Louise had set up coffee service last night. Glancing again—what was that, five times?—at the time on my phone, I headed out the doorway, tote and car keys in hand. This would be a grand day!

Volunteers already waited outside the art center when I pulled up with three dozen donuts and a smile from ear to ear. Within fifteen minutes, after voraciously attacking the donuts, we had people on ladders installing the artwork. Once the walls were done, we'd adjust the lighting.

"Jenny, put the smaller print up a little higher," I heard Louise say to one of the volunteers. "I think it balances the other two pieces better."

"Sure thing."

"Perfect."

I walked around and directed their progress, troubleshooting as the walls went from bare to filled. We had oil paintings, prints, mixed-media pieces, framed photographs, charcoal studies, photographs on canvas, watercolor paintings, and pieces of computerized graphic arts. Then my mother's favorite, the sculptures. Ten of them would go on pedestals arranged in a nice balance, along with several ceramic pieces. I stopped at the coffeepot we'd set up in the middle of the room.

"I'm amazed by the variety of artwork we have." I looked around as I pushed the spigot on the coffee pot to refill my cup.

"I love this oil painting of a working farm. The barn is amazing. It reminds me of my great-grandmother's acreage, well, before all the great aunts and uncles fought over who would get what. That led to several hospitalizations." Louise looked at it again. "So peaceful."

"Jordan, come here a minute if you would, please." Leaving aside Louise's nostalgic family memories, I decided it was time for more intern education.

Jordan walked over, beaming. "It'll be an amazing opening."

I nodded. "Our juror, Debra Montiero, normally would choose which entries to use, but since this is a local exhibit with amateur artists, Louise and I decided every entry would be installed. When it comes to a national exhibit, we'll have a juror who is much pickier. Some pieces won't make the cut. The juror will have to narrow maybe three hundred entries down to fifty."

"Seems sad, but I get it."

"Now, Debra will come in tomorrow to decide on the prizes."

"How does she choose when we have such a variety of media?"

"Wise question. We have several prizes—Best of Show, sculpture, mixed media, painting, ceramics, photography. They compete against other entries in their medium."

"Thank goodness. I'd have no idea how a person could judge, say, a sculpture with a watercolor painting. It's like apples and artichokes."

"That's the point. You're right, although Best of Show includes everything. Some of these artists have entered pieces to get critiques. It's important for their careers as well as their understanding of where they might need to improve." Louise sidled over to us, keeping an eye on a teenager who was balanced precariously on a ladder.

"Think someone needs to hold that ladder?"

"Janet," Louise called. "Could you make sure the ladder Jason's on is steady? Thanks."

"How does the judge figure out what to look for?"

Louise had the answer. "Several areas go into the judging. First, the technical virtuosity and the craft and skill of the artist."

"She'll look at the details, judging how carefully the artist placed them and the quality of the materials she used."

Louise pointed over to the far wall. "Notice the painting over there, the oil whose corner Sandy is touching to make sure it hangs straight. Debra will check on the brush strokes because the details are important."

I turned to Jordan, smiling. "If you watch Debra judge the entries, you'll see her stare at them and study them for a long time. Then she'll back up and examine them from different angles and distances. She'll think about the changes in the details over the months as the artist worked on, say, a painting. Those details, layer upon layer, become a record of the time and process the artist used."

"That makes sense. The process is as important as the final artwork."

"Exactly. How the work is presented is a consideration she'll watch for too. Look at the frame, the matting, the way the artwork is mounted. It needs to show the love and care of the artist."

"Patience. It's what I think about. Whether it's a song lyric, a novel, a painting, or a ceramic bowl, the process—the scratching, sweating, and focus on the far-off goal is all part of the creative process." Louise left that idea hanging in the air and walked over to refill her coffee cup.

I smiled at Jordan. "It's why I wanted to direct this art center. Over time, like a piece of art, it will change. We'll add classes, special events, creative spaces, and joint events with schools in the area. It's important to activate the community and educate them about the arts. Look at all these volunteers working hard, not to mention the people who will come to the opening to see these works. Art has always been my passion, but now, as I look at these walls, I see the passion of others, too, in the eventual outcome of all their inspired work." My lip quivered a bit as I looked at the walls, barren for so long. "It's a miracle." I turned my head and went back to my office for a tissue before anyone saw what an emotional ditz I was.

Everyone stayed through the early afternoon, a few leaving here and there for other commitments or to grab lunch. By three, we were done installing the exhibit, and Debra would have outstanding artwork to judge tomorrow morning. Then we'd put the tags up and prepare for the opening the next night. In between, people could come into the center and see the artwork. They wouldn't know who had won prizes, however, until the opening on Saturday night.

I told Jordan to knock off for the day a little early since we'd worked nonstop. She took off, excited about coming back in the morning so she could watch Debra make her selections. Louise went to her office, and I was finishing last-minute details when Andy showed up to check out the entries, followed by Neal.

"This is like a wonderland." Andy walked from one entry to the next. "You've done it, Jill. The board should be impressed when they see this exhibit."

"We'll see. I'm hopeful. At least it makes me think my job is farther from the clutches of Ivan. All the classes we're setting up to start after the exhibit depend on how well this first art event goes."

"My photographs look great over by those watercolors." He walked around and checked out the rest of the exhibit while Neal came over and told me he needed to ask questions about a couple of bills he'd received from Louise.

"She's still in her office."

"Great!" He took a folder of papers back to her as Andy and I finished wandering past the last wall of entries.

194

"Andy, here's the exhibit program if you want to take it home and show it to Lance. Your photographs are featured." I gave him the exhibit program and squeezed his hand. "Saturday night you must come for the big gala."

"Wouldn't miss it." The bell on the door chimed as he left.

I walked back to my office thinking I would finish a few jobs before I went home. I'd leave when Louise did so I wouldn't be here alone.

Turning in a circle, I could see the whole exhibit, and tears swam in my eyes again. They were tears of joy, however. We'd done it. All the pressure that had weighed down my shoulders was gone, and this exhibit would impress the board. *I will show them success* waltzed through my head. Taking a deep breath, I walked back to my office to list several ideas on paper I needed to remember before I took off. I heard Neal's voice as he talked to Louise and walked down the hallway. He stuck his head in my office door.

"The exhibit looks amazing."

"Thanks. Nothing can go wrong from here on out unless the building burns down. We've managed to get it all done on time, and the juror will be in tomorrow. Then, it's one last push for the opening on Saturday night."

Neal walked into my office and glanced over at my love seat. "You writing diaries now? Where do you find the time?"

I laughed. "Oh, it isn't mine. It belonged to Carolyn Anders. I need to give it to Tom so he can check out her thinking around the time she was murdered."

He looked at the book lying on the love seat. "You know I talked to her quite a bit before she left that night. She seemed pretty happy, as if any problems she might have, like Mitch, were solved."

"My point exactly. She had a plan, a solution to her unhappiness." I almost said, "the baby," but stopped myself. "Tom told me he has a theory about her killer, but he hasn't shared it with me. He's checking out a few more details."

Neal nodded his head. "You think the diary will help?"

I walked over and picked it up. "Maybe. Knowing is one thing, but evidence stands up in court."

"So true. Well, I need to get home. Louise straightened the bills out for me. I'll see you at the opening, I guess."

"Absolutely. Thanks, Neal."

He left, and I heard the alley door shut.

"Louise. You ready to go?"

"Sure," she called out from her office.

My phone rang. Why did someone always call when we were almost out the door?

"Adele Marsden Art Center," I answered.

"Is this Jill Madison?" It was a voice I didn't recognize.

"Yes. Can I help you?"

"I hope so. I'm Debra Montiero's sister, Cecelia. I'm afraid I have bad news."

"Oh, no. What?"

"Debra was in a car accident this afternoon. They're taking her into surgery."

I sat in my desk chair, stunned. "Oh, my gosh. Was it serious?"

"We think she will recover. She's broken a bone in two places in her leg and dislocated her shoulder, but the doctor seems to think the surgery will be successful. She wanted me to call you because she can't make it to some art thing tomorrow morning."

A lump in my throat was replaced by the first idea that came into my head. "Don't worry about it at all. We'll deal with it. Tell her we hope she gets better each day. Where is she hospitalized?"

"She's at the medical center in Sandy Hills."

"I'll get over and see her on Sunday, after the opening."

"I know she'll appreciate your visit. Thanks, and I hope the art event goes well for you."

I punched off the phone and sat in silence.

Evidently, Louise was in the doorway and had heard my end of the conversation. "Jill? Everything all right?"

"No." I explained what had happened.

"How can we get another juror on such short notice?"

"I don't know. I'll think about it tonight and see if I can figure out another potential juror in the area."

"I'll think too. We can put our heads together in the morning."

I nodded. "Sure." Smiling, I turned away toward my desk, my anxiety causing my heart to pound in my head. *I will show them success.*

And hide my anxiety.

Chapter Thirty-One

By the time I pulled into my driveway, I'd made several phone calls to find a juror who could arrive tomorrow morning and judge the exhibit. What did I expect? It was July. Most of these people were on vacation or out of town for various reasons. I sat in my car for a moment. Maybe after I took a shower I'd get a second wind and my brain would be able to come up with more names. I should go by Tom and Mary's house and give Carolyn's diary to Tom, but I was too tired. Tomorrow.

Opening the car door, I grabbed my tote, took a deep breath, and started toward the house. It was still late afternoon, the sun was warm on my face, and it was too beautiful a day to have such a problem. The shower revival plan moved to the back of my mind. Dropping my tote on the bottom step of the deck stairs, I lowered myself to the top step, pressed my lips together, and crossed my arms. Staring at my feet, which appeared to rock back and forth of their own accord, I remembered what Judge Spivey said about no more problems. Great. If I couldn't find a juror fast, all would be lost and the board would fire me. Taking several deep breaths, I stared out at the backyard.

My gaze followed the sidewalk to my mother's art studio. A small wood-framed building, it had been her solitary space to work on her sculpting and leave the world behind. Right now, that was what I needed to do, not the sculpture, but the leave-the-world-behind idea. I stuck my hand in my pocket and found my keyring. Sure enough, pulling out the handful of keys, I recognized the one I'd not used in the years since Mom's death.

Mom and Dad's deaths. After our parents died in that senseless car accident with a drunk driver, we had to decide what to do with all their belongings. For a while, we did nothing. We couldn't bring ourselves to even think about sorting through thirty-five years of their memories. Life, as we knew it, had changed forever. At twenty-five, I didn't understand what that meant. As the years went by, I did. Even our house, the two-story, four-bedroom, full-attic, rambling structure we'd all grown up in, wasn't the same. The heart of it was gone, and when I returned home on holidays from Chicago, it was always a grim journey rather than a joyous pilgrimage. We siblings were now orphans. Tom put a padlock on Mom's studio, and we simply left it.

Andy and Lance continued to live in our house, but eventually, we went through our parents' clothes, papers, and memorable items like the set of golf clubs Mom had surprised Dad with on his last birthday before he died at age sixty. It was as if life had painted a black, final line beneath their names on that date. But, as time went by, I began to come to grips with their accident, and my move back here had helped my sense of life's continuity without them.

I rose to my feet and walked down the brick sidewalk Dad had put in to connect the two buildings. The key fit in the padlock perfectly, and the door opened with a creak since no oil had been applied to counteract the Midwestern humidity or dryness for years. For some strange reason, I expected her to be there, standing next to a sculpture she'd teased into life, but only silence met me. Not the scent of her, nor the sight of her, nor the sound of her greeting. Taking a deep breath, I tamped down my emotions and walked over the threshold.

My mother's studio had one light in the ceiling, and I reached over and touched the switch. The bulb came on, a faint glow of violet-yellow, with lots of white added in, scattering across dusty, sheet-covered ghosts.

There was the modeling stand Mom had used for her sculpture work. A canvas covering indicated the presence of an object rather than a flat surface, and I lifted a corner to see an armature, the framework for a sculpture she must have been planning. A stool was next to the stand, and a small table sat next to the stool, which still contained the sculpting tools used for scraping, detailing, cutting, smoothing, and shaping. I took a few steps and picked one up, expecting to find my mother's warmth. But—nothing.

Dust was everywhere. Even my footsteps left their presence on the powdery floor. I studied the sculpture platform then gazed at the rest of the room. Walking to the far end, I lifted the lid on a storage unit Mom had used for items she wanted to save. Several paint canvases were stacked against each other, mercifully dust-free since the lid had protected them.

I lifted them out and discovered they were my paintings. She must have saved eight or ten of them, relics of my younger years. Two had ribbons on them, and I remembered the days I won those in contests at the local library. She was so proud of me, as was my dad, although he would have preferred a better golf swing or tennis backhand. He hadn't yet given up on the possibility I might become an Olympic champion in some category. I smiled. Dad was forever an optimist, even in the face of my obvious, non-athletic reality.

I pulled out the first canvas, the most recent painting, although I hadn't painted for five years now. It was a street scene I'd done of Chicago with a dark, storm-colored sky, all ivory black, and cobalt violet. People hurried down the sidewalk through the rain, a few with umbrellas, others with newspapers over their heads, their hurried movement palpable. When I brought this painting home to my mother, she'd gasped with appreciation. After discussing the brush strokes and the technique I'd used for the sky, she had hugged me when I told her it was a gift for her and my father. She must not have had time to get it framed. Even examining the brush strokes now, I remembered painting with such confidence. I should try again. If nothing else, my hands would have the muscle memory. Small strokes, small steps.

After closing the lid, I walked back across the dusty floor. I looked at her sculpture platform, the canvas like a ghost covering what would have been another masterpiece.

"Why does it have to be so hard?" I said out loud as if they could hear me. "Each time I reach another hurdle, I find a way to jump cleanly over it. Then, another one looms in the foreground. Now this juror problem. We were home free, but no." I gazed out the window toward the setting sun and hoped someone who could be a juror would answer my phone call in the morning.

I was sure my parents would both say to soldier on. Life treated people unfairly in varying amounts. I would become stronger as I figured these problems out. That was what I would do, soldier on. One foot in front of the other. Tomorrow, I'd get together more names, make calls in the morning, and fix this juror situation, even if I had to pull in a stranger off the street as Plan B. After all, I wasn't a child anymore. No one would fix it for me.

My friend's dead body, stalkers, unset alarms, stolen artwork, murder scenes, angry board members, and now this. I could almost hear my father's voice telling me to get on top of it, not give up, figure tomorrow would be better. On the other hand, I could see my mother's smile and encouragement as she scraped a little more clay off and turned in my direction, a small kid sitting on the window seat looking at a picture book but glancing over at her on occasion, as I watched the sunlight on her glossy black hair.

I turned off the light and locked the studio. My shoulders slumped and my eyes looked down as I plodded down the bricks toward the house.

Tomorrow.

Chapter Thirty-Two

I opened my eyes. My bed covers were strewn all over the floor. It had been one of those nights where I'd tossed and turned, stared at the digital clock changing numbers, and was unable to sleep. The morning sunlight streamed in through my bedroom window, and I lay there for a few moments and thought how relieved I'd feel on Sunday when our first exhibit had been a triumph. But I had to live through today and tomorrow first. Deciding I might as well get up at 6:30, I turned off my alarm, trudged to the bathroom, and took an invigorating shower. Thank God it revived me and I began to think again about possible jurors who could come to the art center, well, today. Only Louise and I knew we didn't have a juror so far. The opening was tomorrow night, so we had to get on this right away.

Yawning my way to the kitchen, I stopped to look in the mirror at my bleary, bloodshot eyes, tiny vermilion tentacles reaching out across the whites of my eyes. Tonight. I'd sleep tonight since we'd have a juror. I hoped. I wasn't worried about the opening tomorrow since I knew we were well-organized. While I was wide awake at three a.m., I remembered a couple of names. My old art teacher who had retired a few years ago was Plan B. One of my mother's friends, who might still be around and had worked in the art department at the college with her, was Plan A. It was too late to try to find anyone from outside the area. I had to wait until a decent hour to call either of them. An hour from now would work. I'd figure this out.

Andy had stayed overnight, but said he was leaving early to help Lance unload a shipment at the store. I could see where he'd left a glass with a milk ring in the sink. Tom would never know, and it was only a brief lapse on our parts. I'd be off to work soon. I popped two bagel halves in the toaster, poured orange juice, and waited for the coffee to signal it was ready. Glancing over at the counter near the back door, I noted the list I'd made in the middle of the night, my tote bag, and Carolyn's diary, which I'd drop off with Tom today. I walked to the window over the kitchen sink and glanced out into the backyard because I thought I might have left the light on in my mother's studio. Nope. Thinking about her and my dad strengthened my resolve to get on top of this today and straighten it all out. If the exhibit went off perfectly, I'd win the approval of the board. I whispered, "I will show them success."

I stood at the kitchen window, watching the first rays of the sun casting shadows on the backyard. The details for the opening tomorrow night were all in place. We had sponsors, food, drinks, mason jar centerpieces with wildflowers, red-checkered tablecloths, and ribbons for the prizes. Louise and I had checked with the volunteers yesterday. Many of those items had been brought in already and were piled in the storeroom. Nothing to worry about, only the juror.

When the bagels popped up, I opened the refrigerator and searched for the butter spread and marmalade. Setting everything on the kitchen table, I figured there was time to eat this morning since it was too early to make phone calls. I'd taken my first bite of bagel when a loud pounding erupted at the front door. Glancing at the clock over the sink, I wondered who could be here at seven-fifteen in the morning and why the pounding?

I walked out to the living room and swung the door open without thinking. OMG, it was Stupid, his face a mask of fury, his fist on the door.

Before I could say a word, he threatened me loud enough for the neighborhood to hear with, "You high and mighty Madisons! You thought you could break into my house and go through my daughter's stuff? Well, you can't! Just because your brother's a cop, you think you can get off like that." He snapped his fingers. "I'll deal with you since the law won't."

I had the presence of mind to shut the front door, but I figured it wouldn't hold him for long. I locked it, but he wouldn't go away. If he'd killed his own stepdaughter, he wouldn't worry about killing me. The pounding continued, and now my heart pounded too.

Where was my phone? I panicked when I saw him pull at the screen door handle. Call nine-one-one. Where was my phone? I checked my pocket. Couldn't reach Angie and her app. What should I do? He would get through the door, maybe even break it down.

Then the door-pounding stopped. I peeked through a window curtain and saw arms come around Downey's shoulders. He fell backward off the porch steps. Now Neal was tussling with Downey on the grass and rolling across the sidewalk. He had Downey on the ground, hitting him. As suddenly as he had started, Neal stopped and told Downey if he ever came near me again, he'd find himself in jail with plenty of bruises and broken bones. He stood up, pulled Downey up, and marched him—holding his arm behind his back—to the curb, where his battered truck was parked at an awkward angle. I watched from the corner of the window, too chicken to be closer. Downey got into his truck, and I heard the raspy noise of an ancient engine as he chugged off unsteadily down the street, his faulty muffler waking up the neighborhood. I took a deep breath, thankful Neal was here. What would I have done without him?

Neal watched Stupid disappear, and I saw him walk toward the driveway. He must have parked behind my car. A few minutes later, he reappeared at my back door with a cardboard coffee tray and two cups.

"Thank God you were here." Opening the door, I invited him in and offered him a bagel.

"Ah, no thanks." He moved over by the sink. "Has Will Downey threatened you before?"

"Well, he's never shown up at my house." I decided it might be better not to mention our breaking and entering.

"And drunk to boot at this early hour. Well, he won't come back after that. Glad I was here when the idiot showed up. I remember him from when Carolyn was in high school. He hasn't changed much, except he's older and crazier."

I gestured to a seat at the kitchen table. My nose recognized the familiar scent. "Why do you have my favorite latte?"

"Oh, I still have to go to work today, but I figured it was a big day for you with your first exhibit and everything. Time to celebrate."

What a kind man. Here he'd worked beside us for the last month for nothing, and he was still thoughtful enough to understand what a great day this was for me.

I sat down, took another bite of my bagel, and chewed it quickly. "Well," I washed it down with a sip of the latte. "Oh, a little hot."

"Blow on it. Mine's okay."

"I was about to say I have to find a juror on the fly. Mine was in a car accident yesterday which put her out of the picture. This means I must find someone else now. Today." I took another sip of my latte, which was a tiny bit cooler. "Figured I'd wait until it was a more civilized hour to call potential jurors." Glancing at the counter, I saw my phone and sighed. When would I ever get organized with my phone's location? I walked over and slipped it in my pocket because this would be exactly the kind of day I'd forget it. Then, sitting back down, I took another bite of bagel.

Neal looked around the kitchen. "Nice kitchen. I like all the counter space." He walked over to the counter, where he studied my pile of to-go stuff, and turned around saying, "Ah, Carolyn's diary. Find anything interesting?"

"Looks to me like her terrifying stepfather is the main topic, but I haven't read all of it." I figured since Tom hadn't seen it yet, I might be wise to keep neutral in any descriptions. Taking several swallows of my latte, I realized I'd forgotten how much I loved these since I hadn't indulged myself in quite a while.

Neal picked up Carolyn's diary and opened it. I noticed he checked out the pages closer to the end.

"Don't think you should read her diary. It's evidence, and I haven't even given it to my brother yet."

He continued to turn pages. Why was he doing that after I told him to stop?

"Hmm...her handwriting. Even after all this time, it's so familiar."

"Seriously? After all these years and students you remember Carolyn's handwriting?" I was about to say something about his long-term memory when an uneasy feeling came over me. Her handwriting. Angie and I had talked about it with those postcards.

"I know she was your friend." He turned more pages. "You didn't know her as well as you think." He still turned pages, not even paying attention to me. Neal's voice had changed—it seemed not so friendly now—and he turned page after page, ignoring me. Weird.

My breathing was tighter, and anxiety rose in my chest.

At that, he turned and looked toward me, a grim expression on his face. For a man who had been all smiles, this was a new development.

"Your so-called 'friend' tried to ruin my life."

"Carolyn? Ruin your life? How?"

He turned and walked toward the table. His presence pressed in a little too closely and I pushed my chair back a bit.

"I was there that night. She didn't head to her apartment alone because I took her to the Rusty Nail. Her request. She wanted me to drop her off where she could meet some guy, but when his car wasn't there, she was disappointed. Then silent. She changed her strategy."

"Her strategy? What are you talking about? Why are you telling me this?"

"Your best friend was pregnant. I'll bet you didn't know."

"Re—ally?" I tried to make it sound like a shock.

"Yeah. Really. And who knows who the father was. When she couldn't blame it on this college guy, she decided I'd be a great substitute."

His face took on a hard look. Narrowed eyes, slash of a mouth. And suddenly it fit together. I understood his interest in the basement and the identity of the body. He always showed up at the art center, keeping an eye on things and asking questions. Now I remembered Tom said Neal had been the last person to see Carolyn alive. But Neal? Carolyn?

"You're not as smart as you think, Jill, and I'm sorry you were so persistent. Why couldn't you leave well enough alone? This baby would have ruined my life. It was only a flirtation at first, and when I tried to cool it, she pushed me against a wall. I suppose it was flattering, but as time went by, she insisted she loved me and we had to go away together."

I looked at him and considered Carolyn's baby. That would have ended everything. A married teacher didn't sleep with a young woman in our small, conservative town, not if he wanted to keep his job.

"Neal, I—" Suddenly, I didn't feel well. I struggled to say, "maybe a paternity test." Then it hit me. Maybe Carolyn's baby *was* Neal's. I could hardly remember his name clearly.

Wyatt started to talk again, but I strained my eyes to see him since his face was getting hazy. I became lightheaded. His lips moved, but I couldn't figure out what he was saying. He looked at me intently, his words all running into each other.

The latte. Had he poisoned me? Holding onto the table, I struggled to get myself under control. Lightheaded and dizzy. Then, nothing.

Chapter Thirty-Three

I didn't know when I started to think again, to be aware I was somewhere dark. Opening my eyes, I turned my neck all around but couldn't see anything. My head banged with a horrible headache, and I was unbelievably thirsty. Hot, it was so hot I sweated through my clothes. Wherever I was, it felt damp...smelled damp. Was I underground? In a basement? I was on something soft, a sofa or bed or blankets. With total darkness, I couldn't tell where I was.

Lying on my side on whatever this was, I became aware my hands were tied behind me, and they were cramped and painful. How long had I been here? As my eyes became more accustomed to the darkness, I saw a few small slivers of light ahead of me, but from where? I took shallow breaths because it was so hot and humid. Should I try to sit up? I hated to think what it might do to the headache. Moving my hands, I tested whether the ropes were tight.

They were.

Then I remembered. Neal Wyatt. My house. He drugged me. Neal. My brain couldn't think right...the drugs...

I must have lost consciousness again because a noise in the darkness was followed by the burst of an overhead light. My head really ached now, and my eyes hurt, the light blinding me. I squinted my eyes, trying to get used to the brightness. Hearing a door open above me, I watched Neal descend a set of wooden stairs. With light now, I could see I was in a room, a sizable one, with lots of boxes piled in various places. A sofa was about the only piece of furniture, except for a small table and lamp. Neal was at the bottom of the stairs now, carrying a sack.

"Awake now?"

"Where am I?"

"You're at my lake house on the lower level."

He had told me about his lake place earlier. It was near the east end of the lake, relatively alone. It was connected to the lake entrance by a service road that encircled the lake.

"Why did you drug me? You did. Right? Drug me?"

"Had to get you out here without any objections on your part. However, I have to say you were dead weight to carry out and in. I'm untying your hands and you can sit up. You can eat something, but you have to promise you won't try to get away."

He pulled me to a sitting position, and as predicted, my head pounded even worse. I thought I might throw up I was so nauseated. Untying my hands, Wyatt moved back and opened the sack he had set on a small table next to the sofa. I noticed a lamp on the table, but he hadn't turned it on since the overhead light was horribly bright. I rubbed my hands together, trying to get the blood to move around in them again.

"Here." He handed me a bottle of water. "Take a few sips. The nausea from the drug will go away."

I looked at him. "You expect me to drink anything else you give me?"

"Check it. Hasn't been opened."

I turned the cap. He was right. It was hard to turn, and the plastic piece on the bottle's neck broke apart, so the lid would turn easier. I put it to my painfully dry lips and took a sip. Better. Taking a few more sips, I stared at him as he pulled out a sandwich and apple from a bag, handing them to me.

"Why give me food?"

"It will make the headache go away."

Maybe he isn't going to kill me.

He sat across from me on a box, shaking his head. "I never thought anyone would use the building again. You see, it was a mistake."

He must have been referring to the Lowry Building. "What do you plan to do with me?"

"The only thing I can do. Isn't it obvious? You haven't left me any choice. Like Carolyn."

"Why didn't you kill me? Why keep me here?"

"I need to make a plan. Figure out what to do with the body. This time I don't want any slip-ups."

Listening to him talk in a matter-of-fact way about my death told me he was out of his mind.

"Besides, I had to talk to you, to explain why. I'm not a horrible person—not a killer. All of this was forced on me. Now you're doing the same. I was a teacher. I helped kids. I have a wife and family, who go to church every Sunday and help with philanthropic projects. I've tried to lead a virtuous life after the situation with Carolyn. Redeem myself. That's why you're here, so I can explain to you. I'm no expert on killing anyone. It was too easy, too fast. I have nightmares about it, sometimes for weeks. Can't sleep. My hands around her neck. Then it was too late, too late to take it back."

"I'm confused about how this murder was forced on you."

He ignored my statement and kept talking. "The art exhibit opens tonight, but I'm sure all is in disarray without you there. If only you hadn't decided to come back and open the Lowry Building. When I saw the story in the newspaper, I couldn't believe it." He pursed his lips and looked off toward a wall. "I thought maybe they won't use the basement. Then my wife pointed out the next article about the basement construction work. Why, Jill? Why did you have to reopen the building?"

I considered the exhibit. This must be Saturday. I'd left the house on Friday morning. Tom would be searching for me by now. It was only a matter of time until he put two and two together. Oh my God, the exhibit. What was happening back there without me? What had Louise done? We didn't even have a juror yet.

"If it makes you feel better, no matter what happens to you now, your days at the art center were numbered. The board didn't trust you, and I gave them little reason to."

"What are you talking about?"

"It wasn't simply Carolyn there where I'd buried her years ago, it was also the burglary and break-in. Your mother's sculpture. I wanted it to seem like theft, but I was checking the basement, trying to figure out where you'd dig." He watched my reaction. "Don't worry. It's in a safe place. The sculpture. You'll never see it again, I'm afraid."

"You? You stole my mother's sculpture?"

"Had a key for the alley door. I used to work at Turnberry's Hardware Store, you know. I made a copy of the Lowry Building key years ago when Jim Lackey, the previous owner, needed copies. While I have a few other keys from various buildings in town, they might not be as useful after this long. Door locks get changed. Fortunately, yours didn't. The alarm was simple since a key turned it off. You should have upgraded the security system. It's so early twentieth century."

I did set the alarm! It might be best to keep still and let him talk.

"And now you force me to kill you. If you'd left well enough alone, I wouldn't have to do this. I tried to scare you away."

Suddenly, I remembered what I had to ask. "The photographs? The stalking?"

He nodded. "If you'd only given up. When I saw her diary at your office, I couldn't take a chance your brother might read it and figure it out. She had a crush on me, and during a weak moment in my life, she took advantage of me. My wife had just had Bree, the bills were piling up, and my future didn't look bright when I was paid so little. We had a brief fling. Carolyn and me."

"Carolyn? This was her fault? Not that an adult like you should have been responsible?"

"She told me she was pregnant the night she babysat for us. She was crying and didn't know what to do. What a disaster. Unbelievable. How could she have put me in that position? It would have ruined me. Don't you understand? I tried to reason with her, but she wouldn't have it. I even offered to pay to get rid of it and give her money to leave town. Once she realized the Evan guy wasn't her ticket out of town, Carolyn said the baby was mine. Who knows? I panicked." His voice became angrier. "How could she think I would do such a thing? Leave my wife? My kids?"

Tom was right when he said Neal was the last person to see her alive. He really was. Mitch or Will Downey had been the two on our radar.

"Neal, what about Mitch?"

"Mitch?"

"Yes. Was that a little mistake too?"

He thought for a moment. "No. I didn't want to kill him, but he'd seen my car at the Rusty Nail and realized the woman with me was Carolyn. He put it together since Carolyn babysat that night. She looks nothing like my wife, Viv. Once her body was found, he remembered. I made an excuse to see him before he could collect any blackmail and heard your message on his answering machine when he played it back. It was a piece of luck, meant to be. Now I knew you'd be there, a perfect situation to put the blame on you. He wanted me to pay him to shut up. I wouldn't. I went back later, after his guys had left, and he was alone."

"And I suppose you took the knife from our shed and tried to frighten me on my way home?"

"Yeah. I was back at your shed the night I followed you home, waiting to see if you'd come out again. I wanted to scare you, to get you to stop asking questions. Just like the photographs."

I didn't say anything else but instead thought about Mitch, who'd met a violent death because he realized Carolyn had an affair with her teacher. He'd not killed her, and, in my heart, I was thankful I hadn't misjudged him. I looked at Neal.

"It was easy to take Carolyn to the old Lowry Building and leave her there because I figured no one would find her. That would've happened except—"

"I showed up."

"You did." He shook his head. "Why? Why did you have to come back? Why did you have to reopen the Lowry Building? Why couldn't you have left it alone?"

Noticing the words he used, I knew what his next plan would be. Somehow, I had to get out of here.

"I'm not a monster, you know. I've worked hard to redeem myself. I coached Little League, helped at the soup kitchen downtown, and worked with kids at my church. Don't you see? Carolyn's death made me a better person. I've forgiven myself and tried to make up for my one little mistake."

One little mistake? Killing my best friend was "one little mistake?" All the soup kitchens in hell wouldn't take away his horrible act. I almost said those thoughts but figured I'd better calm him down. "I understand, Neal. No, you're not a monster. You were simply a man with his future before him and his back against the wall." Andy would be proud of me lying with a straight face. Dad, Mom, Tom, and Mary—not so much.

"Excellent. We agree. I'll tie you up again while I go back. Sorry. Can't afford to have you leave. You shouldn't have come back, you know. It forces me to do something I'd rather not do...like Carolyn. I must appear at the art center for an alibi and to see the chaos without you. Plant an idea or two about your absence. Besides, I need to make sure people see me tonight."

Then later kill me too. However, I nodded, making sure my hands were rolled into fists as he tied the rope around my wrists again. Maybe the ropes wouldn't be as tight. If so, I could squeeze my hands and maybe get the ropes to slide off.

He paused, as if he'd thought of one last thing he wanted to ask me. He turned. "Carolyn's diary. Did it implicate me? You said it was evidence, and that's why I had to have it."

Before I realized what I was doing, I blurted out, "No, Neal. It didn't." Seeing his reaction, I thought, *me and my big mouth.*

Now his shoulders and arms visibly relaxed. Even though I hadn't read all of the diary, I didn't need him to explode. On the other hand, he knew I was relentless and wouldn't have stopped until I found out who'd killed Carolyn. Nor would Tom. I had to get out of here before he came back again. Maybe I could help myself since he figured he was in the clear.

"I know you're a kind guy, Neal. Look at all the good you've done for other people. I wonder if you could do one kind thing for me. Could you leave the small lamp on? I don't like darkness. It frightens me."

He looked at the lamp, a lone little sentinel on the end table next to the sofa. Then he glanced at the shuttered windows.

"'Spose I could leave it on. You stay there. I'll be back later. It'll give you time to put your thoughts in order and ask forgiveness for whatever you've done." He turned on the dim light and scanned the room, making sure he'd left nothing helpful.

I tried to appear scared and vulnerable as he climbed the stairs again, turning off the overhead light and locking the door behind him. It sounded like a deadbolt, a lock that wouldn't help me one bit. My phone. I remembered putting it in my pocket at my house. I couldn't check for it with my hands tied. As I looked around, I worked my hands against the rope. I was right. It wasn't quite as tight this time. There were shutters on two windows on the far side of the door. The light I'd seen before was in places where the shutter boards didn't quite meet. Boxes sat all around, stored here until the Wyatts came back for the weeks before school started. Before I could figure out a way to leave, I'd have to get my hands free. Plan A.

Thinking back to what Neal had said, I realized it wasn't my fault my mother's sculpture was taken. Poor Carolyn. She must have been shocked to discover her pregnancy. Was it Neal's child? Then I considered what he had said. Ask for forgiveness? For what? Wanting to honor my mother's memory? Spending sleepless nights to make sure the building was safe? Coming home to my family or what was left of it? My board choosing a building where my best friend was buried? The more I thought about those coincidences, the madder I became. I would get out of this and see to it that Neal paid the price for killing Carolyn and Mitch.

Rubbing my wrists together, I began to look around for something sharp. I had to get out before he returned. What could I find here that would help?

Chapter Thirty-Four

I walked around the room, looking for an object, anything, that might help me get my hands loose. I constantly worked them back and forth as I examined my prison. Boxes in various groups cluttered the room. If only I could open some boxes and search for a sharp tool.

I had to hurry. He might've been conflicted about Carolyn's murder, although he had solidly blamed it on her—the coward—but he wouldn't hesitate to kill again to keep his secrets safe. Searching in every crevice of the dimly lit room, I couldn't see a single helpful object. Nothing sharp. No knives, no razor blades, nothing. I couldn't break a window because the only two were shuttered and appeared to be locked from the outside. A recent development? Had Neal done this in preparation to kidnap me?

He'd left me an extra water bottle. I examined it and saw the plastic was so useless it wouldn't cut anything. What was in the boxes? I looked at a small pile, three boxes to be exact, stacked on top of each other. Turning around, I used my fingers to feel around the wrappings and twisted and pulled away packing tape on the top box. I managed to open the flaps with my fingers behind me, turning around to see what was inside. Clothing, it appeared, or maybe curtains, but nothing helpful. I pushed the box with my knee until it toppled to the floor and started on the second box. How long had he been gone?

The second box held a hodge-podge of objects, little stuff wrapped in paper I had to unwrap behind my back. My fingers and wrists began to ache. I dropped the various small objects into the box after I unwrapped them, guessing at their identities. They were objects you'd stick on a bookshelf or coffee table like figurines, bookends, small pieces I'd define as miscellaneous. I sighed. How many of these must I open to find something sharp?

I stopped. A car. I could hear it on the road that wound toward the house. Holding my breath, I listened as the sound of the engine got closer. Please, don't let it be him. The car went past the house, and the engine noise disappeared. My breathing was a little easier.

Then I hit the jackpot. A small gadget, round, and metal, turned out to be a flashlight. I rolled it around in my fingers, searching for the button to turn it on. With my luck, the batteries would be dead. No, a light shone out on the wall from behind me. This could come in handy.

By the time I got to the fifth box, over on the other side of the room, I found what I needed. My fingers ached, but I lifted out a framed picture. It appeared to be on a beach with Neal's wife and their two teenagers when they were younger. It couldn't be helped. I dropped it on the floor, but it didn't break. Using my foot and the side of a box, I managed to turn it over, glass-side up, and stomped on it several times. Success. Sharp glass.

It was much easier in the movies to see an actor take a piece of glass and saw through a rope behind his back. I had to lower myself to the floor to find a piece of glass that would work. Holding the glass shard between my right thumb and forefinger, I sawed away, hoping not to cut any major veins in my wrist.

After what seemed like an eternity, the rope was close to breaking and, dropping the piece of glass, I pulled my hands apart, the rope shredding. Free. Moving my fingers and wrists around felt so good that I did a little happy dance around the floor, stomped on the piece of rope, and left it lying in shreds.

Now, how could I get out of here before he came back? I climbed the stairs and checked out the lock on the door. As I had suspected, it was a deadbolt in a well-constructed door. Sitting on the top step, I considered my options. Hit him over the head when he came back? I couldn't even hide and push him down the stairs because the door at the top of the stairs opened into the wall. Besides, I might break his neck, and I'd rather not have his death on my conscience. Too bad he didn't reciprocate my thoughts.

A door and two windows occupied the lake side wall of the cabin. Walking back down the stairs, I examined the windows. Shutters drawn across them on the outside were somehow firmly locked, but not from the inside. He must've planned this. Unlocking and opening a window, I pushed on the shutters as hard as I could. Nothing. Could they be broken? Not without a lot of effort and time, and time was what I didn't have.

Next, the door. Oh, for a screwdriver to unscrew the hinges. Sweat trickled down my neck, and I was worried about the time. He wasn't back yet, although I listened for a car anywhere near the house. I moved over to the other shutter. Remembering the slivers of light when I first opened my eyes, I thought most of the light came from this side of the windows. By now, however, it might be dark outside. Light. It was always a dimension I noticed since it was necessary for shadows in a painting, and it affected the values of the colors. I had seen light coming in through the shutters. Pushing up the window, I felt the shutter on the house, and thought there was a little more give than I'd detected with the other one. The slats didn't fit snuggly, and there was space between several of them. Not much, but perhaps enough.

I got my fingers between two of the slats and grabbed what felt like a piece of wood holding the shutters closed. Pulling on it at an angle, I sensed a little more give. No way I could break it in half, but I could move it. Once I opened enough space to get my hand through, I could feel the piece of wood. He had made a lock by setting a board across the shutters. My fingers moved quickly, back and forth as I tried to figure out how the board was attached to the shutter. It sat in kind of a metal cradle, secure in the knowledge someone inside couldn't get it to budge. Now I understood why he'd let me live long enough to figure out how to dispose of me. He was a planner, all right.

I will show them success. The locking board nestled in the metal cradle he'd made, so if I could push it up, it would fall off. I reasoned if I could get one side up and out, the whole board might fall. Although the angle wasn't easy from the inside, I pushed as hard as I could. I stopped, caught my breath, and planned again. Shaking my head, I figured I had to try again and push harder. I didn't have a hammer or a tire iron I could use as a lever.

I stood back a moment, gathering my forces, and slid my fingers through the opening between the same two slats. This time I had a firmer grasp. I pushed up as hard as I could—maybe a tiny bit of movement. Taking more deep breaths, I tried again, and this time it moved. A little. One more time and I might have it. I worried about Neal returning and considered what it would mean as I stepped to the window again. Pushing as hard as I could, the wooden piece released from the cradle and fell to the ground. The shutter opened. Immediately, the insistent chorus of crickets and the smell of lake water nearby hit my ears and nostrils. It was dark out. A full moon lit up the sky, a situation which would help me see, but it would also make me a target.

I sat on the window ledge and swiveled out. Searching around on the ground, I grabbed the piece of wood that had fallen from the shutters. This might be a weapon if I came across Neal on my way back to town. In the dark? How could I manage that? The lake was several miles from Apple Grove on a two-way highway with narrow shoulders. I didn't want to get loose only to find myself run over by a car. One problem at a time.

Shuster's cabin, now Neal's, was at the far east end of the lake, isolated. His cottage was alone on the end of the lane. I figured I'd walk up to the road and see what I could find in the area. A new event, however, scotched those plans.

A car engine meant a car was approaching the house.

Chapter Thirty-Five

The driveway was on the far side of the house, along with the house entrance. I kept low and ran toward a cluster of tall trees, the ground sloping upward toward the road. Once in the grove of trees, I could move from one to another. The fragrant smell of pine filled the air, and the moon provided enough light for me to see so I could keep from falling over gnarled tree roots. The ground was full of pine needles that softened my footsteps.

Climbing toward the lake road, I pushed myself to move uphill. I huffed and puffed after weeks of sitting at my desk. Despite a chorus of chirping crickets, I heard a car door slam. Almost simultaneously, lights went on in the upper level of Neal's house, shining out the windows onto the lawn. Running to another cluster of trees farther from the house, I moved toward the road. It would be a matter of minutes before he found me gone and came after me.

I had his flashlight and could use it once I was away from the house. I wasn't far enough away yet, so I kept it off and relied on the full moon to show me the road and keep me on my feet. Luck was with me. Usually I wore heels to work, but yesterday I'd opted for flat tennies because we'd have been on our feet all day with the installation. *Thank you, God, for small miracles.* I stayed behind the trees but peered toward the house, at least fifty yards from me. I imagined he'd found me gone by now, the shutters open, and would come after me. A grim idea floated through my head. He couldn't let me get away.

I looked ahead into the darkness. I'd have to run across a stretch of ground to get to the road, and, of course I'd be vulnerable if I tried to cross it. I thought the old mill was somewhere around here, a place with which I was quite familiar. I took off at a run. My heartbeat thrashed in my ears, and I gasped for air too soon. My breath burst in and out of my lungs. I almost laughed. Hysteria. I would have giggled, but I didn't have enough breath.

No other houses in sight. I didn't know how long I'd run along the side of the road before a car engine started in the distance. He could outrun me if he could figure out where I was in relation to his cabin. Glancing over my shoulder, headlights swung onto the road, the lights switching to high beams, and his car came slowly creeping along. I was sure Neal was watching for me in the headlights.

That was when I saw it. The sign for the Cavendish Mill. It was an old grain mill falling apart from disuse, a favorite party spot when Angie and I were in high school. Years ago. One night when the police raided us, lots of underage kids flew out a back window, into a pond. My brother Tom was twenty-five then, a policeman, and he'd have killed me, as would my parents, if I had been arrested for underage drinking. It wasn't that they were puritanical. It meant if I were caught in this small town, it would put a stain on my family's reputation, and that would be worse than the actual drinking. Angie and I had hidden out behind a storage room door, eventually moving up a ladder to the loft. We'd managed to get away, but Tom guessed I'd been there.

I remembered this building as I pushed my way with care through the back door. It was old and crumbling, and I worried I might fall through a floor. Maybe Neal would think I'd run down the road toward town and he'd keep searching for me along the road. He wasn't stupid. He'd backtrack and find me here if I didn't figure out a way to hide from him or get away.

The unpainted wooden building had a dilapidated waterwheel on the west side, where a pond fed into the lake. Inside, huge wooden support beams went from floor to ceiling with ventilation pockets in the walls near the dirt floor. No glass remained in the windows, and on one end of the huge room was a grain shaft, while a set of wooden stairs was supported by the wall at the other end. Moonlight shone in through the windows, so I could figure out precisely what I needed to do.

A catwalk stretched across the top of the building, but it was too dangerous to even contemplate. Beneath the catwalk was a storage room accessed by a first-floor stairway, with a loft near the top of the room where Angie and I had hidden during the infamous high school raid. The rope and the hook from the catwalk must be up there since the rope trailed off somewhere on the loft. The whole rope and hook contraption had been used, years ago, to move grain bags.

Down below, the old machinery of the mill sat rusting in disuse. The runner stone and bedstone that ground the grain were still there, along with a room to store the sacks. The gears and various metal shafts had been taken out long ago. Thank God for illegal drinking in high school. *Sorry, Mom and Dad. Oh, and Tom.*

As quickly as I could, I scrambled up the stairs into the storage room, one rotted wooden step almost breaking beneath me. This room was open on one side clear to the downstairs. Its floor appeared quite stable, so I figured I'd better go higher, but if Neal found me there, I'd have no way out of the loft. If I jumped out of a window into the pond, I'd probably break my neck since it wasn't very deep these days. No plan B. This wasn't good. I was sure there was some book by a Samurai warrior or a Civil War general who wrote, "Always leave a Plan B." Too late. Like Butch Cassidy and the Sundance Kid, I was stuck on a cliff facing a huge drop with no other choice. My resolve wavered momentarily, and then I looked at the ladder in front of me, took a deep breath, and whispered, "I can do this."

I gingerly climbed up the ladder to the loft and tested each board before I put my weight on it. Unfortunately, the ladder was attached to wooden supports, and I couldn't pull it up with me. I'd reached the loft when a car engine rumbled outside, idling, and I held my breath. It stopped, as if Neal thought about whether I'd be here or halfway to town by now. He must've decided on the former. As a teacher, he would've heard stories of the drinking parties out here, and now he figured I could've hidden in a place I knew.

My tongue slid over a bit of dried blood from where I'd bit my lip. I looked around the loft to get my bearings. A pile of wood lay on the loft floor, big enough to hide me from below. I could see through small spaces in this woodpile all the way down to the first floor and even to the front door.

Behind me was the coiled rope which I'd already figured was a hazard to my footsteps. On the end of it was a heavy metal hook. It was the one I'd remembered before. They'd used it to raise and lower bags of grain out the window at the top of the building. The rope was tied to a bracket on the wall. What else could I do? He had me cornered, but maybe he'd give up and leave. Right. Sure he would.

The door at the front of the mill opened with an ominous creak, then silence. I kept my head down behind the wood, but my eyes were used to the darkness now, and the beam of his flashlight swept across the room. Maybe he had one in his car, as my fingers closed tighter around the flashlight I'd commandeered from his house.

"I know you're here, Jill. Might as well come out. I don't want to have to hurt you."

I shivered at the sound of his voice. *Not hurt me? Are you crazy? You plan to kill me.*

Silence again. I put my hand over my mouth, holding my breath, my other hand clutching the flashlight to my chest. My fingers hurt, wound tightly around the flashlight. Could he hear me breathe? Beads of sweat broke out on my forehead, and the hand over my mouth trembled. I peeked out through the wood again and tried to breathe shallowly, my hand still over my mouth. His silhouette was in the doorway, the moonlight behind him. He had a flashlight in one hand and—dear God—a handgun in the other. Neal stood there, totally quiet, unmoving, and listened for any sound I might make. I kept perfectly still, hoping the floor of the loft was as sturdy as I thought it was. Of course, if it gave way and fell on him, it would solve my problem, but it would probably kill me too. It was a long way down.

This was nerve-wracking. My heartbeat raced, almost exploding. How much longer could he stand in the doorway, silent and waiting? The beam of the flashlight swept up the walls and across the loft. I ducked my head moments before it hit the pile of wood and the wall behind me. Sweat poured off my forehead and down to my chin, while its saltiness trickled on my lips. I wanted to wipe it away but was afraid to move even a fraction of an inch. The light swept across the loft another time, hesitated, then moved off in another direction. I lifted my head, barely moving it an inch, and wiped my mouth with my hand.

Chapter Thirty-Six

I didn't move. Maybe Neal was outside or in the main room. Was he under the storage room? I couldn't see any beam from a flashlight. He could've gone out to see if I was anywhere near the outside of the building. I looked around, but the storage room had no windows. Pursing my dry lips, I considered what to do next. If he went outside, I could use this opportunity to move before he came back. But to where? I shivered, my mind on high alert.

Turning my head and gazing around the loft, I considered whether a weapon might be close by...a pitchfork or shovel or barrel, or maybe something I could throw. But no, nothing. The moonlight was quite bright from the windows in the main part of the building. I studied the entire loft, but mostly the pile of wood dominated the floor. I supposed if he climbed the ladder, I could hit him with a piece of wood, although he might shoot me first.

No, that wouldn't be a first-rate plan.

My gaze lit on the dark outline of the rope, and I set my flashlight down in a spot where I could find it again. Inching over to the rope, I unwound it from the bracket on the back wall. The rope was threaded through an O-ring at the top of the building, one end now in my hand, while the rest of the rope lay slack on the loft floor with the heavy iron hook attached. What if I pulled up the slack and laid the hook near the edge of the loft, close to the ladder? The O-ring at the ceiling was almost lined up over the top of the ladder. If Neal climbed the ladder, I might be able to swing out the hook and hit him once I pulled up the slack. I let out a deep breath. Or, with the decades it had been here, the rope might fall apart. This was my last chance, and maybe luck was on my side and the rope would hold. I should make use of my time before he showed up again with his gun.

Picking up the heavy metal hook, I balanced it in my hand and noted its weight. Please, dear God, don't let me kill him. Just knock him out. I promise I'll be kinder to Andy and listen to Tom's conservative advice…well, listen. It was a step forward. I glanced at the hook and shook my head. Okay, I'll *follow* Tom's future advice. Please, let me stop Neal in his tracks so he won't kill me. My brain was already retracting the bit about Tom's advice. I seemed to recall legal jargon that promises made under duress were non-binding.

The door opened again with its now-familiar creak, and Neal's flashlight panned over the loft as I shrank low on the floor again. The light stopped on the woodpile. I squeezed my eyes shut. Perhaps if my eyes were closed, he wouldn't see me. Opening my eyes, I realized the ridiculousness of my idea. When my heart began to race again, I wondered if I could have a heart attack at my age. Calm. Remember your mantra. I whispered it, and my muscles relaxed a little. Setting the hook down on the floor near the edge of the drop-off, I waited.

His voice cut through the darkness, and I held myself tight while I considered a fetal position.

"I know you're up there, Jill. Come down. Don't make me come and get you. A fall from that height might break your neck on the dirt floor down here. Could look like an accident."

Pressing my lips together tightly, I figured the best plan was to keep silent. Let him come to me. I was in my own space here, on higher ground. I had the rope coiled in my hand. Unrolling it, I estimated about how much I'd need to hit him halfway up the ladder. I'd pull up slightly, to get the hook into the air, and then push it out as I lowered the rope. Here was hoping for a lucky trajectory, and I wished I remembered geometry better. Holding my breath, I thought if I didn't hit him, he could at least lose his balance. If he fell into the storage room, it might stun him enough or knock him out so I could get away. If he fell over the edge to the bottom of the mill, the fall would probably kill him. I didn't even want to think about that.

I was sure my contract had a provision that said I'd be fired if I murdered someone. I started to giggle nervously but caught myself.

Footsteps on the stairway, slow...cautious. I counted them as he came up. Seven, eight, nine. *Courage, you can do this. Focus. Be determined.* I waited, held my breath again, and sat perfectly still, leaning forward. Peering over the woodpile, I was all anticipation, the rope in one hand, the hook in the other. My legs trembled, though I struggled to keep them still. My skin was clammy, and my own sweat was overpowering. Disgusting. When the heavy footsteps stopped at ten, I knew he was in the storage room below me. The beam from his flashlight was poised on the woodpile slightly to my right now.

The moonlight was still bright enough that I could see the top of his head as he moved up the ladder toward me. Trying not to remember he was my high school math teacher, I took a deep breath. I counted to three, held my breath, pulled up on the rope, and threw the hook out into space, praying it would find its target.

It didn't, of course.

It swung wildly out in a circle, but, by the time the hook swung back in an arc toward the loft, it hit him with a loud crack on the back of his head. I heard his sharp intake of breath, inches away from my perch, a noise like he was startled. He fell backward, his eyes rolling back in their sockets as he plunged about ten feet to the floor, one arm over the edge of the flooring above the empty space to the bottom floor. The gun had fallen too and was on the floor beside him. I hesitated, looked at him, and grabbed the rope to pull the hook up in case I needed to take another swing. Nothing. He lay there silently on his back, dark liquid spreading out in a slow-moving pool behind his head. Blood. Yuk.

My stomach heaved like a whirlpool, and I worried I might throw up, but I got myself together, stopped thinking about my rolling stomach, grabbed my flashlight, and scrambled down the ladder as fast as I could. I avoided stepping on him, gave the gun a wide berth, and ran down the stairs, out the door, my lungs exploding, my fear pushing me out of the mill. I cried, shook, and ran, my breath ragged in my ears as I landed on the asphalt of the lake road. I fell and skinned my knee. Then I pulled myself up and limped toward the east and the highway. Stopping once to throw up in the grass at the side of the road, I used my sweaty shirt to wipe off my mouth and ran again.

In the distance, car lights came toward me on the lake road. I stopped, bent over to get my breath, and counted to thirty. Then I stood up and watched the lights come closer. It wasn't Neal, but whoever it was might be able to help me if they didn't think I was a lunatic. What if they drove by and didn't stop?

I stood in the passing lane of the road, frantically waving my flashlight toward the car, sobbing, my shoulders and neck aching from fear. I took a few steps back toward the edge of the road as the car approached and stopped a few yards away. Both doors flew open. Two figures ran toward me, and once they were close enough to see, they were Andy and Lance. Another car was behind them, and it stopped now too.

Full-out tears and choking. Strong arms grabbed me before I almost fell to the ground.

Tom ran up behind them and yelled, "Where's Neal?" I pointed back to the west, managing to gasp, "Mill building...hurt...could be dead...I may be...a murderer."

To his credit, before he took off after my renegade math teacher, Tom stopped and pulled me into his arms—despite my sweaty, vomit smell. "Thank God we found you. And you're alive."

I nodded and pointed back at the mill. Tom told Andy to take me to the emergency room and have them check me out, and then he walked back to his car. We heard him call for backup and an ambulance. Once off his phone, he closed the car door and pointed to Lance. "You're my temporary backup. Come on with me." After those preliminaries, Mr. Amazing Detective left on foot for Cavendish Mill, Lance jogging along behind him, while I looked at Andy, holding me in his arms, and I thought I'd never make fun of him again.

Maybe.

Well, not for a week at least.

Chapter Thirty-Seven

"You look considerably better this morning, and..." Andy sniffed the air. "You smell a lot better too. Sweat and hurling do not become you."

I gazed at all the dirty dishes on Mary's kitchen table. "I guess I'll have to let that one go by since you rescued me and you and you." I looked at Tom and Lance.

Mary chimed in. "I'm thankful we got you to the ER for all those scratches and scrapes all over your legs and arms. I'm so relieved you're fine."

"Thanks, Mary. I've decided I don't want to see blood for a long, long time."

Tom poured more coffee into her cup, making the rounds of the table. "You'll be happy to know you didn't kill Neal, but he's in the hospital. His wife showed up in the wee hours when we called her this morning. Nasty gash on his head, a concussion, and blood loss."

Andy piped up with, "Geesh, Jill. Guess we won't have to follow up on our plan to enroll you in a self-defense course."

Angie leaned over and grabbed the coffee cream. "I always liked Mr. Wyatt. He was my favorite teacher, and I thought he was one of the good guys. I wish I'd been there to hear the conversation between Mr. W and his wife last night. I feel sorry for their kids. It won't be easy in a town this size to have a father charged with murder. Oops, make it murders."

Tom set his coffee cup on the table. "Well, he's not going anywhere. He's cuffed to the hospital bed. Officer Simmons is outside the door."

"As for murders, plural, I've put together several pieces, a few of them conjecture for the moment. Neal told me Mitch remembered him being with Carolyn that night after she babysat his kids. He saw her get into Neal's car in the parking lot at the Rusty Nail. After Carolyn's body was found a few weeks ago, Mitch put it together and decided to blackmail Neal. He needed the money. We see where it got him. Neal kept killing to save his reputation and life. Pointing to me was a great way to solve both problems. He made the anonymous call that took Tom to the autobody shop and tried to implicate me for Mitch's death."

Lance gave me a curious look. "How did Neal get you to the lake?"

I repeated the story for the second or third time. Tom told me I could anticipate more questions tomorrow.

After hearing my account of my kidnapping and escape, Lance asked Tom, "How did you know it was Neal?"

"I'd been thinking about him as the possible killer. He had an alibi for Carolyn's murder, but it didn't hold water once I went back over the notes from that night. His wife had had too much to drink at a faculty party and passed out when they got home. She'd never have known if he left with Carolyn. She took his word about him doing schoolwork till two a.m."

I piled a few dishes together. "He must have panicked when Carolyn told him the baby could be his. Hiding her in the Lowry Building was a stroke of genius. She never would've been found if I hadn't decided to renovate."

Tom looked around the table. "As for Jill, a dark SUV was seen at her house the morning of her disappearance. The neighbors described it to me on Friday afternoon and the diary was gone. I knew Jill planned to drop the diary off with me Saturday morning, but it was missing. Neal was the last to see Carolyn alive. He knew her handwriting and either took a trip to send those postcards or had friends he knew in other towns send them. He mailed the cards from places on the acting group's itinerary. Maybe he told them it was a game. He had so much to lose. He must have held his breath and hoped the postcards would arrive and seal the impression Carolyn was alive. Once I talk to him today, I'll see how close those theories are."

"He claimed to have killed her because he thought she'd ruin his life. After her murder, Mitch's death and my planned death were to cover up the initial murder."

"Believe it or not, Jill, her stepfather heard you were missing. He'd seen Neal at your house in the morning. Since Neal had threatened him, he figured he'd put him in the hot seat because he heard you were missing and called me once he sobered up."

I considered the possibility I might have to thank the old goat for saving me, but then I remembered Carolyn's diary.

Angie raised her hand. "Hey, don't forget my contribution. The phone. Remember, Jill, when we set my phone GPS to track your phone because you were always losing it?"

I was puzzled. "But I didn't have my phone with me."

"Right. Neal must have found your phone while you were unconscious and checked it to see if anyone was suspicious. He threw it out the car window into a patch of weeds along the road to the lake. Might have happened when he drove back to the art center. That was a mistake. Forgot to turn it off."

"I'm still so angry he killed Carolyn. Many an unplanned pregnancy has made huge changes in the parents' lives, but murder is rather a drastic step. And then Mitch, poor Mitch."

Angie looked at me. "They could have had the baby adopted."

I thought about her diary. "That would have solved the immediate problem. She needed a man who would take her away from her wretched life in a small town where her stepfather constantly stalked her. She needed a Lancelot. Evan was her first candidate, but when he turned into Mordred, Lancelot's evil nemesis, Neal was her only chance. Carolyn was always such a hopeless romantic about men. I'm sure she believed he'd take her away. Neal saw she planned to tell everyone, ruining his reputation, and causing him to lose his job. It would tear his family apart. He couldn't see any way to solve it other than to silence her."

The doorbell rang, reminding me of the morning Ned Fisher had come to my house with the news of the break-in. It seemed like months ago, but it had only been about five weeks. I pushed my chair back and walked to the front door.

Ned Fisher. "Hi, it's me again."

I stared. He looked at me as if he was afraid I'd slam the door in his face.

"It's—it's good. I have top-notch news this time." He had a huge carton in his arms.

I opened the door for him to bring it inside.

"It's for you."

Setting it on the table, he watched as I opened the flaps. Nestled in some packing peanuts was *Mother and Child*. My eyes filled with tears. It must have been the horrifying experience of the last twenty-four hours that made me so emotional.

"It was out at the Wyatt house at the lake."

"Thank you, Ned." I gave him a big hug and his face turned bright red.

Then, speechless, he did an about-face and left for his squad car.

I turned around and pulled my sculpture out of the box. Staring at my mother holding me, a shudder coursed through me. My sculpture was back.

The exhibit. Tom told me he'd heard it was an unqualified success, but he and the guys were all out looking for me, so they'd missed it. I, of course, had been unconscious for the biggest night of my professional life, the huge event that would seal my job future. Now I really could tell Ivan to stick his head in a bucket.

Tom gently took the sculpture and set it on the table. "I think we should take Mom's sculpture over to your art center. Oh, and we'll make sure the foundation board understands where this sculpture has been and why."

Tom drove me to the art center since my car was still back at my house. Neither of us said a word. The rain fell softly on the car and trickled down the windows. The sound of the wipers on the windshield reminded me of the tick-tock-tick-tock of the metronome back when I took piano lessons—when I was young, my whole life ahead of me, and my mother and father still alive. I wasn't sure why, but I paused, wishing I could hold on to those memories, which seemed so very unimportant and ordinary at the time. I took a deep breath, closed my eyes for a moment, and smiled slightly. They would always be with me.

Maybe it was the emotional drain of the past day, but last night, before I finally fell asleep, I remembered those terrifying moments at the mill. Who had I thought of as I listened to Neal's footsteps in the darkness? My brothers, and Lance, and Mary, praying I would see them again? And Angie. She was family too. Despite the absence of our parents, we were still a family, and we looked out for each other. I paused a moment, the rain falling around the car, and considered how lucky I was.

We were at the art center, and Tom patted my shoulder as I turned to get out. Walking in the alley door, I moved into the gallery. In awe, I saw walls filled with the entries we'd hung, several of them now with ribbons. We did it. Even without me, it all came to pass. I set the box with *Mother and Child* in the children's room.

Thinking back to the week when all this began, my emotions overwhelmed me as I walked around the room studying the walls. "I will show them success," I whispered. *And I did.* Despite Carolyn's dead body being discovered, my mother's sculpture disappearing, Mitch's body with my knife in his back and my bloody self on top of him, climbing out of the Anders' back window with a shotgun full of buckshot aimed at me, our juror having a terrible accident the day before the judging, and the curator being kidnapped, it had still gone off as planned. We had done it!

Think how easy this would be next time without all those…distractions.

Voices murmured back in the office area, and I tiptoed over to see what was happening. Louise was at her desk talking to Jordan, while Jordan looked at something over Louise's shoulder and nodded. They both giggled. I knocked on the door.

They turned. "Jill!" They rushed over to hug me, not the last of the hugs I'd get today.

After all the hugs and relief, we sat in Louise's office.

"I called your house Friday morning around ten because you hadn't shown up. When I didn't get an answer, I called Tom. After he saw the state of your house and your car still in the drive, he called me back. He said we'd have to carry on without you until he found you. Thank God for all those meetings you organized so we knew what to do."

"What about a juror?"

"Louise and I wracked our brains, trying to figure out someone who could come."

"Then I remembered my cousin Patricia. She has an uncle whose best friend knew Sarah who works at the university in Bloomington, a professor in the art department. Patricia connected me with Sarah. When I told her about the bind we were in, she said she'd be delighted to judge our exhibit. She drove here and stayed with me, and even went to the opening."

"What happened at the opening?"

Jordan picked up the story. "Mr. Wyatt was here. He examined all the entries calm as could be. I was shocked when Louise told me she heard he'd been arrested. We told the board you'd been detained, and our instructions were to go ahead and begin without you."

I looked at them, beaming. Our little band of sisters had managed to pull this off. It would be impossible to find better people. In the silence, I quietly thanked them.

Louise patted me on the shoulder. "You should go out to the gallery and look at the walls."

"Absolutely." I left them talking and strolled out to the gallery floor, checking first the free-standing sculptures and mixed-media pieces. One sculpture of a family caught my eye. Maybe I'd try to buy it.

Everywhere I turned, I glimpsed watercolors, photographs, and oil paintings, some with ribbons, some bare, but all of them created with passion and love, the same deep feelings I felt as I created my own works. Right now, my fingers itched to tear into the tubes of paint and canvases back at the house. Maybe my painting block was over. I walked around, checking out each piece, recognizing some I had fixed with a bit of glue or tape. The walls were clothed in bright colors, ingenious patterns, and technical virtuosity any artist would admire.

The alley door opened. Maybe it was Tom returning. No, it was Judge Spivey.

The board treasurer gave me a huge grin, walked over, and hugged me. He was making sure I was all in one piece. "Jill Madison, you've made us all exceedingly proud. This opening ran like a clock. You had Louise and

234

Jordan right on top of every step. As our business expert and board member, Len Walker, would opine, 'A good boss always makes sure she's dispensable so others can step in to carry on the job in her absence.' Exactly what you did." He glanced around at the exhibit. "Louise tells me we had at least five hundred people through the exhibit before the opening, many of them children. Hundreds more came to the opening. I wish you could have seen them. Precisely what you wanted—an art center to pass down appreciation of the arts for the community and its children. I know your parents, my old friends, would have been proud, especially your mother. Next time, we'll have even more visitors, and classes, and all the programs your heart desires."

Tears welled up in my eyes again. When would this blubbering end?

Shaking myself, I realized Ivan was missing. A coward to the end. He couldn't face me. "So, where's my nemesis, the esteemed CPA, Ivan?"

The judge shook his head and a glimmer of a smile passed his lips. "That is quite a story."

"I'm all ears."

"You know the handrail in the basement you two have had a civil war over?"

"I swear he'd pinch a penny till it screamed. That lack of railing is a real disaster waiting to happen."

"Well, it happened."

"What?"

"Ivan came over the day of the opening, and while he was here, he decided to check the work the construction guys had finished in the basement."

"Oh, no. I see where you're headed."

"So true. Yes, I'm afraid he fell—"

"—with no railing to grab." Poor Ivan. I wouldn't have wished this on him. "He did tell me we have great medical insurance."

"I think he's about to find out."

"Is he alright?"

"Well, nothing that won't mend. A concussion and a broken leg. He's in the hospital for another day or two."

I shook my head. "How many times did we argue about the need for a handrail? I guess I'll have to send him some flowers."

"You? Send Ivan flowers?"

"Sure I will. Kill him with kindness. He'll wonder what I'm up to while he's laid up. Now that should really drive him crazy."

"Well, I think the Adele Marsden Center for the Arts will be around for a long time to bring art to the people of Apple Grove, and especially the children. I know your parents would have been joyful to see this day. I'm so glad you decided to come home."

While I had him in a soft spot, I thought I might as well push things a little. "Wait until you hear my plans for a raft of new programs at the art center. I have a list of grants in my head waiting to be written, classes to start, new exhibits, including a national, juried one—and all these items will go up on the whiteboard in my office. I had a lot of time to think about them over the last few days." I pointed toward my office. "You know, Judge Spivey, I may need at least two more whiteboards for my office. Do you think the board will approve?"

He chuckled. "I'm sure you'll have no problem. Buy all the whiteboards you want. And, by the way, Ivan told me he'll be up on his leg for the next board meeting, so don't get too cocky and figure you'll pass lots of expensive bills by the board while he's temporarily laid up. His words, not mine."

"I expect he'll shower me with more advice as soon as he hears I'm back. After all, he can send me emails straight to my computer. His leg won't slow him down."

Judge Spivey smiled. "You have the full confidence of this board of directors even though we all agree you have kept the last six weeks lively." He started to leave.

"But hasn't it been great fun?"

He turned back toward me. "Yes, yes, it has." A twinkle in his eyes, a smile on his face, and he was off and out the alley door.

I thought it was the best day of my life. But then I had one even better.

A week later, my brothers came to the house, and we opened Mom's studio. Andy brought Lance's pickup truck, and we moved Mom's sculpture tables, tools, and supplies to the storage unit we had rented on the edge of town five years earlier, when our world had changed forever.

Shortly after we emptied the studio, Lance and Mary showed up with food and cleaning supplies. Window-washing, dusting, and vacuuming commenced after dinner, followed by several trips to the family room in the house to carry canvases, jars, tubes, and various containers of paint supplies. The easel and a chair were the last additions. Andy set a blank canvas on my easel and lined up the pigment tubes and various bottles on a small table. "There they are, Jill, waiting for you to simply apply paint. A new beginning. An opportunity to create whatever you want."

"Simply?"

Lance laughed. "Tom hopes this will keep you out of trouble."

Andy examined a paintbrush, then looked up. "Jill's like me. Not sure that's possible."

Angie held out the framed picture of the three musketeers. "This photograph will be the first picture we hang on your wall."

Lance took the picture. "I have a hammer and nail."

I stood outside the door of the studio and watched as my brothers laughed, Mary and Angie checked out my old paintings from the storage box, and Lance hung the photo of the three musketeers on the wall. Angie, Carolyn, and me. How fortunate we were to grow up in this small town, surrounded by corn and bean fields, but also by love, affection, loyalty, and devotion. Slow, carefree evenings, summers at the lake, ballgames with the family, bicycling to the park for a picnic, meeting Carolyn at the root beer stand, and always my mom and dad and my two big brothers. They were my universe.

Finding Carolyn's murderer wouldn't bring her back. The rational part of my brain kicked in on that idea. But in my heart, Carolyn would always remain lovely as a summer day, passionate about her friendships, mischievous, and fun. She would rest peacefully now that we'd found her killer, and he'd pay a price for what he'd done.

Now my new universe included great plans for special events and classes at the art center. I had an idea to start a group of seniors who would meet for art talks. They would be intrepid art supporters.

There was yet another new possibility on my horizon, and I hadn't even told Angie yet. I held it close, keeping it to myself for now. When I was in the emergency room getting checked out, a handsome new intern named Sam Finch took my pulse as he checked me over. No wedding ring. Curiosity appeared, and my heart raced a bit faster. Covered with mud, vomit, and sweat, I figured this was a great opportunity missed. Strangely, he didn't seem to mind.

This could be a keeper, a man who saw me like this might be a man willing to hold my hair back while I threw up. That was till-the-end-of-time best friend Angie's puke rule for finding a forever boyfriend. Sparkling blue eyes, wavy brown hair with a hint of blond highlights from the summer sun, and a gorgeous smile with perfect white teeth that complemented his white physician's jacket.

I loved a man in uniform.

Acknowledgements

I owe heartfelt thanks to many people who were instrumental in the writing of this book. First and foremost, thank you to my editors: Anne Brewer at Anne Brewer Editorial, and Lourdes Venard at Comma Sense Editing, who did the same kind of work as my renowned fictional sculptor in this book: shaped, molded, cut away, and smoothed out the ripples.

I also am grateful to my agent, Dawn Dowdle of the Blue Ridge Literary Agency, for her advice, encouragement, and work on this manuscript.

These talented people who are fortunate to work in the art world gave me advice about my fictional art center: Kristyne Gilbert, Executive Director of the Buchanan Center for the Arts in Monmouth, Illinois; Lynn Miller, the BCA office manager and second-in-command; Janis Mars Underlich, Assistant Professor of Art at Monmouth College; and Larry J. Davis, an extraordinary artist. Thank you for the gift of your time and advice.

I owe a debt of gratitude to experts in the "crime world" whom I questioned and often annoyed with "Oh, just another thing…" Those would include Judge Andrew Doyle of the Ninth Judicial Circuit of Illinois; Detective Suzy Owens, formerly of the Ames, Iowa Police Department; and Aloysius J. McGuire, Warren County coroner.

Also, I'd like to give a huge shout-out to Shawn Simmons and Level Best Books for believing in this project and giving it a try. Thanks to you all.

Finally, I must mention my beta group—Jan DeYoung, Hallie Lemon, and Eileen Owens. As always, they were kind enough to be my first readers, and I thank them.

About the Author

Susan Van Kirk is the President of the Guppy Chapter of Sisters in Crime and a writer of cozy mysteries. She lives at the center of the universe—the Midwest—and writes during the ridiculously cold and icy winters. Why leave the house and break something? Van Kirk taught forty-four years in high school and college and raised three children. Miraculously, she has low blood pressure. She's a member of Sisters in Crime and Mystery Writers of America.

SOCIAL MEDIA HANDLES:
FaceBook: http://www.facebook.com/SusanVanKirkAuthor/
Twitter: http://twitter.com/susan_vankirk/
Pinterest: http://www.pinterest.com/sivankirk/_saved/
Goodreads: https://www.goodreads.com/author/show/586.Susan_Van
kirk
Instagram https://www.instagram.com/susanivankirk/

AUTHOR WEBSITE:

https://susanvankirk.com

Also by Susan Van Kirk

The Education of a Teacher (Including Dirty Books and Pointed Looks)

Three May Keep a Secret

The Locket: From the Casebook of TJ Sweeney

Marry in Haste

Death Takes No Bribes

The Witch's Child

A Death at Tippitt Pond

CPSIA information can be obtained
at www.ICGtesting.com
Printed in the USA
LVHW102148260822
726888LV00011BA/65